Waiting To Break

Ruth Madison

Content Includes: institutional neglect, medical trauma, grief, panic attacks/anxiety, power dynamics in caregiving, public debate about "right to die," false accusations, elder death, loss of a parent, difficulty communicating.

Page edges by *Painted Wings Publishing*

ISBN: *979-8-9906859-3-2*

Disclaimer: No part of this book is based on any real person, living or dead. Any resemblance is purely coincidental. Eye-gaze and AAC technology are in no way similar to or related to guided communication.

Art created by the author with a combination of stock images, ai, Canva, and G.I. M.P.

OTHER BOOKS BY RUTH MADISON

Get Bonus Content For All Books At:

ruthmadisonbooks.com/bonus

CONTENTS

1

ANNA

Rosehaven didn't look like what Anna expected. The square weather-resistent sign planted in the gravel announced it was an assisted living facility, but the ornate wooden original was still on the building next to the doors: St. Agatha's Sanitorium. Sun-peeled paint curled like dried petals along the siding. The titular rose bushes were overgrown around the sides, a few lone branches bolting all the way to the row of second floor windows. The glass was so thick and warped that Anna couldn't see in at all.

Her sneakers crunched over gravel as she approached the front door and smiled awkwardly at an old woman sitting in a wheelchair outside the door. The woman didn't respond. Wisps of her white hair floated up in the breeze. Her vacant eyes suggested she was already half living in another world. How was Anna going to do anything to impact these people's lives? What help could she even offer?

The voice in the back of Anna's mind started up again. *You never finished college, you only got this job because your dad called people, you aren't qualified for this. You're going to screw it up like you always do.* She breathed through it, pausing a moment to close her eyes and connect with the sounds, smells, and sensations around her. The mourning dove whose sad cooing she had confused for an owl as a child. The smell of pine sap and too-sweet manure freshly laid around the flower beds. The hot sticky air without a hint of a breeze.

She opened her eyes, nodding firmly to herself like a fool. If she was ever going to get her life back on track, it had to be now.

Why was she just as nervous on her first day as she had been at the interview? She had the job. And probably no one else actually wanted to work at a run-down old nursing home like Rosehaven. The whole place had definitely seen better days.

The square accessibility button sat slightly crooked on the wall, and when she pressed it, the heavy oak door groaned like it resented having to move. The old woman next to her didn't even look up. Anna stepped carefully on the slick polished black and white tiled floor up to the front desk. She felt like a child arriving tardy to school even though she was on time and nearly thirty years old.

"Who are you here to see?" the clerk asked as she picked dirt out from under one long fingernail.

"I'm the new activities coordinator?" Anna said.

"What's that?" the clerk looked up. She hadn't heard what Anna said.

Anna coughed and tried again. "I'm the new activities coordinator."

"Oh. I'm Sylvia."

"Anna."

"Hold on a minute."

Sylvia pushed back in her rolling chair and picked a sheet of paper off a printer then returned and passed it to Anna.

"You know where the resource room is?"

Anna nodded.

"This is a list of the current residents, their room numbers, and basic information. You'll see notes about which ones to look for in your activities and which ones are too far gone."

A lump rose in Anna's throat. She couldn't help thinking of her mother at the end, the point where it was clear she was going to die. But Anna just nodded, took the paper, and proceeded down the hall towards the room that was now her domain.

You could still leave. The thought flared as she passed a bulletin board cluttered with faded holiday decorations several months out of date. Anna pressed her lips together. No running. It was time to grow up.

She passed an archway that opened into a living room space and saw several older people sitting on chairs watching the news at a low volume and one at a table in the back of the room silently clicking puzzle pieces into place.

The cafeteria door on her other side was closed with a note of meal times taped to the outside.

"First day?" asked a nurse who passed, pushing a vitals cart. Her eyes were sympathetic but hurried.

Anna nodded, swallowing hard. "Activities coordinator."

"Welcome to the chaos." The nurse smiled wearily, disappearing around the corner before Anna could reply.

Anna turned the other way down a smaller hallway with only half the lightbulbs working and entered what was called the resource room where activities like art were held.

No one was inside now. Anna plopped onto a chair at the long table in the center of the room and put down the print-out Sylvia had given her.

Anna skimmed the names—Margaret, Henry, Louisa, Doris, Frank, Eleanor, Mary, Harriet. And then, halfway down, one stood out starkly from the rest:

Gabriel Whitlock, 217B. Nonverbal. TBI. SCI.

Beside it, scribbled hastily in pencil: *Don't expect interaction, probably not much left cognitively.*

Gabriel Whitlock. She read the note again, brows drawn together. He couldn't be the same Gabe Whitlock, could he? The rock star guitarist she'd once heard blasting from her high school boyfriend's bedroom? The wild-haired, charismatic frontman whose voice had dripped with honey and angst?

Surely not. What would someone like that be doing in a place like Rosehaven?

"Excuse me?" A shaky voice brought Anna back to the present. There was a woman leaning on a walker in the doorway of the room. Her silver hair was pressed against her head in perfect curls and she wore matching pink pants and shirt with a white cardigan over. "I'm Mary," she said. "I was hoping you might have something for me to do."

Anna smiled. "Of course. It's nice to meet you, Mary. What kinds of things do you like to do?"

Mary walked slowly into the room and sat in another chair at the table. "I like to do crossword puzzles. They keep my mind sharp."

"I can do that!" Anna slid back to the computer and printer that were in the room and searched for some crosswords to print off. Mary pulled a pair of reading glasses that were the same shade of pink as her shirt and pants out of her breast pocket. "I can't wait to tell everyone that we have someone to run activities again," she said.

"How long have you been without a coordinator?" Anna handed her a crossword and a pencil.

"Oh let me see," Mary frowned and gazed into the distance as she thought. "I'm not good with time anymore but it's been a few weeks, maybe six?"

"I'm so sorry."

Mary smiled sadly. "These days no one thinks much about the old folk."

Though she had her glasses on and was looking at the clues, Mary seemed like she wanted to keep chatting so Anna asked, "What do you know about Gabriel Whitlock? Do you see him around here?"

Mary sighed and pushed her glasses on top of her curls. "That's a sad case," she said. "You hate to see someone so young in a place like this."

"Is it the same Gabe Whitlock as the frontman of *Pressure Front*?"

"What's that, dear?"

"A band. It's the same name as a musician."

"Hmmm, I don't know about that. He doesn't come out of his room much. He has a computer voice thing but I don't hear him use it. Maybe once or twice in the years he's been here."

"You're right, that is sad."

Mary nodded.

"No one should be isolated like that," Anna said. For some reason, she thought of the isolation she felt when she had to drop out of college. Like she and her classmates were all on a conveyor belt and she had fallen off the side while everyone else kept moving forward without her. Ever since then she had been clawing at the edge trying to get back on. "I'll go see if I can talk with him on my break."

"That is a lovely idea," Mary said. "Good luck."

Anna watched as Mary very carefully filled letters into squares with a trembling hand. Since no one else came, Anna started working on a plan and a schedule for the next week and making a list of supplies she needed.

At the top of the hour Anna closed up the room and bid Mary goodbye. She looked again at the room number for Gabriel Whitlock and figured out which direction it was.

The door was slightly ajar but she couldn't see inside. There was a light on. She knocked lightly and pushed the door further open.

"Mr. Whitlock?" she said softly, peeking her head in.

At the far end of the room she saw a large power wheelchair and she could just barely see the sides of a head around the vinyl-padded head support and the tops of a man's shoulders over the high back.

She took a step into the room. There was no response from the man. He was seated in front of the window. As she got closer, she could see one stiff hand resting next to a small black joystick on the armrest of the wheelchair and on the other side, a rectangular black box was mounted. He continued to look at the window, no indication that he had noticed her enter the room.

Seeing a wicker chair, Anna dragged it over beside him and sat down. When she saw his face, she had no doubt at all it was him. More gray at the temples, more lines etched into his handsome face, thicker around the middle. But it was the same Gabe Whitlock, frontman and guitarist of *Pressure Front*.

How long had he been here? How had he come to be in an understaffed nursing home in Western Mass? She vaguely remembered hearing about an accident on stage but she had never seen any follow-up on it. That must have been at least five years ago, maybe more.

"Hi, Gabe. I'm Anna, the new activities coordinator. I'll be around quite a bit." She paused, watching his face closely. Not a twitch. "I hear you have a speech device—I'm here whenever you want to talk. Or...just sit. That's okay too."

She could have left. There were plenty of things she could do with her free time here. But again, that memory of being left behind by everyone in her life was pressing on her mind and she was determined to make some kind of connection with this man who had been all but forgotten by the world.

As they sat together she began to talk. "I just started here today and I have lots of ideas for things we can do. Art, music, games. Maybe even trips."

No response. She looked at his hands. One by the joystick and one in his lap. Both were bent sharply towards his wrists and were formed into fists. The right one a bit looser than the left. Maybe the note in the margin of her paper was right, maybe his mind was gone and this body just a shell.

But she continued, "I know you have experience with music. Maybe you can help me with some playlists."

Not even a shadow of a hint that he understood what she was saying.

"I'm getting a fresh start here. I was taking care of my mother but she's passed now." It was still hard to say those words, hard to believe that they were true. Her mother was just in another room, wasn't she? About to come back in and ask if Anna wanted to hit the outlet mall on Saturday. "So I'm getting going with my own life again." Suddenly, Anna wished she hadn't said that. It seemed extra insensitive considering her audience. The life he knew had ended and it didn't appear that he'd be getting on with a new fresh start any time soon.

The tragedy of it pressed on her chest and she recognized the tight feeling of her breath as the first signs of a panic attack. Not now, she told herself. And she used the techniques she had learned to head them off. She took a few deep breaths and she focused her attention on a leaf on the tree outside the window; its shape, its color, its movement. The tension subsided. She wasn't going to solve all the problems of all the people in the world, much as she wanted to. Life was unfair. The sort of statement that you hear a lot, but it doesn't fully register until you experience it for yourself.

Anna kept talking. "I'll have to go home soon but I'll be back tomorrow. I work on the weekdays. I'll make sure you have the schedule so you can come to anything that appeals to you. Seems like you have some nice neighbors here."

She lingered ten minutes. Ten careful, hopeful, awkward minutes. His eyes never flickered toward her, never acknowledged her existence. She fought down disappointment, reminding herself he'd been through enough already without her expectations piled on top.

Finally, she stood to leave. But as she reached the door, a soft click behind her froze her mid-step.

She turned back sharply. Gabe had tapped a button on the AAC device attached to his chair. The screen was lit up and he was slowly moving the knuckle of his left hand to tap something out.

Anna stood still, forgetting to breathe as she waited to hear what he was going to say. She leaned forward, lifting up onto the balls of her feet in anticipation.

Each tap took long seconds of focus and she could see the strain in his face, moving his fist with a shaky, thin arm, slowly pressing each letter one by one. At last, the computer voice spoke a single word into the heavy silence of the room.

Persistent.

Anna blinked at him. Had his jaw shifted ever so slightly? A ghost of a smirk, perhaps?

She raised an eyebrow, feeling an unexpected smile playing on her own lips. "And you're a jackass. Great, we're getting along already."

This time she was sure—the faint twitch at the corner of his mouth was unmistakable.

She left the room, keeping the door ajar just as she had found it. The trip out of Rosehaven was lighter than the way in. Anna had a grin on her face and more confidence than she had felt in years.

She climbed into her mom's old Toyota with scratches on the windshield from a failed attempt to scrape ice off with a bottle and a *Northampton Pride* bumper sticker that was peeling at the edges. Pulling onto the road, she waited patiently for a group of wild turkeys to wander across the road from one set of dense dark trees to the other.

As she drove home in the golden light of dusk, she hummed to herself and tried to remember any *Pressure Front* melodies she could.

The heaviness was waiting for her when she got home. Her mother's spirit lingered here. As soon as she opened the door, Anna could feel the weight on the air. Places there should be sound were now quiet and empty.

Anna dropped her bag by the front door while looking over at the living room that had been turned into a bedroom in her mother's last weeks. At the end, her mother had been so frail she wasn't even recognizable. Now even though it was empty, Anna could almost see a hazy echo of her mother laying on the couch; looking at her, slowly blinking, unable to lift her head. Both the present and the past version of the living room seemed to be competing for the same space.

A clink from the kitchen brought Anna back to only the present. She had things to do and she couldn't afford to sink into grief.

Her father was sitting at the small wooden table in the kitchen with two mugs of tea in front of him. It was the same every day. His white mug with the bioinformatics ad on it, now somewhat gray, and her mother's purple mug with a winking cat face.

Again the grief rose up in Anna's gut and wrapped around her lungs, threatening to suffocate her. But she had to be strong for her dad. She said nothing about the extra cup of tea and went about preparing dinner for them.

It was then her father noticed her, coming out of his reverie. "How was your first day?" he said.

Anna squeezed dish soap onto her hands and bumped the faucet on with her elbow. "Really good," she said. "I think it's going to be a good fit for me."

He smiled brightly, pleased both with her answer and the relief that maybe she had found a place to settle in at last. Both her parents worried about whether she was going to find her way in life and now her father felt twice the weight of that worry as though he had to carry her mother's portion too.

Over dinner, Henry talked about his garden. He had started with sprouts in May so now in June his plants were well established but the weather could be unpredictable and he was thinking about drought and water restrictions. Anna only pretended to listen. Of all the things happening around her, the garden seemed the least important.

She understood why it mattered so much to him. It had been her mother's garden. Her father had never liked things as unpredictable as growing flowers. But as Helen had become sicker and sicker, Henry took over caring for the plants. It made it just a little bit easier for Helen to let go, knowing that her beloved garden was cared for. Now even though she was gone, Henry kept working on it every day.

That night in her room after dinner, Anna pulled out a sketchbook and sharpened a pencil. She sat at her desk and pondered the page. She hadn't felt the urge to draw in weeks. But now she found herself shading gently onto the clean white sheet and Gabe Whitlock's eyes began to take shape. The light crows feet beginning to form around the piercing dark eyes. She leaned in closer, the pencil forming that steely look he had given her. He was still in there, sharp as ever. She was sure of it.

2

GABE

Every day started the same for Gabe. He was awakened at exactly 8:00 (whether he had been asleep or lying awake for hours) and rolled over, checked for pressure sores on his skin, then pulled up to sitting and given his morning pills. His bathroom needs attended to, dressed with ruthless efficiency, and a ceiling-mounted lift beside the bed moved him to his wheelchair. Some time later another aide would arrive with a tray of breakfast and feed it to him, often taking the opportunity to sit and scroll on their phone while he attempted to catch the fork they were waving near his face.

He didn't remember their names anymore. When he first came to Rosehaven there were better aides. People who cared. But this place didn't attract the best and the brightest. The people taking care of him would be the same for a while and then different and new people came without even telling him their names. Now he was mostly just moved around as a job.

They thought he wasn't listening.

They stood over him, around him, speaking in soft condescension or breezy indifference, acting like he couldn't understand. Like he was already gone. Just a body in a chair, a husk propped up by a blinking screen and a list of medications.

But Gabe Whitlock noticed everything.

He noticed the nurse who took extra breaks. The way the walls of Rosehaven grew tiny cracks each winter, left unrepaired. The too-bright lights that buzzed overhead like angry bees.

And he noticed her.

The new girl.

Anna.

She sat with him. Talked to him. Waited.

When she didn't recoil or sigh in frustration at his silence...that had done something strange inside his chest. A little thaw. A flicker of something he hadn't let himself feel in years.

She had stayed a long time, chatting into the silence, unfazed by his non-response. Most staff wouldn't have lasted ninety seconds.

Anna had introduced herself. Even though she had no responsibility for his care. He almost never attended activities and he might never have met her if she hadn't sought him out. Because of his fame perhaps? She was probably old enough to remember him if she paid attention to that kind of thing. Some people enjoy music without ever learning the names of the musicians and some people don't care for rock at all. But she had mentioned knowing he had experience in music so she probably knew who he was. Yet she hadn't acted weird about it.

Today he decided he would go to the activities room after lunch and see if Anna was there. He had no idea if it was a weekday or weekend. Time had lost all sense of meaning and he didn't even know how long he had been living at Rosehaven.

It was a similar feeling to taking an international flight and you can't imagine how you're going to get through 14 hours of flying and yet the time passes in a strange way that feels out of step with how time works on the ground.

Now that kind of time was all there was. Time stretching and compressing and skipping in strange ways and he watched it all, unable to explain it.

He moved his wheelchair to the window as he did most days and gazed out through a glass pane stained yellow with pollen. His window didn't open anymore, hadn't for a long time, maybe years.

He could see the parking lot and noted the new car that had appeared yesterday. Small, blue, and quirky. Anna must be here. Beyond the gravel lot, a shallow dip of wild meadow spread out toward the woods, where black-eyed Susans tangled with high grass. A battered wooden bench sat half-sunk near the edge, weathered gray by decades of snow and sun. No one ever sat there. Often he saw deer, foxes, and occasional coyote. Once he even watched a bald eagle sit at the top of a tree and devour a squirrel.

He had a lot of time to think, but not a lot of ability to save those thoughts. In the past, he would write songs and dig into thoughts, preserve them, pin them down like rare butterflies, and share them with the world.

Now his thoughts were his own, and he wondered if they still had meaning if they were never shared with anyone else. Did having the thought create its own vibration? Its own impact on the world, even if it was never spoken aloud? Like a mantra in a meditation, a sound that vibrates only within you but still changes the world. Supposedly.

For a hot minute, *Pressure Front* had been into yoga and meditation but he'd never been sure it was doing anything. Probably because in those days, he was in constant motion. He hadn't had much time for things like meditation before but now it was, in some ways, all that he did. Like a contemplative monk, cloistered away from the world. Those monks must believe that silent thought and prayer behind locked doors mattered in some way, impacted something.

Kind of ironic that he felt like a monk now, considering the wild and fast-paced life he used to live. The cities, the drugs, the women. So many beautiful women and sex that was like music.

The songs he could write now would be better than the ones he did before because before he didn't have time to listen. Now he had so much stillness and so much realness that surfaced in his brain. Was it a shame that the world would not know the new music that he would be able to write today? He didn't even know what Ray and Tommy were doing now. Perhaps they had solo careers. Perhaps they had replaced him. Perhaps *Pressure Front* was still out there, creating and performing, as though he were dead. He hadn't seen them since he came to Rosehaven.

In a way, he had to be grateful for the stillness. The accident was the only thing that slowed him down and he would never have stopped moving otherwise. By the time he was doing tours around the world and constantly flying and moving and partying he never had time for the contemplation that it took to write meaningful lyrics. The songs that he had written when he was a young man still trying to find his place in the world were performed again and again and again because he never had time to stop and create new ones.

And now all he had was the contemplation of life and whether his was meaningful in this state. The thought was raw and hot like a live wire. Instinctively, he wanted to write about it, bring it out in music, to share what he felt with the world. He would never be able to do that again. There were times when it was overwhelmingly maddening, and there were times when he was at peace with it. There were times when it felt like an inside joke between him and the universe.

He had never been religious and he couldn't see God the way that Mary did, but he felt something meaningful, something that he might call divinity, humming around him in the world. And it was only in this intense stillness over meaningless amounts of time that he had begun to feel it.

How do we find meaning in our lives? So many of us strive and climb and run forward without really knowing where we're going and as long as we keep moving, we think that it's all going in the right direction.

But now Gabe couldn't move and so he had to face how meaningless the moving could really be, how it masks our fears, how it keeps us from having to think about the vastness of the world and time and whether anything we do lasts or matters in the long history of the world. How long does memory live? When the world burns itself to death, is there a memory where it lives? Is there a memory that God holds?

And from his personal experience, Gabe knew that even being famous around the world, even having people everywhere know your name, was not the same as being truly known or remembered. The Gabe Whitlock that was famous was a two-dimensional character and a projection of what people wanted him to be. Even if his name lived on in history, it would be a story, a character, an interpretation, and not who he really was.

It all came back to time again.

Time as he used to experience it and time as he experienced it now. And how it was now, it seemed entirely meaningless. The only sense of linear time was his hair getting a little grayer, people around him getting older, dying...even that didn't fully feel linear. It felt like it was all happening at the same time and yet also not happening at all. Every change just an illusion and meaningless minutes and hours, days and years existing all at once in one tight space.

Time must have been passing, but it all seemed a static moment from where he sat.

And now there was a new person, a break in the clouds, letting in the faintest hint of sunlight. Would something change? Would something shift? It seemed that she had brought something new to this world that was removed from time and what it would be, he still couldn't see.

A perfunctory knock at his open door. It was lunchtime. The morning was somehow gone already.

While he was being fed, Gabe slowly entered a couple words into his AAC device for later.

After lunch, Gabe took a few moments to relieve the pressure on his spine and take weight off his skin by engaging the tilt function on his wheelchair and adjusting the angle until his back was stretching out. Then it was time to go see what everyone was up to. He wished he had something better to wear than black jogging pants and a twenty-year-old band tee but he didn't, so it would have to do. He didn't even own shoes anymore. His feet were placed on footrests each day in only socks. Why bother with shoes?

He used the side of his right fist to gently push the wheelchair joystick and move down the hall. The hum of conversation and the sound of plastic Bingo chips clacking against the table met him as he approached the resource room. Frank was arguing with Ellie over whether G-52 had actually been called. Gabe rounded the corner and saw into the room.

There she was.

Anna. Standing in front of the group, turning a tiny cage of bouncing orange Bingo balls. Her ponytail of slick black hair bobbed as she laughed at something Frank had said.

When she saw Gabe, her whole face lit up. Not polite-surprised. Not staff-smiling. Real joy.

Gabe drove himself in, his fist pushing awkwardly on the joystick, and stopped just inside the door. The whir of his chair attracted attention and all the noise in the room stopped, everyone shuffling and turning to stare at him.

Oh great. He hadn't wanted it to be quite so obvious to Anna that he never came to activities. Why he was trying to play it cool with her, he couldn't say. It wasn't like you could really give off cool vibes in a big tank of a wheelchair with no ability to hold up your own head and no voice.

Speaking of which, he pushed his left fist into the machine and the computer on his side said:

No autographs.

Gabe cast his gaze down to his tightly curled hands and then winked at her.

Anna blinked, then burst out laughing. "Damn," she said. "Now no one will ever believe that I met THE Gabe Whitlock."

He smirked and made his way further into the room.

The satisfaction of making Anna laugh didn't last long. He couldn't participate in any activity she planned. What had he even been thinking? His stomach felt sour as he could vividly picture how Anna would look at him when she realized just how very disabled he was. If only he had a rearview mirror and could just back out of the room right now. It was too late for that. Old people were crowded all around him and the exit was blocked.

Ellie, a former drama teacher who wore so many colors and bangles at once that it was hard to look at her, clapped her hands together, beaming at Gabe. "Wonderful! Gabe can join us. We'll just move Frank's cards over—"

Frank shuffled slowly over, always agreeable to whatever the ladies said to do.

Mary cleared her throat delicately. "Now Eleanor, perhaps we should first see if Gabriel even wants to play Bingo. We shouldn't assume—"

"Nonsense, Mary," Ellie retorted, waving her good hand. "Everyone enjoys Bingo. Gabe just needs a little assistance—"

"Assistance is one thing," Mary interjected softly yet firmly, "but presuming to speak for someone is quite another. Let's allow Gabriel to decide for himself."

Ellie pursed her lips, shooting a pointed glance at Mary over the tops of her bedazzled reading glasses. "Well, Gabe, would you like to join our thrilling Bingo adventure, or do you prefer the riveting pastime of spectating?"

Time to fully humiliate yourself in front of a pretty girl, he thought. He was here now so he may as well enjoy himself. Gabe tapped his machine:

I'm in.

Ellie grinned triumphantly. "See, Mary? Some people just need a little encouragement."

Mary gave a gentle sigh, shaking her head slightly, "If you say so, Eleanor."

"Anna, get Gabe a card, dear!" Ellie called out in a sing-song voice.

"Gladly," Anna said, already pulling one from a stack. She smiled warmly as she put it down on the table where Frank had made room for Gabe to drive his wheelchair up.

"I'll mark your squares," Ellie said, her glasses sliding down to the very tip of her nose, hanging on by a miracle of physics. "You just make a noise when you have one."

Gabe nodded. After a long moment as Anna was getting his place set up, the computer voice said:

If you cheat, I bite.

Ellie hooted with laughter. "Oh, *he's* going to be trouble."

Mary narrowed her eyes. "You'd better be careful, Gabriel. She bites back."

They all waited a moment while he pressed the device:

Hot.

Anna choked on her laugh, eyes wide. "Gabe!"

He grinned at her.

"I like him," Ellie said brightly, as if addressing a room full of guests at a party. "He's got more spirit than the rest of you corpses put together."

Frank blinked slowly. "What'd he say?"

"Nothing, Frank," Mary said primly.

Gabe was starting to wonder why he never joined in. He didn't even know they all knew his name. That surprised him more than it should. It might be a bunch of old kooks around here but it was turning out that old kooks are a lot of fun. The game hadn't even started yet and he was already highly entertained.

Anna started twirling the little cage and reading the numbers on the orange balls. It all suddenly reminded him of fundraising nights at his Catholic high school. Like the moms who organized the events, Anna had that gift of making a community around her instantly. Gabe had seen it before. His old bandmate Tommy was the same way. Never met a stranger, as they say.

Mary won the game and said "Bingo" with a quiet self-satisfaction, only allowing herself a small smile to celebrate.

The air in the room was fizzy with laughter and teasing. Gabe felt something strange in his chest—a warmth, light and unsteady. This. This was the old him. Sparring with an audience. Making people laugh. Holding attention without needing to shout for it.

And Anna was watching him with a look that made his stomach clench—like she saw all of it. And liked it.

Gabe watched as Anna packed the game away and the other residents made their way slowly past. He wished he could help clean up. It would be the gentlemanly thing to do and it felt awful to just sit and watch someone else do all the work. But this was just one of those daily frustrations he had to live with.

"That was fun, wasn't it?" Anna chirped as she tapped the stack of cards against the table to straighten it. "I'm glad that you came." She paused and smiled at him. He smiled back.

He was glad that she had come too. Her kind energy was exactly what Rosehaven needed. Everyone seemed more relaxed already. Even Mary and Ellie bickering had less sting to it, he thought.

But something in him still pulled back. If he let himself enjoy her company...what would happen when she left? Everyone did. Most sooner rather than later. A job like this was a stepping stone to something better. No one lasted long except maybe the residents. There had been several activity coordinators in the time he had been here. She would do her time, get some credentials, and move on to better things. And she deserved better things. He really did want that for her.

"See you next time!" Anna said. She followed him out and locked the door of the resource room.

Was it a law of the universe that no good experience could exist without a horrible one to balance it out? It certainly seemed that way.

After dinner Gabe drove back to the quiet hallway of the resource room to check the schedule Anna had posted on the door. But when he tried to go back to his room, he nudged the joystick on his wheelchair, moved two inches and came to an abrupt halt, his body jolting.

The wheelchair battery was dead. Not for the first time, staff hadn't charged it last night and now he was stranded in a hallway where hardly anyone came in the evenings. Unbelievable. He tried to get more juice out of the chair but it stayed stubbornly off like a PR agent that hadn't been paid.

Lights clicked off around him. The night aide was supposed to be doing rounds and making sure every resident was in their bed. Yet no one came for him. No loudspeaker announcement desperately trying to locate him. Just forgotten. Again.

He tried to make some sound, to call attention from the staff but all he managed was a soft growl deep in his throat. No one came. The muscles in his neck tightened painfully, reminding him that he had been sitting in the same position for far too long and his body was not about to let him get away with it.

Maybe his AAC device? The volume didn't go very high but maybe it would be enough for someone to hear him.

He strained, jaw tight, trying to angle his head, neck muscles tight as stone, toward the device to see if he could get it on. Spasms pulsed through his arms and then into his legs, gripping him in painful constraint like a tightening vice around his limbs. His hands and arms were seized up too much and no matter how hard he tried, they weren't going to move. *Damn it, body.*

The AAC sat mere inches away—*impossible inches*. He stared desperately at the button he needed, unable to press it, unable even to tap out a simple "help."

Sharp pain hit in one hip and sent waves through his limbs. He squeezed his eyes tight, trying to breathe through the pain. There was something extra *fuck yo*u about being able to feel his body but not move it. If the light rig was going to take his ability to move, couldn't it have at least also taken his ability to feel?

He longed to stretch out his back. Without a charged battery he couldn't even tilt his chair to relieve the pressure. How long had he been stuck here? How long would he be stuck here? At this point his blood pressure had to be rising and he could die of autonomic dysreflexia before anyone noticed he wasn't where he was supposed to be.

The indignity. What would happen in the morning if they found him dead in his wheelchair? He almost smiled at the thought but it turned into a grimace as spasms wracked through his neck and back.

And then sudden warm moisture soaked his lap as his bladder released and urine soaked through his pants and into the wheelchair cushion.

Is this your idea of funny? he thought to the version of God he imagined in his head. *Go pick on someone your own size.*

Trying to figure out some way to move, he rubbed his head against the headrest of the wheelchair, but nothing happened. If he wasn't strapped to this thing he would have tipped his head forward until he fell onto the floor to at least not be sitting in his own pee. But even that he couldn't do.

His legs had gone rigid, his feet no longer on the footrests, the metal edges were now cutting into the skin of his ankles even through his socks. If he survived tonight, he'd need to get someone to treat the skin on his ankles or he could lose his feet. What total insanity.

Wait...was that the sound of a soft-soled footstep around the corner?

Gabe gathered all his remaining strength to make the loudest gurgling groan he could.

He heard a mutter of, "What in the world?" and then a face appeared around the corner. "Oh goddamn it, Ken," the night nurse muttered with a heavy sigh. She spoke into a radio. "Ken skipped his checks again...I know, but now it leaves me with a mess to clean up. He can't keep doing this. I don't care what he's dealing with." She clicked the radio off, clipped it to her belt, and took hold of his wheelchair, pushing it towards his room without ever saying a word to him.

Her fury was palpable as she stripped off his wet clothes. She roughly loaded him, naked, onto the lift and dropped him onto his bed. The jerky motions were triggering more muscle spasms in his thighs and he gritted his teeth. This time it was more an uncomfortable feeling than actual pain. Sighing and muttering, the nurse got a washcloth from the bathroom and cleaned him with ruthless efficiency. At least she knew to be relatively gentle on his skin. The last thing he needed was an open sore. That would be a trip to the hospital for sure. Next time he saw Nurse Becky he would tell her to check his ankles. No way was he going to try to communicate with this one.

The night nurse pulled the radio out again and barked, "Bridgette, get to room 217B. You need to get this cushion cover into the laundry ASAP."

Finally she covered Gabe's naked body with a scratchy, thin sheet that had been bleached far too many times but he couldn't relax until he finally saw her plug the wheelchair in. The light turned on and he closed his eyes at last.

What a brutal reminder of his reality. The Bingo game had been fun, being around people had been fun. But did the lift of his mood make the later crash even worse? He had felt almost normal again for a little while and the universe wasn't going to let him forget for long that he was living in a nursing home and needed more care than the oldest residents here. He couldn't open himself up like that again. Far safer to do what he had been doing and live silently within his own room, contemplating the bears and eagles outside the window.

He sank into sleep, the events of the last hours leaving him utterly drained. But he was alive. Alive to fight another day.

3

ANNA

The next morning in the parking lot Anna felt completely different. She hardly noticed anything as she eagerly hurried to the entrance of Rosehaven. She was already thinking about the activities she could do with the residents today and only at the last moment saw that the same old woman was sitting outside the door, just as yesterday and the day before, still as a statue, as though she hadn't moved. Like a pin prick to her mood, Anna deflated a little. She felt the air of hope slowly leaking out of her.

But she focused her attention in front of her and built her enthusiasm back up as she walked past Sylvia at the front desk. The same nurse who had rushed past her on her first day was standing next to the desk, making notes on a clipboard.

As Anna approached, the nurse looked up and smiled. She was a young woman, probably younger than Anna herself, a thought that twisted in her stomach. Her honey-blonde hair was twisted along the back of her head and held with a claw clip.

"I'm Becky," she said warmly. "The residents all call me Nurse Becky."

"I'm Anna."

"Great to meet you, Anna. Glad to have you on the team. I'm off to check some vitals! I'm sure I'll see you around soon."

Even after Nurse Becky left, it seemed that her energy hung in the air, a bright shimmer.

Sylvia muttered to herself, "That girl needs less coffee."

That was who Anna should have been. If her life had stayed on track, gone the way she planned, she would have a degree and a career and maybe even a family of her own. Becky was bright and confident and everything Anna wished she could be. The past threatened to drag her back down, the same old thoughts circling around and around in her head. But before she was completely overwhelmed by her own thoughts, she looked up and saw through the open archway that led into the living room and she couldn't help smiling when she saw Mary and Ellie facing off. Anna headed that way.

The two ladies were seated opposite each other near the fire-place and the aftermath of an elementary school performance still lingered in the room. Glittery construction paper back-drops leaning against the wall, the smell of school glue in the air, a construction paper flower abandoned on a side table. Frank was sunk low in a recliner by the window, arms crossed, mouth hanging open in theatrical slumber—though one eye cracked open at Anna's approach before sliding shut again, accompa-nied by a faint, clearly deliberate snore.

Anna looked around for Gabe, but he wasn't there. She felt a little tug in her chest, a tinge of disappointment when she didn't see him. She tried to ignore it. Of course she wanted everyone to participate, that was part of her job. Hopefully he would show up for her group this morning.

"—and I'm only saying," Ellie declared, "if you're going to put on a musical number from *The Sound of Music*, you might try casting someone who can carry a tune! The poor girl playing Maria sounded like a teakettle left on the stove too long."

Mary blinked slowly, hands folded neatly in her lap, her walker parked next to her, floral ribbons wrapped around it. "They are children, Eleanor. And they volunteered their time. It's not Broadway, it's a parish school."

"And that's no excuse for making the Von Trapps sound like a chorus of asthmatic squirrels," Ellie shot back, undeterred.

Mary drew in a breath through her nose. "It is our responsibility to encourage, not to critique."

"And how exactly are they going to improve if no one tells them the truth?" Ellie asked, lifting a well-manicured eyebrow. "What if that poor Maria grows up thinking she's meant to sing professionally? We'd be unleashing a menace on the public."

"They were *eight*, Eleanor."

"An eight-year-old is perfectly capable of singing well. I've heard hundreds of them in my time. Their teacher didn't care a whit or she wouldn't have let them out in public like that."

Frank snorted and muttered without opening his eyes, "I've heard better yodeling from my garbage disposal."

Mary pressed a hand to her chest. "The children tried so hard."

Ellie turned to Anna so quickly her glasses fell from her face down to her chest, caught by their beaded chain. "You agree with me, don't you dear? Bad enough all us old folk are stuck here, they have to torture us too."

Before Anna could say anything, Mary muttered, "I like seeing the children. Fills me with hope."

Ellie rolled her eyes.

Both women looked at Anna and she laughed. "I'll tell the director to get more talented children next time. In the meantime, do you know who that woman is that sits outside every day?"

Ellie's face softened. "That's Harriet," she said. "She likes to listen to the birds."

The room fell silent, each of them reminded of what it was like to see someone's life slowly fading to gray.

Then Mary said, "Remember when Harriet used to finish all the crosswords in the newspaper before anyone else could see them?"

Even Frank chuckled. "Always used pen too," he added.

"She was smart as a whip," Ellie said. "And she never let you forget it."

"Is there anything we could do to include her?" Anna asked.

Mary patted Anna's hand and said, "Just let her enjoy the birds until her time comes."

Anna swallowed a hard lump in her throat. Just like caring for her mother, there was only so much she could do to hold back the inevitable. At least she wanted to provide what joy she could but Mary was right, the birds were what brought Harriet joy and Anna couldn't do any better than that.

"I'm going to go set up," she said. "See you all there, I trust."

"So long as no one cheats today," Frank grumbled. "I'm not going again if you guys aren't going to play fair."

"I'll keep an eye on the troublemakers," Anna said with a wink to Ellie.

As she left the room, she heard Frank say with a sigh, "What a spitfire Harriet was."

Passing by another open door, Anna caught a flicker of movement from the corner of her eye. She slowed. The woman inside looked younger than most of the residents—maybe in her early sixties, with neatly combed gray hair and a pressed blouse. Papers were scattered across the bedspread in careful but overflowing stacks, and the woman was hunched over, tapping and swiping at a cellphone held inches from her face, her brow furrowed in concentration.

Anna paused at the threshold and glanced at the name-plate beside the door. *Doris Carver*. She knocked lightly on the wooden frame. "Doris? You doing okay?"

The woman looked up. Her eyes were startlingly clear and alert, a small smile lifted her face.

"Oh yes," she said. "Just...trying to get in touch with some people, and it's more challenging than I expected."

Anna took a step into the room, careful not to disrupt the careful terrain of folders and notebooks. "Are you going to come down to the group today? We're playing Bingo. Frank's already accusing people of cheating and the game hasn't even started."

Doris chuckled softly. "I wish I could. I really do. But everything happens during business hours, and I have to be available in case one of these calls comes through. Contractors, lawyers...you know how it is. I'm just chained to this phone all day."

Her voice caught for a second, and Anna noticed the fraying edges in her tone.

"If I could just get everything sorted," Doris continued, brushing a hand over a yellow legal pad beside her, "I might be able to go home."

Anna's brows lifted. "Oh wow. That's...that's amazing."

"Yes, well, that's the hope." Doris's smile flickered again, then dimmed. "But I already upset my daughter trying to get her to help. She says I'm being impossible. So now it's all on me. It always is."

Anna shifted her weight from one foot to the other. "Maybe I can come back another time? Sit with you and go over the list?"

Doris shook her head with polite dismissal. "There's not much you can do. I just need to line up the right people. The right permits. The right insurance. It's all just...logistics. And timing." She tapped her phone again and squinted at the screen. "And patience. Which I'm rapidly running out of."

"I get that," Anna said quietly. "Well, I'll leave you to it. I hope you'll come to an activity sometime. Even if it's just to yell 'Bingo' really loudly and scare everyone."

That got a real smile. "Tempting."

As Anna turned to go, Doris was already bent over her notepad again, writing something in small, methodical letters.

The Bingo game was underway and there was no sign of Gabe. Anna pulled out the next Bingo ball and found that it was partly crushed like a ping pong ball that's been stepped on. She wasn't sure if that made it more likely or less likely to come out of the rotating cage, but one thing was certain, this game was far from fair and balanced.

"O-50," Anna said.

Frank picked up his fraying card and brought it up to his nose to look at his numbers, forgetting that he already had a chip down and it plinked lightly onto the floor.

"Frank!" Ellie yelled.

"Huh?"

"You dropped a chip."

He frowned and looked around in confusion. Anna picked it up from the floor and handed it back.

"Anyone know what number that was on?" Frank asked, squinting down at his card.

"Oh for goodness sake," Ellie muttered.

"It's just a game," Mary said. "We aren't even playing for any stakes."

Bingo again?

Anna startled at the sound of Gabe's device and everyone who had been crowded around Frank's card looked over to the door of the room.

There he was—his head resting in the curve of the chair's black headrest, his eyes hard and glinting. They seemed darker than Anna remembered them being.

She caught his gaze for a second, raised her eyebrows in greeting.

He didn't blink. Didn't smile. Just slowly looked away.

Anna's fingers tightened on the dry-erase marker. She turned back to the board where she was writing down the numbers in big block letters as they were called.

"I guess you'll be glad to hear we're doing a different activity next week," she said, trying to keep her voice light. "I just need to get supplies."

He didn't answer except to roll his eyes.

"Joining us today, Gabriel?" Mary asked.

Rather than a reply, he drove his chair out of the room and disappeared down the hallway, the sound of his wheels on the floor squeaking in the silence.

"Well," said Ellie after several moments.

"What bee got in his bonnet?" Frank muttered.

The soft crepe paper skin of Mary's face seemed to crumble and it made Anna's heart wrench.

She clapped her hands. "If he doesn't want to have fun, that's his problem. The rest of us have a game to play."

The sky was the color of dishwater. Gray and flat. Anna's little blue car rattled over the familiar dips in the back road that led to her neighborhood, the air already thick with early summer humidity. She cracked the window anyway, hoping it would cool her cheeks.

Unbidden, the image of Gabe kept looping in her mind. His eyes—sharp, unreadable—and the way he turned away like she was a mistake he didn't want to make twice.

She gripped the steering wheel tighter. "It's fine," she said out loud. "He doesn't owe you anything."

What had she expected? That they'd trade smirks and jokes? That he'd light up just because she was there?

She exhaled hard, fogging the windshield. "Get over yourself."

She reached over and turned up the volume on the radio, hoping for distraction. Some light indie pop flooded the car. It only made her feel lonelier. She flipped the station and froze when a *Pressure Front* song burst from the car speakers.

You kissed me like venom / Sweet and sharp on my tongue.

Her breath stopped short and she had to pull the car onto the side of the road with trembling hands. That was his voice.

Every whisper was a warning / But I crawl back every time.

Heartbreakingly raw and powerful. You could hear the control he had over his voice and you could hear the moment he let it go, breaking in pure emotion.

If loving you is poison, then pour me another glass.

I'll drink 'til I forget my name, and laugh as the world turns black.

She reached for the volume but couldn't turn it down. Couldn't turn it off. She just sat there with the music pouring over her and it was like she was hearing a ghost. This was the voice that used to be his and now it was gone. This voice was reaching out to her from years before, an echo of him that never faded.

Was he still in there? The man who'd sung like that—fierce and vulnerable and so alive? Or had she imagined the connection between them entirely?

"I'm such an idiot," she whispered.

By the end of the song Anna's cheeks were damp, though she hadn't noticed she was crying.

She hit the off button at last, the sudden silence making her ears ring. The sound of birds returned slowly, the faint hum of insects from the trees. Her heartbeat was still too loud in her chest.

Anna leaned forward, resting her forehead against the steering wheel. The plastic was hot from the sun.

She replayed the scene in her mind again. The way the others had stared. How Mary had crumbled. How the silence had stretched between them after Gabe rolled out of the room like a one-man storm cloud.

"You don't owe me anything," she said again, but now it sounded less like self-incrimination and more an acceptance of how things were.

Eventually, she put the car in drive and rolled slowly back onto the road, the tires crunching over loose gravel.

That voice—*his* voice—was going to haunt her all night.

She made one last sharp turn toward home, up a hill. The houses peekabooed between dark green leaves and ropey brown vines. The flash of a red cardinal darted from one tree to another. Once she turned into her driveway she could finally see her mother's garden in the side yard and her father was crouched beside the delphinium beds in the dying light of the day.

He wore his usual uniform: tan slacks, a button-down with the sleeves rolled just so, and his frayed sun hat casting shadows over his brow. He moved with that familiar, deliberate precision, fingers pressing soil around the base of a stalk that drooped in quiet protest. One of the plants Anna's mother had insisted on including, even though they never lasted through the summer. Even now, Henry planted them.

Anna stood still, halfway up the walk, and watched.

The layout hadn't changed. Not in years. Not since before the diagnosis. Coneflowers still flanked the wooden trellis. Snapdragons clustered by the fence. The rosebush near the birdbath bloomed wildly on one side, bare on the other—like it missed her mother's pruning shears. And in the center, the curved bed of delicate columbine, wilting under too much heat, too little shade.

Out of season. Out of sync. But untouched. Her mother had always had unrealistic optimism. Helen's hope and passion could make anyone believe that an orange tree would thrive in New England. She never let reality get in her way. Henry didn't have any of that on his own, he had entirely depended on his wife to create the world for him.

Anna cleared her throat gently and stepped closer. "Need help with that?"

He didn't look up. "It's late for planting, but the nursery had one last tray."

Anna crouched beside him and saw the cluster of delphiniums he'd just buried, already wilting. She shooed away a mosquito by her ankle.

"They won't take," she said softly.

"I know."

They knelt in silence. Bees buzzed near the lavender. Her father adjusted a stake beside a spindly stalk and wiped his hand on his knee. His hand hovered over the next hole, soil dark and soft, waiting. Without looking up he said quietly, as though to himself, "Just because something doesn't bloom doesn't mean you stop trying."

Her chest tightened. She nodded once, too full to speak. Then, quietly, she reached for the trowel and helped him plant the next one.

When they went back inside, sticky with humid sweat, Anna realized she had missed a call from her best friend. Her phone was great at telling her after she had gotten a call instead of when it was coming in.

Somehow Rachel had the time to reach out despite a husband, a career, and a child. While Anna rarely made the first move. Rachel didn't let her fall between the cracks and Anna appreciated that. She texted and they made plans to get together over the weekend.

4

GABE

The air reeked of sweat, beer, and that static charge of electricity that only came after a perfect set. Gabe leaned against the wall of the green room, a towel around his neck, guitar calluses still tingling. His voice was raw in the best way. His heart still pounding from the final chorus of *Paper Crown*. The crowd had screamed his name like it would save them.

Tommy was already halfway through a bottle of something brown and slurred, and Ray was on the phone with his wife, pacing in a circle near the catering table.

But Gabe?

He was glowing.

This was the life. The pulsing throb of a bass line still ringing in his bones. Adrenaline high. A girl's phone number written in eyeliner on his arm.

"Jesus Christ," Ray muttered, finally off the phone. "You really lit them up tonight."

Gabe smirked and took a swig from a bottle he didn't remember grabbing. "I always do."

Ray dropped onto a lumpy beige sofa and dragged his fingers through his hair. "You ever think what comes after this?" he asked.

Gabe raised an eyebrow. "Death, probably. But hopefully not before the Vegas show."

Ray laughed, but it sounded hollow.

Gabe threw the towel at him. "Why the hell would I think about 'after'? This is it, man. Don't let your wife get in your head."

But later, alone in his hotel suite, with the silence pressing in around him after the high had worn off, Gabe sat with his guitar and plucked out a slow, aching riff that didn't belong in any of their songs. A private sound. A softer thing.

He'd always have the music. That was the one thing no one could ever take from him. Whatever future was out there for them, the music would always be there for him. His voice would always be there for him.

But here he was sitting in the stuffy living room of a nursing home in the middle of nowhere listening to Wheel Of Fortune, unable to play his guitar, unable to sing, or even to speak. The universe loves irony, he was certain of that. An old box fan rattled in a corner. Gabe's eyes were closed but he was aware of Mary shuffling in and settling into a chair with her spy novel.

She tended to accidentally read out loud in a mumble and some days he listened to the story, though he never told her that.

Today he continued to drift into memory. He had preserved certain memories in his mind to come back to and relive over and over. And he had no shortage of them to keep him company. He was lucky he had experienced all that he had.

Like the very first time that he heard a *Pressure Front* song on the radio driving in the car. The way he and Tommy and Ray whooped with delight, turning the volume all the way up and rolling the windows all the way down.

Or the time the three of them got matching tattoos. He could still see his on his hip when he was being bathed, roman numerals of the date of their first album's release. The lines slightly faded from black to dark gray.

Once they all got high and recorded total nonsense then played it back in the morning and laughed so hard Tommy fell off a chair.

The hundreds of concerts all blurred together in his mind but he remembered the feel of them. The way you could get high without any substances at all just from the energy of the music and the crowd. Music itself was intoxicating.

He couldn't think about what his life would be if the accident hadn't happened or if he had recovered, it was too painful. He kept his thoughts firmly in the past or in imagination. When the TV wasn't on Wheel of Fortune it was reruns of Murder She Wrote. Those stories fueled his daydreams.

Gabe glanced at the clock on the wall. Mary was still here reading. No activities so it must be the weekend. It had been a long time since he paid attention to what day of the week it was. Not that he was planning to go back. He had to keep his boundaries tight and his emotions in check. It would be too easy to fall apart and never get put back together again. At most he would see the new girl around the halls. He wasn't sure if he was glad he wouldn't catch a glimpse of Anna today or disappointed.

But as he thought about it, traced the feeling around his gut, a sickening realization dawned on him. *Oh you stupid sod, you've got a crush on her.* His face flushed but no one noticed.

What a goddamn cliche. Aging rock star drooling over a beautiful young woman. No, worse than that. Severely disabled aging rock star who can't wipe his own ass drooling over a beautiful young woman who has been hired to entertain. How did he let his guard go down so fast? He felt shame and embarrassment burning through him. *Are you as delusional as all the other creepy old men? She's not even 30 if she's a day and you're...I don't know, probably 48 or 49.*

Mary put her book into a bag on the front of her walker and got shakily to her feet. Instead of walking past Gabe, she stopped when she got to him.

"It was nice having you participate with us in Bingo," she said. "It's good for all of us to have young blood in there. We all liked having you. I hope you'll join us again soon." She smiled and then walked on. He watched her slowly make her way through the arched doorway across polished dark wood floors.

It had been fun, for a few moments during that Bingo game he felt like part of something again. He had nearly forgotten what it was like to have friends and he had definitely forgotten how fun it was to make people laugh. Was it worth the self-hatred he felt now to be that man again?

Enough ruminating. He clicked his wheelchair back on and drove to the dining hall for dinner. After that the independent hairdresser would be in to trim his hair and shave his beard. Routine ruled everything in this world.

That evening, after the aides had hoisted him with the sling and lowered him awkwardly into bed—his limbs bumping against the nylon straps, his pants tugged wrong at the waist—Gabe stared at the ceiling trying to imagine he was anywhere but here.

It wouldn't hurt anything to imagine meeting Anna in another time, another place, another life...would it? He had promised himself to never daydream about a life where the accident didn't happen and yet tonight that's exactly what he did.

The bass still pulsed in his ribs even though the set was over an hour ago. Gabe leaned back on the cracked leather booth, bottle sweating in his hand, stage sweat still clinging to his shirt and the creases of his neck. The club was dark and packed, sticky with beer, but familiar. Safe in its chaos.

Tommy was at the bar, probably talking someone into bed. Drummers are a type. Ray was rambling through some drunken story about hotel shampoo bottles and European customs agents. The drunker he got, the more worried about logistics he got. Gabe was only half-listening.

Until he saw her.

She didn't belong in a place like this. Not in the usual way.

Too bright. Too *real*. Her ponytail was crooked and her oversized tee-shirt had a smear of something green on the sleeve—paint maybe? She looked like she'd stumbled into the wrong scene and decided to stay just to see what happened.

Anna.

He didn't know her name in this version of things. But he *felt* it. Like déjà vu from a forgotten dream.

She was by the wall, sipping something with a straw, eyes scanning the crowd. She wasn't flirting. She wasn't posing. She looked like someone watching from a distance because getting close would make it too loud to think.

Gabe rose before he realized he was doing it, bottle forgotten on the table. His boots thudded on the sticky floor as he walked toward her. The lights shifted—reds, purples, golds—and she turned just as he reached her.

Her eyes met his like she'd been expecting him.

"I liked the second-to-last song," she said before he could speak. "The one that wasn't on the album."

"Oh you noticed that, huh? I didn't peg you for a *Pressure Front* superfan." He leaned against the brick wall beside her. In this reality he was still his full height and he towered over her.

"Appearances can be deceiving."

"I have heard that."

She smiled, a moment of silence in the crazy noise around them.

Then he said, "You're not going to ask for a selfie?"

"Nope."

"Not even an autograph?"

"Should I?"

"Nah," he said. "This is nice."

He wanted to tell her something stupid and earnest. That she made this whole chaotic night feel like it had been leading here. To her.

Instead he said, "You want to get out of here?"

She raised an eyebrow. "That's a strong opener."

"I've got stronger," he said. "But most of them are lyrics."

She laughed. Not loud. Not dramatic. But real. And that sound was the best hook he'd heard all night.

"Alright, Rockstar," she said, finishing her drink. "Show me who you are when no one's watching."

He followed her out into the night like someone chasing a song he hadn't written yet.

The hum of the overhead light interrupted his fantasy and the pain in his neck wasn't helping either. It was going to be a long night if this pain kept him awake. He didn't have a call button in reach and his AAC device was charging on the table. He couldn't ask for pain meds even if he wanted them.

He wasn't expecting anyone else tonight so when Nurse Becky appeared in the doorway, clipboard in hand and her smile bright but soft, Gabe blinked in surprise. He wanted to say, *To what do I owe this pleasure?* But all he could do was shift his eyes toward her and raise one eyebrow.

"Hey stranger," she said, stepping in. "Don't worry, nothing scandalous. I'm just here to check your muscle tightness."

What an opening for a dirty joke. All he could do was roll his eyes.

She laughed. "What, no comeback?" She set down her clipboard and tugged on a pair of gloves. "Let's take a look at those traps."

She pressed her hand into the knot of muscle at the top of his shoulder and immediately sucked in a breath. "Oh my goodness, Gabe. You're *so* tight."

He groaned in his head. *Really? That's the line we're going with?*

Becky was all business now, though. Her fingers moved with practiced pressure, finding the places that had stiffened into something close to stone. "Has no one been stretching you?"

He fixed her with a look that clearly communicated, *what do you think?*

She sighed. "Right. I'm sorry. I'll talk to them again."

He didn't even blink. She'd said that before. Others had too. It never changed much. His chart said "stretch daily." His reality was once a week, if that. And it showed. His limbs had grown stiffer, more uncooperative. His spasms got worse. No one wanted to work that hard. No one thought he mattered that much anymore.

After the accident, he'd clawed through every therapy imaginable—speech, PT, OT. They all stopped when the insurance did. He had plateaued. Which was code for *we're done trying*.

They'd given up on him.

So he had given up on them, too.

Now he barely used his voice device. Most of the aides didn't wait long enough to listen anyway. He was just the silent one in Room 217B. The rockstar who'd fallen. The man who wouldn't die and wouldn't recover. Just stuck. A relic. A burden. A body with a beating heart no one knew what to do with.

And yet.

He was still here.

Night after night. Month after month. Year after year.

He couldn't say why, couldn't put it into words or even thought, but he knew his life still mattered. Even if his observations and thoughts were just for him, they still mattered. If a man thinks a thought that he never shares, is it still meaningful? That was Gabe's Zen kōan.

Becky gently rolled him onto his side. The mattress creaked beneath him, the sheet pulled taut under his body. Her hands moved to his neck, fingers pressing deep under the base of his skull, just where the tension collected like storm clouds. He closed his eyes. It was painful but the good kind of pain.

"You've been locking up in your back again," she murmured, almost to herself. "No wonder your hips are angry."

She worked lower, digging her thumbs carefully into the muscles along his spine. When she hit a pressure point in his lower back, his whole body spasmed slightly, then slackened. A soft moan escaped him—part pain, part relief.

"Sorry," she said, without slowing. "I know it's a lot. But it'll help."

It already was. The deep ache that had hollowed out his ribs for days loosened just enough to let him take a full breath. It felt good.

She rolled him onto his back again and braced a hand under one knee, slowly bending and stretching his legs. He could feel the fibers stretch and pull, like dry rubber bands. He imagined dust lifting off his joints.

Her radio beeped. A long, urgent tone.

She ignored it.

She moved on to his arms. Each elbow cracked softly. Each wrist needed coaxing to uncurl. When she got to his hands, she paused and gently pried each finger open. His palms were damp. She used her thumb to massage the base, then worked each stiff digit and gently wrapped them into night-splints, his fingers trying to curl again against the foam and Velcro.

Finally, she crossed his arms over his chest with a tenderness no one had given him in weeks. Months. Maybe longer.

"Okay, stud," she said, rising. "I'll check on you later."

She gave his shoulder a little squeeze. Then she was gone, tugging her radio from her belt as the door clicked softly shut behind her.

Gabe stared at the ceiling again. But now the light seemed less harsh. Becky was a good soul. An ally in this harsh world and despite how busy she was, she made time for him when she could. It wasn't enough but it was something.

5

ANNA

It was Saturday afternoon and Rachel was standing at Anna's kitchen window with a mug between her hands, looking out at Henry in the garden.

"Well, he certainly is determined," she commented, then came back over to the table where Anna was sitting, laptop open but untouched in front of her. "You know what else takes determination?"

Anna looked up, suspicious. "Don't say it."

"Online dating."

Anna groaned. "Rachel…"

"I'm just saying," Rachel said, setting down her coffee and slipping into project manager mode, eyes already scanning Anna's screen. "You're almost thirty. You've been living with your dad, working at a job that doesn't pay you enough for the amount of finger paint in your hair—"

"It's chalk pastel," Anna muttered.

"See? Even more expensive. And when was the last time you went on a date? Like a real one. Not counting your awkward coffee with that guy from grief group who cried into his muffin."

Anna winced. "He *offered* me a bite of the muffin."

"That's sweet and all, but did you ever see him again?"

Anna reluctantly shook her head and Rachel said, "We're fixing this."

Before Anna could object, Rachel had grabbed the laptop and slid it around to face her. She began typing. "Okay, what are we working with here? Let's make a profile. Name: Anna. Age: 29. Interests...art, kindness, listening to elderly people complain about pudding."

"Rachel!"

"Fine, fine." She typed with speed and confidence. "Art therapist and accidental Bingo champion. Fond of indie music, overwatered plants, and people who say what they mean." She glanced up. "Too much?"

"I hate you."

Rachel grinned. "That's going in the 'what I'm looking for' section."

"What? That I need a new best friend?"

Anna tried to reach for the laptop but Rachel pulled it closer. "Nope. You lost your veto privileges when you admitted you've only been kissed twice in three years."

"That's not even—how did you—?"

"I guessed. But thank you for confirming."

Anna buried her face in her hands. "You're evil."

"I'm your best friend, it's in the job description." Rachel said cheerfully. "Now smile."

Anna looked up just in time for Rachel to snap a photo with her phone. "There. You look adorably annoyed. Men love a challenge."

"I swear, if you post that—"

"Already uploaded," Rachel said. "Now let's swipe."

"Oh my god, you're doing this now?"

Rachel was already gleefully scrolling. "This one's holding a fish. Immediate no. This one has a baby in his arms. It says 'not my baby' in the caption but it's still weird. Ooh this one has a dog and a book collection that includes Murakami. Possible literary bro. Thoughts?"

Anna leaned over warily. "Too many rings on his fingers."

Rachel nodded solemnly. "Wizard cosplay vibes. Next."

Anna gave in with a laugh that surprised even herself. "Okay, okay. But you are not allowed to actually message anyone pretending to be me."

Rachel's grin was mischievous. "Absolutely. Definitely not gonna do that."

Three minutes later, Anna's phone dinged with a message notification. She narrowed her eyes.

Rachel didn't even look guilty. "Just a little icebreaker. I said you were too charming to ignore and that you secretly wanted someone to argue about movie endings with. You're welcome."

Anna sighed, already bracing for the awkwardness. But underneath it all, a tiny part of her—the part that had stopped hoping a long time ago—felt...curious. After all, she had been watching Rachel's life with at least a bit of envy for years now. It looked nice to have someone to partner with in life. Someone who was there when you got home, someone to talk about your day with, someone to listen to all your silly thoughts and stories.

She looked out the window where Rachel had been standing. Her dad was still out there. Quietly tending. He didn't do very much else these days. He had lost his purpose when her mom died. He was an untethered string with nothing attached to the other end anymore.

That was the big risk when it came to putting herself out there. Maybe she wouldn't find someone. But maybe she would, and maybe she'd fall in love, and then she'd be making herself vulnerable to the kind of loss and pain Henry was feeling now. This was the part of the love story no one liked to think about.

Yet the way Henry kept working the garden even though it had never been his passion, trying to coax out the beauty in the flowers her mom loved, that seemed like a love worth striving for.

Maybe it was okay to want something to grow again.

"You okay there?" Rachel asked, her voice quieter than before.

"Yeah," Anna said. And she was. She returned to the table, a new contentment settling over her. She might be behind but she wasn't out for the count yet. "Let's message a few more of these guys."

The late afternoon sun poured in through the kitchen window, hazy and golden, catching on the edges of Anna's scattered papers like a spotlight she hadn't asked for. Activity schedules, messy hand-drawn flyers, a half-drunk cup of tea gone cold. She sat at the kitchen table, hunched in a way her mother used to gently scold her for, pencil tapping against her teeth.

She made a note to research chair yoga instructors to bring in. Maybe an art project with a local school could build community. Perhaps a puzzling tournament for Mary. A talent show for Ellie. Something energizing to take Doris's mind off her troubles. A dessert-making class for Frank, who loved food more than anyone she had ever met. There were so many ideas Anna couldn't even keep up with them.

From outside came the faint crunch of boots on gravel. The back door creaked open a beat later, and Henry stepped inside, smelling faintly of damp earth and marigolds. He moved with the careful quiet he always did now—like sound itself might crack something.

He washed his hands at the sink, methodical. He dried his hands with the towel, hung it back exactly straight.

"What are you doing there?" he asked gently without turning around.

"Planning activities for the residents," Anna said. "Trying to make sure Bingo doesn't conflict with Jeopardy again. That was apparently a crime."

He gave a small laugh, but it sounded empty. He turned just enough to look at her, then nodded. A pause.

"You're enjoying this job," he said slowly. "It seems like a good fit."

There was nothing casual about the way he said it. The words hovered—like he was afraid if he breathed too hard, they'd dissolve. Or turn out to be wrong. Again.

Anna lowered the pencil and looked up. "Yeah," she said. "I think it is."

He nodded again, but it felt more like bracing than agreement. His eyes lingered: measuring. Guarded. Like he wanted to believe her but couldn't quite risk the weight of believing.

"I'm glad," he said. It sounded like he meant it. And also like he didn't trust it.

She couldn't blame him for the doubt, she felt it too. It had been a long time since she trusted herself. Every plan she had for her future had crumbled in the slightest breeze. She didn't know how to build something that lasted, something strong enough to hold her above the storm. What she used to think was solid had turned out to be made of sand. How could she ever believe anything was solid again?

The panic attacks hadn't started until after she went to college. Away from home, even if it was just two hours, she had lost her mooring. The first time it happened, she was walking back to her dorm after a late studio session, the air thick with the smell of rain on hot pavement. One moment she was fine, the next her chest seized up, her heart jackhammering against her ribs. Her breath went thin, as if the oxygen had been pulled from the air. Her vision tunneled, the sidewalk swaying like she was underwater. She dropped her portfolio—charcoal sketches spilling across the grass—and clutched the wall of a nearby building, convinced she was dying.

She remembered the other students glancing over, hesitating, not knowing what to do. And all Anna wanted was to disappear. To not make a scene, to not have everyone know her just for this.

The campus EMTs arrived, their radio static and clipped voices bouncing off the buildings. They said her vitals were fine. That she was fine. Her body didn't believe them.

After that, the attacks came more often. In class, at the grocery store, halfway through a critique. She learned to feel them coming—a prickle at the base of her skull, the heat rising in her face, her breath shortening—and she'd bolt before anyone could see. Eventually she stopped going to critiques at all. Then she stopped going to class.

By the end of sophomore year, her transcript was a graveyard of withdrawals and incompletes.

She hated herself for not being stronger, not able to power through. All the hope her parents had in her, everything they had poured their energy into...amounting to nothing. Anna failed in her first flight from the nest and that was it. For the rest of her life she would be nothing more than disappointment and failed expectations.

It wasn't like her parents were all that happy about her wasting money on studying art anyway. Her mom might have been a creative free-spirit, but she was also second-generation Chinese-American and her rule was always art after practical matters were taken care of. Technically Anna had been majoring in psychology but her plan was to do art therapy to bring her creative side to it. Even that she hadn't been able to follow through on.

She had come home feeling like a prototype that should have worked but didn't; a waste of money, energy, and resources, to be stored away and forgotten on a shelf in the attic.

Years later, Anna still felt like that girl on the way back to her dorm room—back pressed to the wall, watching everything she'd worked for scatter at her feet.

6

GABE

Ellie sat near the windows in her favorite corner—the one with a clear view of the garden, even though she complained about how the roses were trimmed wrong. She was radiant today. Her gray curls had been freshly set and her lipstick was darker than usual, a bold plum that matched her suit jacket. A pair of long earrings danced whenever she turned her head. She'd even swapped her usual pastel blanket for a deep violet shawl folded neatly across her lap.

Gabe knew what that meant. Company.

Sure enough, five minutes later, a voice sliced through the air like over-polished silver. "Mother! I hope we're not too early."

A woman in a crisp slate-blue pantsuit swept into the room with two teens trailing behind her like they were tied to her purse by invisible string. Ellie's daughter looked like someone who ran a consulting firm or chaired a neighborhood committee with Sylvialess efficiency. High heels. Blowout. Designer tote. Her energy was composed chaos, barely held together by practiced charm. Reminded Gabe of his sister.

Ellie straightened in her wheelchair and lifted her chin. "Of course not, darling. You're precisely on time."

"We brought photos from Jackson's robotics meet," the daughter said, already unzipping her bag.

"How nice," Ellie said. "What does the robot do?"

The granddaughter sniggered while the grandson said, "I told you last week, gran. It picks up rocks and throws them."

"Oh." The look on Ellie's face was so baffled that Gabe almost laughed. He could just hear her later saying they don't need robots to do that, little boys do it just fine.

The girl leaned against the wall with her arms crossed and earbuds half-hidden under her hair. Her thumbs moved rapidly over her phone screen.

Ellie attempted small talk, voice high and overly bright. "You know, we used to build papier-mâché sets when I directed the school plays. Nothing moved on its own back then, except the actors."

Her daughter smiled tightly. "Yes, well, times change."

The grandson said nothing. Just fidgeted while his mother quickly flipped through the photos in front of Ellie's face.

Gabe watched Ellie's smile strain at the edges. She adjusted her shawl with her left hand. "How's work?" Ellie asked.

"Busy," the daughter replied. "We just rolled out a new training protocol for our volunteers. I don't know if I told you, but I'm overseeing onboarding now. It's exhausting, honestly."

Ellie nodded politely. "You always were a leader. I remember when you organized that fundraiser for the drama club. What did you call it—'Broadway or Bust'?"

Her daughter blinked. "I don't remember that, sorry."

Ellie looked away for a second, then down at the shawl in her lap. She smoothed it gently, over and over.

"You were brilliant in *Our Town*," she said softly. "Do you remember?"

The daughter glanced at her watch. "I barely remember being in that play, Mom. It was like twenty years ago."

Ellie smiled again, but her eyes were somewhere else now.

Gabe felt the tension like pressure behind his eyes. It was too familiar. The way someone could be *present* and still not really be *with* you. The polite duty of it. The soft, clumsy betrayal of forgetting the most important things.

He thought of his sister again—the saccharine voice, the way she turned every conversation into a project. The way she talked about him like a task to manage. And his mother, always arriving with fresh-baked guilt and a handpicked charity program to involve him in. Lately his parents didn't even come at all. They left it to Vicky to manage him. Vicky, the little sister, who had always been jealous of his success and delighted in having power over him at last.

Once, they'd raced through the marble halls of their South Hadley house—he was ten, she was seven. He remembered the echo of their footsteps on the polished floor, the way she shrieked with laughter but also fury when he reached the library door first.

"You always cheat," she had panted, slamming into his back. "You started before me."

"You said 'Go,' dummy."

"I wasn't ready. You only win 'cause you're older."

"Or better."

She'd gone still then, her face puckering into a thundercloud. He remembered the sting of her palm against his arm—how hard she slapped for such a little kid—and how she stormed off, crying, "I *hate* having a brother!"

He'd laughed it off then, but years later, backstage before a show in L.A., he'd found her there again—older now, perfect manicure wrapped around a clipboard, barking instructions into a headset like she owned the place. "You need me to run this, Gabe. You suck at organizing."

She had started to use his accomplishments to pull herself up. But now that he was broken and hidden away she could claim the spotlight directly. Her new performance was "that poor woman whose brother had the terrible accident. Isn't it so sad for her? She's so strong to carry on after that tragedy."

He kept watching Ellie and her daughter. No one introduced him so the only name he knew was the grandson, Jackson.

"We've got to head out," the daughter chirped, standing up and straightening her jacket. "Traffic on 91 is no joke this time of day."

"Of course, darling. You've given me so much time already."

The granddaughter bent down and gave Ellie a one-armed hug without eye contact. The boy muttered "Bye," barely audible. The daughter leaned in with a quick kiss on the cheek.

"I'll send you the link to the photo gallery. If you can't open it, just ask the staff to help."

Ellie nodded. "It was lovely seeing you," she said.

The three of them swept out of the room in a flurry of handbags, phones, and half-hearted promises.

"We'll come again soon!"

The room felt ten degrees colder when they were gone.

Ellie didn't move for a while. She stared out the window, but her reflection in the glass gave her away. Her shoulders, once lifted with effort and hope, had slumped slightly. Her chin had lowered. Her hands were still.

Gabe wanted to say something like "that sucked" or "they don't deserve you." But he didn't. He slowly tapped out:

You look nice.

His voice box delivered it in that blank, mechanical tone. The words felt too thin.

Ellie turned slowly. Her expression was unreadable for a second. Then her eyes softened.

"Don't you start," she murmured.

But she smiled. Really smiled. Small and true.

He wasn't sure which was worse: that Ellie had expected the visit to be more, or that he'd expected nothing at all.

The TV was on, some crime procedural Gabe wasn't really watching, just letting the noise fill the edges of his day. The artificial brightness of the screen cast flickering blue light across the frame of his wheelchair. His head was tilted back against the padded headrest.

He heard her footsteps before he saw her. Anna was back. There was a flutter of happiness in his chest and he hated himself for it.

"Hey," she said softly. "Hope I'm not interrupting the...murder marathon?"

In another life he would have made a joke. But now, embarrassed by his feelings for her, he made no movement. One thing to be said for losing your ability to speak was no one expected you to fill in the silence. He could watch and wait, see what the other person was going to do. He could get away with not responding to people.

Anna, however, was as persistent as she had been that first day. Definitely one of the things he liked about her. She was young but she had grit. She said, "We were going to do some painting in the resource room. I thought you might like to join us."

He thought of what Mary said. It had been fun spending time with the others in this strange dormitory-like situation. But having fun was going to make him even more vulnerable, open him up to deepening feelings that could never go anywhere. Besides, while Ellie had found a way to include him in Bingo, what was he going to do for painting?

Slowly, he moved the knuckle of his left hand to the screen.

Hard pass.

"Oh come on, Gabe. Could be fun. You don't have to paint a landscape or anything. You could just hang out. Throw stuff at me. Metaphorically. Or literally. I've got smocks."

Hearing her say his name made his heart leap up into his throat and he swallowed hard. He couldn't let her see how she affected him.

Do I look like a finger painter?

She grinned, not backing down. "I don't know. You've got the broody tortured artist vibe. Could be a whole new era. You and a bunch of angry sunflowers."

He couldn't help it, he laughed. A strange choked sound but unmistakable. Anna's face lit up. "I knew it!" she said triumphantly.

He let his head roll just slightly in her direction, his eyebrow raised to convey, *You're ridiculous.*

Anna pretended to misread it completely. "Oh, was that a yes? Great. I'll get your beret."

He tapped again.

Stop.

"Too late," she said, stepping closer and resting her hands on the back of the sofa in front of him like she might actually be considering pushing his wheelchair to the resource room regardless of what he said. "I already pictured it. You, brooding in a shaft of afternoon light, tragic yet majestic. Paint streaked across your face. Women weeping in the hallway."

His lips twitched into a smirk. He slowly lifted his hand back to the device.

You're insane.

"Not certified," she replied with a wink, "but give me time."

For a moment he imagined them again in another life, out at a bar talking about art and music late into the night. Her face aglow with passion and excitement, ruddy from alcohol. He would put chords to what she drew. *You're art and I'm music.*

"So?" Anna said, dragging him back to reality. "You coming?"

He hesitated. It already hurt to not be the man talking art with her over beers at a bar. It would only hurt more if he let her in more. Better to shut things down. Better to be the bitter asshole everyone expected than to let his guard down.

He looked back to the TV.

Anna sighed. "All right, Vincent van Nope, you know where to find me if you change your mind."

He listened to her footsteps leaving the living room. He was alone now, everyone else was probably going to paint. *It's for the best,* he thought.

7

ANNA

The conference room was so humid, Anna felt a sheen of sweat form along her forehead the moment she walked in. Panels of LED lights overhead clashed with the preserved historical elements of the room. Rosehaven was a strange mix of old and new everywhere she looked.

The executive director, Patricia, was sitting at an oak conference table that had a hand-crocheted doily in the center. A few other admin staff were already there.

Anna set her notes on the table, including printouts with bright Post-it flags marking potential guest specialists: a music therapist who brought her own harp, a retired drama teacher who did improv with memory care residents, a visiting dog therapy team that made people light up like Christmas morning.

"I know we can't afford everyone," Anna said, trying to keep her voice steady, upbeat. "But even one a month would make such a difference. I talked to a few—some of them don't even charge. They just want to give back."

Patricia tapped her tablet with the end of a stylus. "We already offer Bingo twice weekly, holiday events, and the art sessions. That's well above minimum state guidelines."

Anna blinked. "But this isn't about guidelines. This is about *quality of life*. About giving them something to look forward to."

There was a pause. Anna looked around the room and no one would meet her eye except Patricia, who said, "Your enthusiasm is noted. But we have to allocate funds where they'll make the most measurable impact."

"I'm not asking for much," Anna said. "Just a little more flexibility. These residents, some of them barely leave their rooms. If we brought in the right people, it could change that."

"Activities," Patricia said coolly, "are not treatment. We are not a therapy center. We are a long-term care facility. Maintenance, not miracles."

Anna's stomach knotted. "Then why even have a programming department?"

Patricia gave a small smile. "Families ask. During tours. It's reassuring."

Anna opened her mouth, then closed it again. She hadn't expected that.

Patricia closed her notebook. "We'll keep doing what's been working. You're free to pursue volunteer options on your own time. But there's no budget adjustment."

There was a long silence.

Anna gathered her papers more slowly than necessary, her throat tight. "Of course."

As she left the room, she felt like she was walking on shaky ground. She had come in full of hope this morning. She left feeling like she'd just seen behind a curtain she hadn't meant to peek through.

Well she wasn't going to let Patricia get in the way of giving the people at Rosehaven everything she could. Flipping through her notes, her eyes landed on a nearby Y that offered private water aerobics classes for groups like theirs. Of all the possible activities they could do, that one stood out as the most fun and impactful. Plus it was something Gabe could participate in too.

There was a small inheritance from her mom. Would it be crazy to use some of that money to purchase this class? Honestly, Anna already knew that was exactly what she was going to do. She felt the obligatory guilt about spending on something like this when she should probably be using it to go back to school but in her heart she already knew she was going to call the gym and set up a water aerobics field trip.

Anna tapped lightly on the doorframe of Doris's room. "Hey, Doris? I brought reinforcements."

She held up her notepad with a grin.

Doris looked up from a pile of papers on her lap and smiled. "Ah, good. I hoped you'd come back."

"I said I would," Anna said, stepping inside. "You said you had a list of things to get in place before you could go home?"

"Mm-hmm." Doris gestured to the chair. "Sit, sit. We've got a lot to get through."

Anna dropped into the seat, flipping open the pad. "Ready when you are."

Doris adjusted her glasses and pulled a folded sheet of notepaper from beneath her crossword book. "First, I'll need to confirm with the pharmacy that my prescriptions will transfer. I want everything delivered weekly, like before. The new girl—Tanya, or maybe it was Tanya's friend—she said they don't do that anymore, but they always say that until you ask twice."

Anna nodded, writing: → **call pharmacy re: weekly med delivery**

"And I need someone to check the stairlift. Last time it stalled halfway up and I had to sit there yelling for fifteen minutes. The cat was no help at all."

"Stairlift. Got it," Anna said, scribbling.

"Oh—and I'll need my dresses from the cedar closet. I told my daughter where they were but she brought me the winter ones. In June. Can you imagine?"

"Cedar closet. Summer dresses."

Anna looked up and smiled. Doris was so calm, so assured. This wasn't chaos or desperation, it was just logistics. A project. One with a beginning, middle, and end. Anna could do logistics.

"I can follow up with your daughter, if you want," she offered.

"Oh, she's impossible," Doris said airily, then softened. "But she'll come around once she sees I'm ready. I just need to show her that I've got everything handled."

By the time Anna stood up, her notepad was full of stars and arrows and phone numbers.

"Same time tomorrow?" Doris asked, already reaching for another list.

"You got it," Anna said, squeezing her shoulder gently. "We're getting you home."

And she meant it.

Evenings at Rosehaven had a rhythm. Post-dinner quiet, the clink of trays being collected, the low murmur of televisions playing game shows or reruns in the living room. Most of the staff were already moving like ghosts through the halls, eyes on the clock, counting down to shift change.

Anna was walking back to the resource room after checking the mail for a new set of knitting needles she ordered when she saw the back of Gabe's wheelchair in the dark dining hall.

She poked her head in.

"You're still here?"

No answer. Not exactly surprising but she felt compelled to double-check.

She stepped further in, came around to see his face. He wasn't moving at all. He sat rigid, his mouth set tight, the wheelchair in stand-by.

"You know they'll be looking for you soon," she said, trying to keep her voice light. "Night meds, catheter checks, all that fun. Did you shut your chair off out of pure rebellion, or...?"

No response.

No blink. No button press.

The smile faded from her lips. Something wasn't right. She walked closer, crouched beside him.

"Hey," she said, softer now. "Gabe? What's going on?"

His eyes found hers. A slow blink. The tension in his jaw deepened, visible now—like it hurt just to be.

Anna scanned him. His fingers were curled tighter than usual. The bones of his forearms were visible under his skin. His legs looked like they were braced against something invisible. His jaw was clenched, his breathing shallow. His arms were locked in place. His knees twitched ever so slightly.

Her heart kicked. "Are you...stuck?"

One blink.

"Oh God." She sat back on her heels, her hand covering her mouth for a moment. "I thought—" her breath shook, "I thought you were being a stubborn ass."

From his throat came a faint sound—half breath, half laugh.

She let out a breath, nearly a laugh herself. "Okay," she said. "Well, now I feel like the ass."

She touched his shoulder and felt the tightness through the fabric of his tee shirt, the bracing of muscles that would not let go.

Anna ran to the kitchen and turned on the hot water then dashed back to Gabe's side while waiting for it to heat up. She wasn't entirely sure what to do but she took one of his elbows and began moving it in small, careful circles. Not pulling. Not forcing. Just coaxing.

"Okay," she murmured. "Passive range-of-motion. We did this with my mom."

His breath remained shallow, his body vibrating with effort, but his eyes tracked her. Sweat dripped from the sides of his face.

She moved to his wrist. Rolled it. Flexed his stiff fingers one by one. She could feel the tension like a live wire beneath his skin.

"You're going to be okay," she whispered. "I'll be right back."

She dashed over to a staff intercom and pressed the call button, trying to sound calm.

"This is Anna in activities. I need assistance in the dining hall. Gabriel Whitlock is experiencing severe spasticity. Can I get Nurse Becky, please?"

Then she ran back to the hot water and soaked a cloth, dripping water behind her as she ran back to him and pressed the warmth gently to his forearms one at a time, watching his face for signs of relief but there was nothing. His eyes were squeezed shut and his forehead was shiny with sweat.

Anna looked at the chair controls trying to figure out how to turn it back on and tilt it but she had no idea how and Gabe couldn't direct her. Since she couldn't move him with the chair she tried to adjust the pressure on his body in other ways. She gently slid her fingers under his seat cushion and adjusted the angle.

Nothing was working. Anna was starting to feel desperate. She couldn't stand to see him in so much pain.

When Nurse Becky arrived Anna was back to trying to gently stretch and move his arms. Becky rushed to Gabe's side, breathless.

"Thank God you caught this," she said, kneeling beside them. "Hey, Gabe. I'm gonna help now, okay?"

He blinked once.

Becky gave him a soft smile, already pulling out a small bottle from her med pouch. "You've got a PRN dose of baclofen on file. That's going to help."

As she administered it, Anna stayed close, using the damp cloth to keep sweat out of Gabe's eyes. She remembered hearing that his blood pressure had to be monitored closely and a whole new wave of worry crashed over her.

"Here," Becky said, "Lift under the shoulder, not the elbow. Let his body tell you where the resistance is."

Anna followed her lead, feeling the subtle difference as they shifted him together. The weight and heat of his body made her breath catch in her throat even in a moment like this. She hadn't touched a man in years and now she was so close to a rock god that she could feel his breath on the delicate skin of her neck.

Focus, Anna, now is not the time.

After a few more minutes, something finally gave. The tightness eased, slowly, the tension draining away. His jaw unclenched. His fingers twitched. And his eyelids relaxed. After one quiet moment he opened his eyes.

Becky breathed a sigh of relief and patted Gabe's knee.

"You did good," she said to Anna. "Most people panic."

"It's okay, I scheduled my panic for later," Anna said but her voice was shaky.

Becky gave her a look that Anna didn't know how to interpret. "I'll get him to his room," she said.

Anna looked at Gabe and said, "Don't get used to this. I still think you're a stubborn ass."

As Becky pushed his wheelchair through the door Anna heard the AAC respond:

Fair.

She shook her head with a smile. Same old Gabe.

Of all things, Anna had to rush home for a date. As she was throwing her papers into a bag, Nurse Becky appeared again, touched her elbow and nodded her head to a side corridor. When Anna followed, Becky said in a hushed tone, "That shouldn't have happened."

"What do you mean?" Anna asked.

"They're not taking proper care of Gabe. Or any of the residents. I don't think it's malicious but I think Patricia burned out a long time ago. The budget is so tight and the people they hire just don't care enough to do the whole job. If Gabe was getting the right care he wouldn't be having episodes like that."

Anna's throat felt tight. "So you're saying that he's in a lot more pain than he needs to be?"

Becky nodded. "I'm doing my best to prevent it but there's only so much I can do myself."

Helplessness clouded the edges of Anna's vision. The familiar feeling rising through her core. As she had promised, a delayed panic was starting to grip her. There had been so little she could do to ease her mother's pain and there was literally nothing she could do to ease Gabe's. But his was unnecessary which made it even worse. Her breath sped up and she gripped a grab bar on the side of the wall. Do not have a panic attack, she told herself. Becky was saying something but Anna could no longer understand the words.

She forced herself to do the grounding exercise.

Five things I can touch. The metal bar I'm holding. The fabric of the pocket of my jeans. My hair on my neck. The air from the box fan on the floor. The textured wallpaper behind the bar.

Four things I can see. Becky's manicured fingernails. The door to the resource room. Knots in the woodgrain of the floor. My sneakers.

Three things I can hear. A vacuum cleaner running. Staticy beeps from Becky's walkie-talkie. A television on.

Two things I can smell. Citrus cleaning spray. Mothballs.

One thing I can feel. Tightness in my stomach.

The cloud started to clear and now she could make out that Becky was saying, "I can see how much you care about him and I thought you should know."

"Thanks," Anna said, even though she still didn't know what she could do about it. "Does he have any family who could put pressure on the admin?"

"I don't know," Becky admitted. "If he has visitors, I haven't been around to see them. Unfortunately, a lot of the families just want a relatively safe place to store someone it seems."

Anna's chest sank and she had to admit to herself that before she started working here she saw a nursing home and old people the way most do, as ghosts or shadows of a former life with nothing really left. But now that she spent every day here, she saw that they were the same people they had always been and their lives had been stripped away from them. Maybe it had to be that way but it didn't mean they had become less.

The whole drive back she couldn't stop thinking about Gabe. How scary it had been to see him like that. He had looked so vulnerable and so alone; trapped in his body and unable to even say he was in pain. Anna had wanted to touch his face, brush the damp hair back from his forehead with her fingers. She hadn't. She didn't know if he would want that. She didn't know what he wanted.

He never said. And she didn't know how to ask without making it worse.

You're just the activities coordinator. Not a therapist, not a nurse, not his girlfriend, not anything. What are you even doing?

Except—except the way he looked at her sometimes. Like he was examining her soul. Like he was testing her with those deep, brown, too-aware eyes. And when he didn't want to be seen, he went cold. Shut down. That little smirk vanished and he became stone again.

How much he was able to convey with the slightest changes in his facial expressions was remarkable. There had been a moment, right after Becky gave the meds and his limbs started to ease again, where he turned his head, barely a few degrees, and looked at Anna like...like he was surprised she was still there. And that—*that* look had undone her.

As soon as she got home she had to rush through the world's fastest shower and put on a fresh plain shirt and a jersey skirt then run right back out the door for her date.

The restaurant was one of those trendy fusion places Rachel had picked from a list—dim lighting, faux rustic wood beams, and Edison bulbs hanging in clusters like overripe fruit. Anna tugged self-consciously at the hem of her tee-shirt as she walked in.

The hostess led her to a small booth near the back. He was already there. Liam.

He looked...too familiar. Same kind of easy, flannel-shirt-and-good-teeth charm her first boyfriend had. The one she'd ghosted in college when the panic attacks got so bad she couldn't leave her dorm room without vomiting.

"Anna, right?" Liam stood and gave her a quick hug. He smelled like laundry detergent. "You look just like your photo."

She smiled, unsure what to say. "Thanks."

They sat. Small talk came surprisingly easily at first. He asked about her favorite food, favorite movie, if she liked hiking. His voice was warm and practiced, like someone used to first dates going well.

"So," he said, leaning forward a bit, "what do you do?"

And there it was.

The question that always snagged.

At least now there was an answer even if it wasn't a five year career plan. "I work at a long-term care facility," she said. "As an activities coordinator."

He smiled politely, then cocked his head. "Oh, that's cute. Like finger painting with old people?"

"Only when we're not too busy overthrowing the jigsaw puzzle cartel."

Liam gave a slow blink. "Huh. Interesting."

Not even a smile. Did he not realize she was joking? She took a long sip of water. She could feel the pressure rising in her chest.

"I used to be in school for psychology," she said, too suddenly. "I had to take some time off. Family stuff. Health stuff. I'm—just now getting back into things."

Liam gave her a smile that didn't reach his eyes. "Well, hey, that's great. You're finding yourself. That's important."

The words hit her like a slap. Finding herself. As if she'd been on some whimsical journey of self-discovery instead of wiping her mother's fevered brow and cleaning up vomit and forgetting who she was because grief ate holes in her brain.

She laughed softly, but it came out brittle. "Yeah. I guess."

Liam had moved on. He was telling a story now about refinancing his condo and taking his dog to Vermont. She nodded, but her eyes were starting to sting. Would Liam even notice if she started crying at the table?

She stood abruptly. "I'm sorry—I have to go."

Liam blinked. "Wait, what?"

"Sorry," she said again, already grabbing her bag. "It's not you. I just...I thought I was ready for this."

Anna sat in her parked car in the lot behind the restaurant, the glow of the dashboard casting soft shadows on her face. She hadn't even started the engine. Her hands were still in her lap. She stared through the windshield where a couple was laughing near the valet stand, arms casually looped together like they belonged there. Like people who knew how to keep moving forward.

She turned toward her phone, lying screen-up in the cupholder.

Rachel: *How's it going??*

Anna swallowed.

She picked up the phone and opened the thread. Typed.

It was fine.

Backspaced.

He was nice.

No. That wasn't it.

I left early.

Her thumb hovered. Deleted that too.

She tried again.

I think I'm not built for this. Or I missed the part where everyone learned how to be normal.

She stared at it, heart thudding.

Then she deleted the whole thing and dropped the phone into her bag.

What could she even say?

The silence inside the car was thick. Her throat ached with words she couldn't give shape to. There was nothing big or dramatic about what happened. Nothing she could point to and say *this is why I left*. It was a thousand small things: the way he smiled when she stumbled through explaining her job, the way his words skimmed across the surface of everything.

She leaned forward and pressed her forehead to the steering wheel.

This was when she most wanted to have her mother. That was who she could talk to about dating and life and fears. Everything. "You would know what to do," Anna whispered into the silence. "You could tell me how to get moving except that it's you I have to move from." Even alone she couldn't quite say "move *on* from."

After a long while, she started the car. The engine rattled to life with a familiar hum. She flicked on the headlights, backed out of the space, and drove home in silence.

Without thinking about why she was doing it, at home she pulled her laptop onto her bed and typed *Pressure Front* into the search bar on Spotify.

Album covers appeared in a neat line, years of his life frozen in squares of color. She scrolled to the very bottom and clicked on the earliest one. A raw guitar riff split the quiet house wide open and she scrambled for her earbuds, afraid she would wake her father. It felt almost obscene, how alive this sound was compared to the sterile quiet she'd left behind at Rosehaven.

Then his voice came—reckless, full-throated, aching. *If I burn down the road, at least it's my fire. If I choke on the smoke, I'll be my own pyre.*

It went on and on, the voice raw, fierce, and angry. The emotion pouring out of him was almost unbearable to hear, to hold. Anna hugged a pillow to her chest, stunned. This was Gabe? This furious, hungry man? She played the whole album straight through, then queued up the next. One after another. Midnight slid into one a.m., then two, but she couldn't stop.

The songs were wild, desperate, searching for meaning. He wasn't just singing—he was tearing himself open. Fans must have screamed those choruses back at him with tears in their eyes. And now that same man sat quiet in a wheelchair, his words rationed one knuckle-tap at a time. The contrast startled her but it didn't feel like a contradiction—it felt like the wholeness of both sides of a coin.

She had heard his songs before but usually in the background, as part of a milieu around her, or just one-off on the radio. She heard them in a completely new way when she played them in order one after another, giving them her full attention.

When *Nowhere but Here* began, the melody caught her instantly. Simple, haunting, unforgettable. By the second chorus—*If I'm lost, I'm lost with you / If I'm found, it's only true / That there's nowhere, nowhere but here / Nowhere but here to belong*—her eyes stung. She replayed it twice, then a third time.

When she finally closed her laptop, Anna felt that she knew him in a whole new way.

That night she dreamed about him. In the contradictory logic of a dream, nothing about him had changed—his gaze still held that quiet, devastating intensity, that way of listening with his whole being, still and focused as if the world outside them didn't exist—but here, he moved. He touched her. His fingers curled against her skin, warm and deliberate, sliding along her jaw, down her throat, leaving trails that made her breath catch.

He leaned in close, his mouth brushing her ear, murmuring words she couldn't quite make out but still felt, low and rough, sending a shiver through her center. She woke confused and shivering.

Maybe Rachel was right. She did need to get out more, date more. She couldn't let this disaster of a date with Liam put her off. She was clearly longing for closeness and connection. And starting tomorrow she was going to remember that Gabe could be a friend and nothing more. There were so many things she admired about him as a person and they were all great qualities in a friend.

8

GABE

Nurse Becky had given Gabe something to help him sleep last night after the incident but instead of sleep he had stayed in a half-dream state for a long time. His body had finally released the tension but despite how exhausted he was from the attack, sleep didn't come.

Most of the night he was deep in thought. Anna had come through for him in a way he never expected. She was at Rosehaven to run activities. She wasn't a nurse or a caretaker or an aide. As far as he knew, she had no reason to recognize a medical problem like that.

But she had noticed. She had somehow seen when something was wrong though no one else had.

He had never seized up that badly before and he was rattled from the experience but he was also intrigued by Anna's tenacity. Once again she had stayed when anyone else he knew would have run away.

She moved towards problems instead of away from them. It was an unusual quality and he respected it.

Over the course of the night he came to the conclusion that he was done trying to avoid her friendship. It would be what it would be. He would enjoy her bright company while she was here and miss her when she left. It was the nature of life. He didn't have it in him to fight against human connection any more.

She seemed to have decided on a similar truce as she burst into his room shortly after he got out of bed.

"You look better," she said as she hopped up onto his bed.

He used the joystick to turn his wheelchair toward her and smiled. A real smile. She grinned back.

"You know," she said, "I've been wondering how you came to be here in Western Mass of all places." She pulled out her phone. "Let's find out."

He wondered if he should try to stop her, knowing what inevitably came up if someone searched his name. Instead he watched her face as she started scrolling. "Oh, you are from near here. I never knew that," she said. "I always think of musicians as being from Florida or Seattle."

Then her playful expression turned suddenly somber and he knew she had found the video. After a few moments her face drained of color. She gasped and then looked back up to him.

It was a fan video shot on an old iphone but it clearly showed the moment the rigging came loose above him on the stage. Anna didn't have the sound on but Gabe knew every second of the brief video. The spotlight crashed down directly on his head and then the video turned into a mess of blurry movement and screams.

"I'm so sorry," Anna said, her voice shaking.

Gabe shrugged one shoulder as best he could.

"I should have known that would come up." She stared down at her phone silently for several moments. Then she said, "I can't believe it was eleven years ago. Feels like it couldn't have been more than five."

Gabe tapped a few words on the AAC:

Tell me about it.

Anna smiled. "Time does get away from us, doesn't it?" she said.

Gabe nodded. He didn't know it had been eleven years either. A quick calculation. Oh God that meant he was 51. What a gut punch. And no one had even celebrated his 50th. His sister never mentioned it.

He couldn't help wondering if there had been any medical advances in that time that might help him. After the accident he had tried everything there was but since then he had just been kept stable as much as possible. Were there new therapies, new drugs or new surgeries that could give him back a little of what he had lost? Who could he even ask about it?

Anna was watching him and he saw the pity and sadness on her face. If anything was going to illicit pity it would be that video. Time to lighten the mood. She kept watching him patiently as he tapped on the AAC device.

Crushed it. By it I mean my skull.

Anna blinked in surprise. "Wow, Gabe. That's a whole new level of dark. Respect."

He nodded his head as though tipping a cap and she laughed.

"I suppose you have always been known for the intense lyrics, haven't you?"

He didn't have to answer that, everyone knew it was true.

"So, will you come to activities today?" she asked. "It's music themed. No more Bingo until next week."

He smiled and gave a slight nod.

The resource room buzzed with the clatter of chairs and walkers shuffling and scraping. Anna knelt near the Bluetooth speaker, her phone open with a curated playlist of "Songs You Loved in Your 20s." Some of the residents were already grumbling that their twenties involved Glenn Miller, not Fleetwood Mac.

"Let's make this interesting," she said, standing and clapping her hands. "Whoever can guess the most songs gets to pick the next playlist theme."

"If I win, it will be showtunes," Ellie declared, raising one eyebrow. Her wheelchair had a freshly draped scarf across the back like it was about to make a theatrical entrance.

"No showtunes!" Frank barked, crossing his arms. "Last time I had *Memory* stuck in my head for a week. Felt like the damn cat was stalking me."

Gabe was parked just inside the edge of the group, his eyes watching Anna intently.

With a small smile, she walked over to stand by his chair. "Want to be on my team?"

"Not fair! You can't have a professional musician on your team!" Frank shouted. "No teams."

Gabe didn't answer but after a brief moment he made a low, brief hum in his throat.

"Oh my god," Anna said, pretending to gasp. "Are you making *sounds*? From your vocal chords? Sir, we didn't authorize that."

Mary blinked. "Oh, my."

Gabe hummed again, this time adding a few more notes. The room fell quiet.

Frank squinted. "Wait a minute...I know that. That's—Springsteen?"

Ellie's eyes lit up. "Yes! *Dancing in the Dark*! Good heavens, I haven't heard that in years."

Anna turned back to Gabe, eyes wide. "You can hum tunes? Like...whole melodies?"

He gave the slightest nod, head tipping gently on the headrest.

"You are full of surprises! Okay, we're playing a new game now," Anna announced. "Gabe's in charge. Guess That Tune, Whitlock Edition."

Frank leaned forward. "You telling me Rock Star's gonna test us now? Bring it on."

Gabe hummed again—this one slower, with a heavy rhythm. Mary tilted her head.

"That's... oh, it's on the tip of my—*House of the Rising Sun*, isn't it?" Her voice sounded a little breathless, almost triumphant.

Gabe's brows lifted just enough to register a silent "well done."

Ellie clapped. "My goodness, Mary! Who knew you had a jukebox brain?"

Mary just gave a modest smile. "My husband played it on guitar. Every Saturday morning."

The next round brought chaos. Gabe hummed something fast and erratic.

"That's nothing!" Frank shouted. "That's just noise."

"No," Anna said. "It's something but I can't put my finger on it."

She looked at Gabe as he stopped humming, waiting for an answer. "You're judging me."

He blinked, and that faint smile grew.

"You are! You're doing the condescending rock god smirk. Don't think I can't see it."

Still silent, but the gleam in his eyes was unmistakable now.

"It's Queen," Ellie said. "*I Want To Break Free*. He's just not doing the chorus part to trick us."

Gabe rewarded her with a cheeky grin.

The next one made Anna clasp her hand to her chest. "No," she whispered. "You're kidding me. That's *Pressure Front*, isn't it? That one with the weird tempo change? Um...*Lucky Ones*."

He hummed again giving her exactly that part. His own song.

Anna sat back, grinning wide. "Now you're showing off."

Gabe didn't deny it.

They kept playing. Anna was laughing, face pink from joy, as Gabe's eyes sparkled with wicked humor. Ellie mimed air piano. Frank shouted, "This is a circus," but didn't actually move.

When the game finally wound down, Anna knelt again beside Gabe's chair. "That was amazing," she whispered.

He locked eyes with her and time changed again, slowing to a crawl around them. He had the urge to hum one more thing. *The Air That I Breathe* almost rose up in his throat. But that was a step too far. He blinked to break the spell and Anna came back to herself.

"Okay, you name the winner," she said.

Gabe nodded toward Ellie, who called out, "Next week: showtunes. I'll bring the feather boas!"

Frank groaned. Gabe hummed the first few notes of *Memory* and the whole room broke into laughter again.

9

ANNA

Anna balanced a tub of paintbrushes on her hip as she nudged the resource room door open with her foot. "Okay, art crew," she called. "Let's make some questionable masterpieces."

Ellie rolled in from the hallway. "Are we creating *art* or just humiliating ourselves again in public?"

"Why can't it be both?" Anna grinned and handed her a palette.

Frank sat at the table, arms crossed, glowering at the setup like it had insulted his wrench collection. "This crap smells like the glue the nuns used in school."

Mary took her seat more delicately, adjusting the cuffs of her soft pink sweater. "Let's hope there's no glitter this time. My scarf is still sparkling from last week."

"No glitter," Anna promised. "Just paint and the unspoken judgment of your peers."

Ellie cackled. "So, like high school art class. Excellent."

As Anna handed out supplies, Frank muttered, "Won't be here long tomorrow. My son's dropping by."

The room quieted, just briefly.

Anna blinked. "Oh! That's...nice?"

Frank shrugged. "Sure. Whatever. Probably wants to check if I'm still breathing."

Ellie tilted her head. "We didn't know you had a son."

"I don't talk about him much," Frank said, too quickly. "He lives out in Boston. Real busy."

Anna watched him pick at the edge of his paper. His voice had gone tight around the edges, more brittle than usual.

"Is he coming for a special reason?" she asked gently.

Frank didn't look up. "Suppose he thinks it's been too long. Wants to talk. Whatever that means."

Mary murmured, "Well, that's something, isn't it? A long drive just to visit."

Frank gave a noncommittal grunt.

Gabe, watching from the edge of the room in his chair, tapped slowly on his device:

Hug or lecture?

That drew a sharp huff from Frank. "Neither, if I'm lucky. Just wants to talk. And you know what that means."

Gabe's reply came slower this time but everyone waited.

Guilt trip. One way. No refunds.

Ellie raised an eyebrow. "Frank, do we need to rehearse your lines? I've got cue cards and passive-aggressive facial expressions ready to go."

Frank smirked. "Nah. I've got my own script. 'Yep, still here. Yep, still eating the pudding. Yep, not dead.'" He flicked some dried paint off his brush. "That should cover it."

Anna felt a flicker of unease in her chest. The way he'd said *he*, the too-flat tone. No fondness. No warmth. No specific name. Frank, who could talk for fifteen minutes straight about the best way to fry a porkchop, couldn't seem to form a full sentence about his kid. She didn't push. But she glanced at Gabe. And Gabe—who missed nothing—was already looking at her. He gave her the faintest nod, just once. They'd both noticed something was off.

Still, Anna moved on, keeping the tone light. "Well, Frank, in case you need an emotional support painting to get through the visit, now's the time."

Frank grunted again but picked up his brush.

"That's the creative spirit," Anna said, slapping a piece of watercolor paper in front of him. "Paint your feelings."

"I did that once," Frank muttered. "Came out looking like a busted carburetor."

"Modern art would love you," Anna replied cheerfully.

Mary smoothed her lilac skirt. "I do hope the brushes have better bristles this time. Last week mine shed like a golden retriever."

Anna laughed. "New brushes. Specially selected for holy ladies and grumpy gentlemen alike."

"Saint Luke was a painter, you know," Mary murmured, dipping her brush into sky blue. "Though I doubt he used plastic palettes from the dollar store."

Anna turned to Gabe with a sly grin. "Don't think you're exempt from this activity, Mr. Whitlock," she said.

He squinted suspiciously at her and she pulled out a small table easel with a flourish. "I saw this online," she said. "People who can't hold a paintbrush with their hands can use their teeth."

Gabe's eyes opened wide and everyone else stopped what they were working on, looking over.

Anna started setting up a canvas close to the edge of the table and pulling out paints. Eventually Gabe's AAC said:

You've got to be kidding.

"Not even a little," Anna said. She dipped a paintbrush in a dab of blue paint and held it out to him, handle towards his mouth.

At first it didn't look as though he was going to take it. Anna and Gabe stared at each other for a long second. But then the intensity of his gaze shifted back to playful and he bit his teeth down onto the paintbrush handle.

Everyone cheered and he rolled his eyes.

Anna ran around to the back of his chair to make sure he could reach the canvas. Gabe leaned forward, his arms braced on his armrests. The paint touched the canvas, but the brush wiggled and fell from his mouth, hitting the side of the table and splattering blue on the floor.

Ellie clapped once, delighted. "See? He's a natural. Picasso had his Blue Period—Gabe's having his Blue Floor Period."

Anna was already wiping up the splatter. "You're just getting warmed up. Let's try again."

He gave her a mock, long-suffering look but opened his mouth for the brush anyway. This time, when the tip met canvas, he was able to make a stroke. A thick stripe of blue slashed across the canvas.

Frank, watching from his seat, snorted. "Kid, if you were painting a car like that, you'd be fired in five minutes."

Anna swapped brushes for a thinner one. "Okay, finesse this time."

The brush wobbled, wavered, then dropped again, this time landing bristles-down in a cup of rinse water, which immediately tipped and spread a diluted rainbow across the table.

Ellie slapped the table with her good hand. "Abstract expressionism! He's channeling Pollock now!"

Tell museum I'm available.

"Well then, you'll need to sign this masterpiece when it's done," Anna said.

Gabe tilted his head, eyes glinting.

With my teeth?

Everyone laughed and Anna definitely noticed Gabe's delight whenever his jokes landed. How different he was now from the first few days. It was like he decided to flip a switch and Anna was glad he did.

She was cleaning up while everyone else painted. She was hyper aware that Patricia could show up at any moment and object to the mess of this activity. But then she caught Gabe's eye and the paintbrush fell again, this time directly into his lap.

"Oh no! Your best sweatpants!" Anna teased. Even Gabe laughed in his unique way.

Anna went to retrieve the paintbrush for him but it was laying directly across his crotch and when she touched his inner thigh trying to grasp the brush, Gabe inhaled sharply.

Her eyes flew to his and their gazes locked. Her hand froze where it was and Gabe groaned softly. Against her fingers, she felt the push of his cock hardening and that's when she snatched her hand away with a gasp. No one else seemed to have noticed.

She tried again to retrieve the paintbrush and plucked it from his lap as quickly as she could. She swallowed and held it back out to Gabe's mouth, blushing as his lips wrapped around the handle, his dark eyes never leaving hers.

Anna retreated to the other side of the room and sat down in a wooden chair, trembling. She had assumed he was paralyzed but clearly he could feel even if he couldn't move. She didn't quite know what to do with that information. Against all reason, she was fighting off thoughts of touching him more.

He's a patient where you work, she reminded herself. *He is deeply vulnerable. What is the matter with you? You shouldn't be feeling things like this.*

While Anna tried to become a professional again, everyone else was focusing seriously on their painting. Including Gabe, who was getting a hang of how to hold the paintbrush not too tight and not too loose.

Eventually Anna walked back around and when she came to Gabe's canvas, she gasped.

The scene was unmistakable. Blue and black circles gave the feel of a crowd of people, the strokes full of energy. The edge of the stage in the foreground. Dark black lines across the top giving the impression of the light rigging.

Slowly everyone else gathered around behind Gabe's wheel-chair to look at the painting. Every single person recognized the significance of the scene.

"You remember it all, don't you?" Anna said softly.

He used his teeth to drop the paintbrush to the table and lay back in his wheelchair, his face drained and exhausted. He tried to speak but since his brain no longer had the wiring to do it, the sound he made was only a moan that almost had the cadence of a word. Anna saw the frustration and she wanted to do something to make it better. She wished there was some way she could give him his voice back. She hated to see how hard he worked for every single word.

That night Anna couldn't stop thinking about the rough image Gabe had painted the moment she gave him the tools to do it. Raw and so full of emotion, it took her breath away. He was an artist just as much as she was; they both used anything and everything in front of them to pour out all their thoughts, feelings, and vision of the world. They both hungered to com-municate what was in their thoughts. But since every medium was imperfect, they kept on creating and creating and creating in every new way, trying to find that transcendent method to finally create sense out of the mess of life.

The next day Anna was organizing the supply cabinets in the living room, searching for forgotten materials to use in further art projects. Partly because she had been meaning to do it and partly because Gabe was here and she was finding herself wanting excuses to be near him. She didn't want to think too hard about that.

Frank was in his usual recliner but his pretending to sleep was working even less than usual because he was waiting for his visitor. Finally a figure appeared in the doorway and Frank sat up a little straighter.

"This is my son, David," Frank said gruffly, announcing it to the room in general.

Anna and Gabe glanced at each other. This explained some things. "David" was wearing a tulip-sleeved pink shirt, a white silk circle skirt, and diamond earrings.

"Deborah," she corrected without malice and smiled as she reached out a hand to shake.

"It's wonderful to meet you," Anna said, accepting the hand. "I'm Anna. And this is Gabe."

"Oh, it must be family day," Deborah said brightly. "Are you visiting your father too?"

Anna was stopped in her tracks but Gabe was surprisingly quick on the AAC.

Wife.

"Oh, I'm so sorry to have assumed," Deborah said while Anna glared at Gabe and he grinned back.

"She's the activities coordinator," Frank said.

Gabe shook his head as though to say *ruining my fun.*

Deborah looked more confused than ever.

"Sorry," Anna said. "Let's start over. I'm Anna, the new activities coordinator for Rosehaven. Gabe likes to kid. Should we give you and your dad some space for your visit?"

"He's just here to check that I'm alive," Frank grumbled.

"Well I could just check off the box on my list," Deborah said, "But I was thinking we could go to the rare car show that's going through Worcester right now." She winked at Anna as Frank began hemming and hawing about how he might be able to do that.

"You going to wear that?" Frank asked at last.

"Yep. Take it or leave it," Deborah said.

"I'll get my coat," Frank said, heaving himself up out of his recliner and heading to the door.

"Dad, it's 90 degrees out," Deborah called after him. She paused and smiled at Anna and then Gabe. "It was nice to meet you both." To Gabe specifically she added, "Cool shirt."

It was a *Pressure Front* tour tee-shirt from 2005. Deborah was gone before either Anna or Gabe could figure out if she had recognized him.

10

GABE

The living room was the perfect place to go when you wanted entertainment. You could count on at least an episode of Murder She Wrote but more often than not it was some kind of improv comedy that ended up happening. Especially when both Ellie and Mary were there at the same time.

"I once organized a talent show here where our lead singer lost her voice halfway through her number. Did she quit? Of course not. We swapped her song for interpretive kazoo and turned the whole thing into a comedy sketch," Ellie was saying as Gabe drove his wheelchair into the room. He had no idea who she was talking to or what had preceded this comment and it didn't matter at all.

Mary looked up from her needlepoint with a smile. "Is that when you borrowed my good scarf for a prop and ruined it?"

Ellie didn't blink. "It was red. It was dramatic. And it had fringe. Worth the sacrifice."

Gabe's lips twitched.

Mary spotted it. She turned slightly toward him, smoothing her blouse. "Well, I think some of us mistake chaos for creativity."

Another twitch. Gabe didn't even try to hide it.

Ellie leaned closer. "Don't encourage her, Gabe. She still thinks the Vatican has a hotline for modesty violations."

Mary pressed a hand to her chest in mock offense. "As if I would ever call the Vatican on a Sunday."

Gabe gave a low, slow blink but didn't say anything.

Mary sniffed. "He's judging us."

"He's judging *you*," Ellie said with glee. "Which means I'm winning."

"I let you win," Mary replied. "I was being gracious."

"You don't know the meaning of the word."

"I taught third grade for 37 years," Mary said primly. "I define the word."

God help me.

Ellie howled with laughter. Mary tried to hide her satisfaction, but Gabe saw the faintest hint of smugness behind the lace collar.

They were both ridiculous and he loved it. The room was already humming with ridiculous triumph when Anna walked in, a canvas tote on her shoulder and her sneakers squeaking faintly on the waxed floor.

She stopped cold just inside the archway. "Why does it feel like I just interrupted a cage match?"

Mary folded her hands neatly in her lap. "We were simply having a polite conversation."

Gabe touched his device and everyone waited several moments just watching as he painstakingly moved his knuckles to type. Finally the flat computer voice said:

About the Vatican's emergency modesty line

Anna's eyes widened. "I'm sorry—what?"

Ellie grinned and waved her good hand like she was announcing the second act. "Your boy here thinks I'm ridiculous. I told him, you haven't even seen ridiculous yet."

Anna tilted her head, a slow smile forming. "Oh no. Are we trying to win Gabe's reactions now?"

"Trying?" Ellie said, indignant. "Succeeding, thank you very much."

Mary gave a small, innocent shrug. "We were just talking. And some people," she nodded toward Ellie without looking at her, "don't know how to not make everything a competition."

Anna dropped her bag on a chair and stepped into the fray. She turned toward Gabe. "You realize you've created a monster, right? You encourage them with your tiny smirks and now they're locked in a permanent battle for the Sacred Twitch."

Gabe didn't deny it. Why should he? It was the most fun he'd had in days.

Ellie leaned forward conspiratorially. "You know what he really likes? A little Shakespeare. Gets him every time."

Mary sniffed. "And here I thought he preferred psalms."

Anna laughed, then dramatically cleared her throat. "If music be the food of love—"

No.

The room exploded in laughter.

His body still ached, stiff and twisted in ways he couldn't fix, but for this moment, he wasn't on the outside. He was right there with them—at the center of the ridiculousness. And he didn't mind being the prize, so long as they kept playing.

Anna crossed her arms, mock-stern. "All right. This is getting out of hand."

"Because Ellie's cheating," Mary said primly.

"I am not!"

"You used jazz hands and a fringe story. That's basically a bribe."

"A bribe would be slipping him whiskey. I'm saving that for the encore!" Ellie crowed.

Gabe actually laughed at that one.

"See?" Ellie said, "He'd take it."

Anna held up both hands. "Okay, okay. We need order. We need structure. We need..." She reached into her tote bag and began rummaging with exaggerated purpose. "...an official scoring system."

She pulled out a handful of random craft supplies—buttons, a stray pipe cleaner, a glue stick, a crumpled sheet of stickers shaped like woodland animals. "I hereby declare this the first annual Rosehaven Gabe Reaction Games."

Gabe's brow furrowed, but his eyes were already gleaming.

Mary squinted. "That's not very dignified."

Ellie clapped. "Oh I love this."

Anna picked up a bear sticker and slapped it dramatically onto the front of Ellie's sweater. "That's for making him laugh."

Ellie beamed. "I'd like to thank the Academy."

Mary looked horrified. "You're giving stickers?"

Anna nodded solemnly. "Badges of Honor. For Outstanding Contributions to Gabe's Facial Amusement."

She slapped a squirrel sticker on Mary's walker.

Mary peered down at it. "Is this...mocking me?"

"Nope. That's the Badge of Pious Shade."

Gabe snorted.

Ellie whipped her head around. "That's two points!"

Anna was now fully leaning into it, pulling out a sharpie. "I'm gonna start a scoreboard."

Gabe quickly tapped:

Hostile takeover.

But he was still smiling when Anna put a sticker of a fox on his cheek over the stubble and said, "This one's for putting up with us."

Ellie leaned over. "Fox for 'sly little devil,' right?"

"Obviously."

Mary sniffed again, but even she was smiling this time.

Gabe had just earned a second fox sticker—this one affixed by
Ellie to the armrest of his chair with a whispered, "For quiet
suffering"—when the air in the room shifted.

The laughter was still echoing, Anna doubled over and gasping for breath as she held up a chipmunk sticker with mock
gravitas.

Then the door opened.

And there she was.

Vicky.

Gabe's sister stepped in wearing an expensive blouse in muted taupe and oversized sunglasses perched on her head like a
tiara. She stopped just inside the threshold, a leather bag still
slung over one shoulder, frozen as if she'd walked into the wrong
room.

Which, emotionally, she had.

"Oh," she said, blinking at the scene: Ellie in a feathered scarf
and a sticker on her forehead, Mary with a pipe cleaner crown
that Anna had just bestowed upon her with an exaggerated
curtsey. Gabe surrounded by fluttering stickers and the unmistakable afterglow of joy.

"Is this—" she cleared her throat, clearly grasping for some
polite phrasing. "A...program?"

Anna straightened slowly, still holding the chipmunk.

Ellie turned with the grandiosity of a Shakespearean queen. "Darling, it's a spectacle."

Mary said quietly, "You must be his sister. You have his eyes. Though his are warmer."

Vicky looked like someone had slapped her with a wet fish. "Yes. I'm...Victoria." She turned to Gabe, her expression flickering between confusion and irritation. "I wasn't expecting... whatever this is."

Anna took a small step closer to Gabe's chair, instinctively feeling protective. "We were just having a little fun," she said, her voice still light, but quieter now. "A sticker war. Totally sanctioned."

Not true at all but Anna had no way of knowing how close his sister was to the administration here. Gabe kept his eyes on Vicky. She blinked at his chair, at the silly decorations, at the women smiling around him like they liked being here. Like they liked him. It seemed to disorient her. She couldn't quite comprehend that even without a voice, Gabe was still charming. Something she had never been.

"Well," Vicky said briskly. "I didn't mean to interrupt. I just thought I'd stop by." Her voice had that polished, affected tone she used in front of lawyers and real estate clients. Gabe hated it.

I'm busy.

He had to keep the sentences extra short with Vicky. She would be onto the fifth topic before he got a single word typed. He stuck to the pre-loaded words.

Vicky flinched, then tried to cover it with a brittle smile. "Right. Clearly very important."

Ellie leaned toward Mary and stage-whispered, "She's losing the sticker round. Badly."

Mary murmured, "You can't earn one if your soul leaves the room."

Vicky cleared her throat sharply. "Perhaps we could have a moment?"

Gabe didn't move.

Anna hesitated. "We were just heading out anyway," she said gently, even though they hadn't been.

She gave Gabe a look—quiet, apologetic, a soft brush of her fingers on the back of his hand as she gathered the stickers and nonsense supplies.

"We'll leave you to it."

And just like that, the joy left with them. The air settled into something colder, more formal. Vicky sat down stiffly beside his chair.

"I see they're keeping you entertained," she said, reaching into her purse for something. Probably a document. Probably a favor she wanted.

Gabe didn't look at her. He looked at the fox sticker on his armrest. It suddenly seemed a missed opportunity that he hadn't covered his entire chair in stickers. It should be a collage.

Vicky crossed her legs like she was settling into a brunch meeting.

"I spoke to Patricia yesterday," she said. "She mentioned you've been more...animated lately. Participating in things."

Gabe didn't blink. Didn't move.

It was always easier, with her, to go still. To disappear behind the silence. Though he was tempted this time to bring up the fact that she never acknowledged his 50th birthday. His miraculous survival seemed worthy of celebration.

"She's not concerned, of course," Vicky added. "She just said some new staff are getting a little...over-invested. Which, honestly, isn't surprising. These young, bleeding-heart types always think they're going to save someone."

She gave a little laugh, the kind people use when they're trying to make something sound like a joke.

"They don't understand," she said, turning to face him more directly, her eyes scanning his face like he was a damaged painting. "You're not really...there anymore. Not in the way you were." Her voice lowered. "And that's okay. It's not your fault."

He stared at her. That perfect hair. That flawless makeup. That practiced look of composed pity. He felt the heat rise in his chest. That slow burn he'd learned to smother under layers of inertia.

She looked away, digging in her bag. "Anyway. I'm going to be working with Patricia to get a few legal matters straightened out. We'll need to have you sign some things."

She pulled out a manila folder and placed it gently on the coffee table beside them. How did she think he was going to sign anything? With his teeth? The memory of painting with the paintbrush in his mouth almost made him smile right then and there but there was too much imminent danger when Vicky was here. Anything she had planned was going to be bad.

"You don't have to do anything," she added. "I'll speak with Patricia. We'll get someone to help. We need to set up a guardianship arrangement. Just a formality. We'll make sure everything's taken care of. I'm going to leave this at the front desk for when Patricia can get someone in to help you sign."

Guardianship arrangement. That phrase immediately rang alarm bells. Still, he didn't move. Didn't press a single word. Didn't give any indication of the fear that was wrapping itself around his chest.

Vicky reached out—tucked a piece of his hair behind his ear and he flinched. "I know you'd thank me if you could," she said softly. "For keeping everything from falling apart."

His jaw clenched.

She didn't notice.

Or maybe she did and chose to ignore it. Either way, she stood up with a rustle of her crisp linen blouse and took the folder back. She hadn't even shown him what was in it. What was the point of her coming? Just to disturb the little peace he was managing to carve out in his life? Remind him that she was in control now?

"I'll check back in a few days." She kissed the air near his cheek and left the room with her heels clicking in neat, calculated rhythm.

The silence she left behind was different than the one before. Heavier. Edged.

Gabe could still hear the click of her heels echoing down the hallway, then stopping just a few paces outside. A brief rustle, a chirp of a ringtone, and then her voice—sharp, clipped, meant for someone else.

"Hey. It's me. Yeah, I just saw him."

A pause. Paper shuffling.

"No, he didn't say anything. He never does. Just stares like a vegetable." A brittle little laugh. "I mean, come on—his brain was squished. He has massive brain damage. There's nothing left but the instinct to breathe."

Gabe's breath caught in his throat. He wanted to shout. He wanted to slam his fist into something, push over a chair, shake Vicky by her shoulders. Not that he could shout. Not that he could throw anything or slam a hand on a table.

All he could do was listen.

"It's outrageous," Vicky went on, voice rising just enough to carry. "That they're keeping him like this. Just prolonging everything. I mean, for what? So some art therapist can feel good about herself? He's not Gabe anymore."

There was a pause—just the tinny sound of the person on the other end responding.

Vicky sighed. "I'll talk to Patricia again. No judge is going to argue once they see the reports. He's got no quality of life. It's cruel, honestly."

Her voice faded as she walked further down the hall.

But the words stayed.

Nothing left but the instinct to breathe.

Gabe stared at the door. At the space where she'd stood. At the spot on the table where the folder had rested, like a gift wrapped in paperwork and mercy killings. His fingers curled tighter, the nails digging into his palms painfully. The edge of one knuckle brushed the screen of the AAC. Not to press anything. Just to remind himself that he could. That he was still here. And that Vicky, for all her perfect posture and high-level connections, didn't know the first goddamn thing about him. And she never had.

A moment later Anna peeked in, half-smiling. "Hey. I forgot my chipmunk."

Gabe didn't turn his head.

She stepped in slowly, the playfulness fading from her face as soon as she saw him. "That bad, huh?" she said, sitting down on the armrest of the couch beside him.

He didn't know what to say. If it wasn't so exhausting to type out even a few words he would be ranting to her right now. He imagined all the things he wanted to say. "Can you believe that bitch? It's never enough for her. I'm out of her way, the accident was super convenient for her. Worked out perfectly. She couldn't have planned it better if she tried. Except that I lived. And now she wants the money that I earned. All she really wants is for me to die. Her own brother."

He said none of it. The only sound was a chickadee somewhere in the trees outside.

"I can come back," Anna said gently. "If you want some space."

He blinked once, knowing that Anna was somehow able to understand every tiny bit of communication he could manage.

She lowered herself the rest of the way onto the couch, hands resting in her lap.

"I know family can get weird," she said. "Especially when they think they're being helpful."

Another long pause.

"You don't have to talk about it. You don't have to do anything right now. But I'm here. Okay?" She leaned against the arm of the couch, folding her arms and resting her head on them. She wasn't looking at him but just sat comfortably in the silence with him.

Anna didn't expect anything from him. She didn't prod or ask. She was still wearing a hedgehog sticker on her sleeve. Crooked. Silly. She hadn't even noticed.

Gabe let the vibration rise through his chest and into his throat, listening as the note hummed through him.

She turned and looked at him, her chin on her hands. She didn't say anything but just waited for the next note.

He hummed a few more notes. She blinked once. Then smiled.

Her lips parted. "Is that...Johnny Cash?"

He held the next note a little longer. Let it shape itself. A pause. Then the familiar rise and fall of the opening.

"*Hurt*," she said quietly. "The cover."

He didn't look at her—not directly. But he let the corner of his mouth lift. Just a little.

She caught it anyway.

"I knew it," she said, voice low. "God, that one guts me. You always pick the emotional assassins."

That just sounded like a challenge so he switched tunes. Something looser. Brighter. Playful.

Anna squinted. "Wait, wait, don't tell me—" She leaned toward him, her ponytail slipping over one shoulder. "Is that—*Bennie and the Jets*?"

He hummed a little louder. The odd staccato rhythm was unmistakable now.

Anna burst out laughing. "Oh my God, it is. You dork. You went from devastating Johnny Cash to Elton John in under thirty seconds."

Gabe's lips twitched wider.

She grinned. "Do it again. Come on. One more."

Another hum. Slower. Bluesy.

She wrinkled her nose. "Hmm...Fleetwood Mac?"

The hum deepened. Wrong.

"Ugh, I lose a sticker," she said, peeling the hedgehog off her sleeve.

He hummed again, same melody.

She gasped. "Wait. Otis Redding? *Sitting on the Dock of the Bay*?"

He gave a single breath of a hum—upward, triumphant.

She threw both arms up. "Yesss. I'm back in the game!"

She was looking at him now—really looking. The hum faded. Her head still tilted near his, eyes soft and unreadable in the dim light of the room.

Without speaking, she reached over. Fingers light, she brushed his hair back from his forehead. It was a similar gesture to what Vicky had done and yet it was entirely different when Anna did it. He felt it down every nerve in his body. Her hand lingered for a second longer, fingertips grazing the side of his temple like she wasn't quite ready to let go.

And then she seemed to realize what she was doing. Her hand snapped back like she'd touched something dangerous. Which, to be fair... maybe she had.

"I—" she started, but no words followed. Her eyes widened, and a flush rose along her throat. She stood too fast, bumping her knee into the coffee table. "I shouldn't have—"

Gabe's mouth was dry. His pulse hammered.

She backed up a step. "I'm so sorry. That was..."

He tried to blink something to her. Tried to soften his eyes, give her something—anything—that meant don't go, please don't go.

But she was already halfway to the door.

"I shouldn't be—"

She was gone.

And he was alone again.

He rested his head back, tilted the wheelchair until he was looking at the ceiling, ears still ringing with the echo of her footsteps and the phantom warmth of her hand against his face. He could still feel it.

He wished he couldn't.

He wasn't stupid. He'd seen that look before. That flash of panic in someone's eyes when they realized what he was. What he wasn't.

Gabe's jaw twitched. Eleven years and he hadn't so much as jerked off. He couldn't wrap his fingers around it, didn't have enough control of his hands to stroke. So much he couldn't do.

God, he wanted—

No. He couldn't want. What he wanted didn't fit inside this life.

Anna was young and warm, alive and messy in all the ways he couldn't be anymore. She made chaos out of order, sunshine out of sterile white walls. She gave chipmunk stickers to cranky old women and talked to him like he was a person, not a project.

And for one impossible second he let himself believe she saw him. Not the chair. Not the machine. Not the ruined silence where his voice used to be.

Him.

He should have known better. That kind of closeness never stayed. It cracked the surface just enough to let the cold in and leave him alone and freezing.

He let himself feel the sting of wanting what he couldn't have and then he straightened the wheelchair and got on with it.

11

ANNA

Anna sat in her car in the Rosehaven gravel parking lot and stared blankly through the windshield not really seeing what was in front of her. She had touched Gabe Whitlock. Touched him. Felt his skin beneath her fingertips. She saw the moment again and again in her mind. Her hand in his soft, wavy hair. The endless depth of his eyes. The sharp stab of shame.

She'd crossed a line with bare feet and no plan. Now she was standing in a place she didn't belong.

He was a rock god but it wasn't even about that. The intimate moment touching his face had been so electric she almost felt as though she had been burned. And the relentless pull toward him hadn't eased even now.

It's wrong, she chastised herself harshly. *You cannot be having these feelings about a resident at the long term care facility where you work. God, Anna, what are you thinking? No, you aren't thinking at all. As usual you just plough through life on impulse and then act surprised when you break everything in your path.*

Hot tears rolled off her chin and hit her hands but she was angry at herself for that too. *No, you spoiled brat, you do not get to just cry and have that make everything all better. You need to be a professional. He deserves that.*

And think about your dad. He put his neck out to get you this job and you're about to fuck it up. You don't get more chances after this. You've already had more than your fair share.

By now Anna was shaking with fury and there was no way she could safely drive. She was going to have to calm down at least long enough to get home.

Pull yourself together. She yanked on the sleeve of her tee-shirt to wipe all the tears from her face and sniffed in a deep breath. *You can be his friend but you cannot be crossing lines like that ever again. Got that?*

Why did he have this effect on her? She had never before felt like this around a man. She had had boyfriends, she had had dates. She never experienced the kind of pull that she felt around Gabe Whitlock. It was like walking past a magnetic field, every atom in her wanting to veer toward him. Was that just part of the charisma that made him famous? No, it had to be more than that.

In all brutal honesty, he didn't have much going for him at the moment. How many women could he bring to their knees when he lived in a nursing home and couldn't move or speak? And yet...somehow he still made Anna feel like she was on a date and not at work. It was really quite remarkable.

Finally Anna had calmed down enough to turn the car on and begin her brief commute home. She resolved that tonight she would call the gym and get the water aerobics outing set up. She would be professional. She would be normal.

And if something inside her felt like it was straining toward him anyway—she would ignore it.

She had to.

Anna came in the next morning with her sign-up sheet for the pool outing. She held it against the bulletin board and firmly pushed the thumbtack in like it was the finishing touch of a senior art project. She stood back a few paces and admired it. Behind the sign-up sheet, a construction paper shamrock from St. Patrick's Day still peeked out. Maybe she should consider clearing the board since it was now July.

> *Water Therapy Outing: Thursday! Bring your suit and towel! Transportation provided*

She could already picture the look on Mary's face, the way Frank would grumble but secretly enjoy it...how Gabe might look in swim trunks. *Shit. No.*

"Miss Lin."

The voice made her flinch and she instantly turned bright red as though Patricia could read her thoughts. Her boss stood a few feet away, tablet hugged to her chest, glaring at her.

"Yes?" Anna pasted on a smile.

Patricia's gaze flicked to the flyer, then back. "What exactly is this?"

"Water therapy," Anna said, too brightly. "I booked time at the gym. They have a lift and trained staff. It'll be safe. I thought it might be really good for everyone's bodies, and for morale too."

Patricia didn't move. "And who approved this?"

Anna only stuttered a little when she answered, "You told me I could schedule things as long as they didn't require a budget."

Patricia inhaled sharply.

"I paid for it myself," Anna added more meekly than she had intended.

"I see," Patricia said. She paused for a long moment and then she said, "You're not going to last if you don't learn some boundaries."

She knows. How does she know? Somehow she knows. "Wh—what?"

"In this job, people come and people die. Then more people come. And they die too. Nothing changes. You are going to burn out fast if you don't learn to accept that and not get so emotionally involved."

Anna was speechless and Patricia took that as a sign the conversation was over, walking away past the bulletin board.

But she hadn't said to cancel the outing...

Anna moved like a woman on a mission: chipper, brisk, breezy.

Too breezy.

A frantic, manic energy was radiating off her. What Patricia said had shaken her but the truth was Anna already knew that caring too much was part of who she was and she wasn't going to change that for anyone...not even herself. It might bring more pain and suffering down the line but Anna knew in every fiber of being that it was worth it. If she ever gave up on caring, she might as well give up on living.

"Okay!" she called, clapping her hands, as she strode into the resource room ten minutes late, "Listen up, Rosehaven rascals—because I have *news.*"

Mary looked up from her crossword. "You're too cheerful. That's suspicious."

"How much coffee did you have this morning?" Ellie asked but Anna ignored her.

"This Thursday there is going to be a pool excursion."

"Excersion? Like leaving the premises?" Ellie said.

"Yes! Like a field trip. There will be a bus to bring us over to the Y where we have a private water aerobics class."

Ellie's face lit up. "A pool excursion? Oh, darling, I am in." She spun her chair halfway and clapped her hands. "I need a hat. Something with flair. And I am not wearing one of those hideous cover-ups from the donation bin. I want color. I want drama. I want sequins."

"Pretty sure sequins aren't pool safe," Anna teased.

"Neither am I," Ellie shot back. "But here we are."

"How lovely!" Mary murmured. "I haven't been to the Y in...goodness, at least ten years." She reached for the pen tucked behind her ear. "Do we need to bring towels? Should I make a list?"

Anna smiled. "I'll print everything out, don't worry. There's a sign up sheet on the bulletin board but I'll also make a list here so who can I put down?" She had a notebook out. "Mary? Yes? And Ellie. Frank?"

Frank snorted. "Excursion, she says. Like we're going to summer camp."

"Would you prefer I call it a heist?" Anna asked, her pen poised above the page.

"Someone better bring snacks."

"I'm taking that as a yes." Anna wrote down his name and then she looked at Gabe. She had been avoiding looking directly at him and he had been completely silent all morning.

She met his eye and he still said nothing, gave no indication of his thoughts. He simply looked back at her.

"What?" she said finally, "You got somewhere better to be?"

That got the slightest hint of a smile from him. She leaned in and tapped the paper lightly. "C'mon. It'll be good. Hot water. Floatation noodles. Me pretending not to stare at your shoulders." Her face flushed instantly. She covered it with another too-loud laugh. "Kidding. Obviously. Totally professional."

The room was quiet for just a second too long.

Then Ellie, bless her, muttered, "Someone's had more espresso than sense."

Mary just raised an eyebrow and said, "Well. That's certainly a choice."

Anna ducked her head and scribbled a doodle in the margin of her notebook like she just thought of something very important.

Then they all heard the sound of Gabe's device.

I'm in.

"Yes!" Anna grinned and wrote his name on the notebook page.

Since she was on a roll, Anna stopped at Doris's room next.

"How are we doing on the list?" Anna asked. She flipped to her notes ready to update the to-dos.

But Doris waved the notebook away. "Just a few more things and I'll be on my way home."

"Lay it on me," Anna said. She sat down again and flipped to a fresh page.

Doris adjusted her glasses and pulled a folded sheet of notepaper from inside one of the catalogs. "First, I'll need to find out if the kitchen timer still works. The one with the loud bell. I can't trust myself to remember cookies anymore."

Anna nodded, writing: → test kitchen timer / find loud one

"And someone needs to check the gutters. There was a whole mess of leaves last fall, and if they're still clogged it'll drip on the walkway and I'll go sliding like Bambi."

"Gutters. Got it." Anna scribbled.

"Oh—and I'll need the quilt from the cedar chest. Not the pink one. The yellow with the blue edging. It's the right weight for early fall and I won't sleep without it."

"Yellow quilt. Cedar chest."

Anna looked up, her pen hovering. "I can call your daughter if you want," she offered cautiously. "To ask about the quilt, and the gutters—"

"Oh, she'll fuss," Doris said, waving a hand. "But she'll come around once she sees I've thought everything through."

"Any progress on the other things we talked about?"

"Don't worry about that." Doris's voice was sharper than Anna had ever heard before but it was quickly smoothed over with a cheerful laugh.

Anna nodded slowly, glancing at her notes. There was no mention of pharmacy transfers. No stairlift. No dresses. This list was entirely new.

By the time she stood up, her notepad was once again full of stars and arrows and side comments but she had no idea if Doris was any closer to getting home.

Rachel leaned across the café table, pushing a laminated kids' menu out of the way like it was an obstacle in a project timeline.

"Anna. You are going," she said with the same tone she probably used on contractors at work. "Saturday night. I already set it up. He's cute, he's single, and he owns a condo. A *condo*. That means stability."

Rachel's toddler, Lena, pulled every crayon out of the little cardboard box and lined them up on the sticky tabletop.

"Sweetie, remember rainbow order?" Rachel automatically moved a purple crayon to the far end while taking a sip of her latte.

Anna leaned back, amused and a little exhausted just watching. "She's two, Rach."

"Two and a half," Rachel said firmly. "Which is why she can already sort by color family. Right, pumpkin?"

The little girl banged the orange crayon like a gavel and stared at Anna.

Rachel smiled—tired but determined. Then her project-manager voice snapped back into place as she turned to Anna. "Anyway. Saturday night. Seven o'clock. Bistro on Main."

Anna groaned. "Rach, you don't have to—"

"Yes, I do." Rachel looked at Anna with that familiar mix of affection and exasperation. "You're wasting your twenties hiding in your dad's house and your nursing home job. You need to get back out there. Date. Live."

Anna's chest went tight. She stared at the swirl of foam in her coffee, wishing she could disappear into it. She didn't disagree and yet she was dreading Saturday night already.

Across the table Rachel's daughter shrieked happily, waving the blue crayon in triumph. "Ta-da!"

"Exactly," Rachel said, seizing the moment as if her daughter had just endorsed her plan. "Ta-da. You're going. Saturday."

12

GABE

Gabe couldn't stop thinking about what she'd said. *Me pretending not to stare at your shoulders.*

He wasn't imagining it. The pull went both ways. As unlikely...as crazy...as it sounded. This happy little chickadee who brightened up every room she entered was into him.

If it weren't for the situation he was in, he would be asking her out right now.

He let his eyes close and the walls of Rosehaven dissolved. No antiseptic smell. No random beeps of medical equipment or half-finished snores or the squeak of tires on hardwood floors. Just the soft purr of cars in the rain and chatter that belonged to another life.

She walked close to him but not quite touching, her hand brushing his now and then like she was testing the idea. He wanted to catch it, hold it, lace their fingers together—but he liked the not-knowing, too.

The city's noise stretched around them, neon lights humming, taxis darting past. He felt her watching him as much as he was watching her.

For a second, he let himself imagine her in his apartment—charcoal smudges on her fingers, sketchpad balanced on her knees, sunlight spilling across the floor while he strummed chords that didn't need words.

He swallowed hard, shoved the image down. Too much, too soon.

Instead, he nodded toward the flickering marquee across the street. "Want to see something weird?"

She narrowed her eyes playfully. "Depends how weird."

"Indie film theater. Midnight horror double feature. Absolutely terrible."

She laughed, quick and bright, and before he could second-guess himself, he caught hold of her hand and they ran across the street together.

After the movie they stood outside, the air beginning to chill.

"Well," she said, "that was...definitely cinema."

He chuckled.

She looked down, a blush racing across her cheeks. "My place is a few blocks away. I've got tea and—" She glanced up at him with a nervous smile "—way fewer exploding rubber monsters."

Her apartment smelled like turpentine and jasmine tea. Sketchbooks were stacked haphazardly on the couch, a stray paintbrush had rolled dangerously close to the edge of the coffee table. She was sitting cross-legged beside him on the couch, close enough that her knee was touching his.

"Draw me," he teased, tipping his beer bottle toward her sketchpad.

She wrinkled her nose. "Too obvious."

"You scared?" he asked.

Her eyes glinted. "Of you?"

He leaned closer, close enough to catch the faint citrus on her skin. "Of what you'll see."

That was when she shifted, slow and deliberate, unfolding her legs and climbing across to straddle his lap. The world tilted with her—her hair falling against his cheek, her mouth only inches from his.

"You want honesty?" she whispered, her breath warm against his jaw. "Fine."

Her hand slid slowly up his chest, fingers learning the shape of his body through the thin cotton fabric of his tee-shirt. His breath caught in his throat, every nerve sparking. He'd forgotten what it felt like to be studied that way—not as a performer on a stage, but as a man in the half-light of someone's living room.

She kissed him then, slow at first, then hungrier when he pulled her closer, his hands around her back. Her knees tightened around his hips.

He grabbed her suddenly and flipped her so she was lying flat on her back on the couch and he braced above her, his weight pinning her down. The cushions dipped beneath his knees, his arms steady on either side of her shoulders.

Her eyes widened at the sudden shift and he grinned at her.

"God," she whispered, her fingers lightly teasing around his neck, "you're heavier than you look."

He bent to kiss her throat, his mouth finding the flutter of her pulse. She clutched at his shoulders, nails grazing, pulling him closer, wordless and hungry.

He shifted lower, pressing his mouth to the edge of her collarbone, tasting her skin, breathing in paint and soap and something sweet that was purely Anna. She trembled under him, laughing breathlessly when his stubble grazed her.

"Hello! Good morning, Rosehaven!"

Gabe's eyes snapped open to the familiar sagging floral couches and the TV silently broadcasting a game show. He was in his wheelchair again, his neck stiff against the headrest, his fingers tightening into his palms with disappointment and frustration.

A plump kid had just blown through the archway: messy black hair, thick glasses slipping down his nose, socks covered in cartoon flamingos. He was hauling a backpack, a clipboard, and—Gabe blinked—a ukulele case?

"Guess who's your brand-new intern?!" he announced to the room, as if he were on stage. "Max Chen, reporting for—uh—service? Duty? Friendship?"

A few residents blinked at him. Frank muttered something about circus clowns.

Gabe watched him bounce through the room, making the kind of small talk that sounded rehearsed. Mary got a chirpy

"How are we feeling today?" and gave him a polite, noncommittal "Isn't that something," which should have warned him to slow down.

It didn't.

Max plopped into an armchair and said to the room in general, "So! Who's up for icebreaker questions? Favorite song of all time—go!"

He looked around brightly. His eyes landed on Gabe but didn't register a flicker of recognition. No oh-my-God-you're-him moment. Just another old man in a wheelchair. Once, women had screamed Gabe's name in arenas. Now some kid with flamingo socks thought he was a trivia partner.

Max looked closer at Gabe's AAC. "Cool setup. I've never actually seen one of those used in person. Do you like it? Does it work okay for you?"

Questions stacked one on top of the other until they teetered. Gabe let them fall, answering none. He held the kid's gaze instead, long enough for the bounce in his posture to hitch. A moment later Max laughed—soft, awkward—like he'd realized he'd stepped into the wrong rhythm of the song.

Gabe decided the kid needed breaking in. He waited for the right opportunity and pretty soon Max was asking everyone if they needed anything. When he got to Gabe, he responded.

Red pen.

Max blinked. "A...red pen? Sure." He trotted off toward the front desk.

Five minutes later, Max returned, pen in hand, looking proud. Gabe tapped:

Blue pen.

Another trot, another return.

Stapler.

That took longer—apparently Sylvia guarded them like gold—but Max came back holding it like a trophy. Gabe studied it for a long moment, then tapped:

Tiny paper clips.

"Tiny... paper clips?" Max repeated. Gabe nodded seriously.

It went on—rubber bands, tape, a yellow notepad, three paper towels. Each time Max came back slightly more rumpled, glasses smudged, hair even messier from pushing it out of his eyes.

Anna had abandoned any pretense of working, openly staring. Ellie and Mary were pretending not to notice but the pile of items on the table next to Gabe was getting too large to ignore.

Max was just returning with rainbow thumbtacks when Patricia appeared in the archway to the living room behind him.

"Mr. Chen," she said in that clipped tone that struck fear in everyone's hearts, "what exactly are you doing?"

Max stammered, "He—uh—Mr. Whitlock—needed—"

Patricia's gaze slid to Gabe, cool and assessing. Gabe's expression was pure innocence.

"Your job does not involve..." Patricia looked down at the mountain of items. "Fetching office supplies. Put all these things back. Mr. Whitlock has no ability to use any of this."

"Yes, ma'am," Max muttered, retreating a step. When Patricia swept out again, he glanced at Gabe, flushed and defeated. "You think you're pretty funny, don't you?"

Gabe hit the AAC with one knuckle.

Very.

Anna's laugh escaped before she could stop it, bright and uncontained. Max groaned, but even he was smiling now.

Gabe rested his head against the support, satisfied.

After lunch it was time for Anna's pool excursion.

"Okay, Rosehaven, it's pool day!" Anna said, though everyone knew that since they were crowded together in the lobby by the front desk already dressed in swimsuits.

Nurse Becky had helped Gabe with his. He felt exposed and ridiculous sitting in his wheelchair wearing only swim trunks. When he caught an unfortunate glance in the mirrored wall of the lobby, he saw how flat and pale his chest had become, a lot of the muscle atrophied over time. Above the seatbelt of the chair he had a small gut poking out that never used to be there. The muscles in his abs had gone the same way as the muscles in his chest and arms. Thin legs emerged from the swim trunks and his bare feet felt the cold bite of the wheelchair's metal footrests. He was starting to regret saying yes to this.

But it was just too hard to say no to Anna.

She was wandering through the crowd checking off names and she practically glowed. She was in her element. Gabe smiled in spite of himself. He already knew that he would let her talk him off a cliff.

A bus pulled up to the front of the building. Anna guided people one at a time through the front door and Max went down to the bus to get them situated.

Gabe was the last one out the front door. The wheelchair lift on the bus was already out, lowered to the gravel, waiting for him to drive on.

It creaked under his chair as it rose, jolting slightly as it met the bus floor. Gabe felt a jerk of motion reverberate through the headrest into his skull. Max steadied the base of his chair and unhooked his wheels from the lift's straps.

The inside of the bus was full of chatter and the rustle of bags, sunhats, and reusable water bottles. Mary had a zippered pouch that said *Jesus is my Lifeguard* and Ellie had already started narrating their departure.

"Act One: The Voyage Begins. Will our heroes make it to the pool before their bones dry into dust?"

Frank snorted. "I've been marinating mine in cholesterol, I'll be fine."

The bus smelled like summer. Plastic seats, sun-warmed vinyl, and a faint trace of chlorine from the pool bags. The windows were streaked from yesterday's storm, and the sunlight slanted through in long strips, cutting across Gabe's lap and casting hard shadows on the floor. He blinked slowly, letting it warm the left side of his face. He couldn't actually remember the last time he had left Rosehaven. It felt strange to be driving away from it, even knowing he'd be back that evening.

The gym pool was quiet when they arrived—not silent, but gentle. Echoes softened by water and tile. The smell on the air reminded him of indoor hotel pools that invariably had a family screaming in the shallow end and a vending machine just outside the glass doors.

Gabe watched as the other residents shuffled slowly down the steps into the water. A staff member held Ellie's arm to help her stand. Then Anna was at his side.

"You ready?" she asked quietly.

Her eyes were wide with anticipation. Not just for him, for all of them, but he could see that little flicker of nerves, too, the *please let this go okay* that she never said out loud. He wished he could tell her she was doing fine.

The transfer to the pool lift was slow. A staff member crouched beside Gabe; big guy, quiet voice. "I'm Mateo. I've got you, Gabe."

Gabe eyed the machine skeptically. It was a hard molded plastic chair attached to some kind of large machine arm that would bring him from the deck into the pool. Well, he had come this far, there was nothing for it but to put his trust in Mateo.

The big man undid the seatbelt on Gabe's wheelchair, then lifted Gabe's arms over each of his shoulders. Before they even had a chance to think of sliding off, Mateo locked his fingers behind Gabe's back and heaved him up, pivoting him immediately to the seat of the pool lift.

As usual, Gabe's limbs decided to lightly protest the disturbance with a few tremors. One spasm in his foot got particularly strong and lifted his entire leg up into the air for a few moments. Mateo waited patiently for it to subside then strapped Gabe to the lift.

The motor whirred louder as the seat started to move horizontally over the pool. Gabe's chest tightened with instinctive panic but he breathed through it. For a moment he was suspended above the pool and he could just barely feel the water lapping at the tips of his toes where they dangled from his dropped feet.

And then, Frank's voice, echoing in the tiled room, shouted, "Would you look at that? He's strapped to a forklift! Like one of those claw machines from the arcade."

Gabe narrowed his eyes. A slow, death-ray glare that would have withered plants but Frank's eyesight wasn't good enough to notice it.

Mary, floating nearby in her pink swim cap and pastel bathing suit, arched one brow and gave a pointed sniff. "Don't be rude," she said firmly, adjusting the noodle beneath her arms with all the elegance of a duchess on a gondola.

"I'm not being rude," Frank protested. "I'm just saying..."

Gabe's chair vibrated with the machinery as he descended, the straps snug around his ribs and thighs. His feet broke the surface first—then his legs, knees, hips. The warmth of the water reached up like a living thing, curling around him inch by inch, cradling him like something ancient. Something that remembered.

The lift paused at shoulder-depth. Mateo reached under Gabe's arms and helped him slide slowly off the seat. Gabe's arms floated upward to the surface of the water, twitchy and bent, but weightless.

"I'm gonna support your back here," Mateo said gently, and then there were hands, one at his spine, one at his shoulder blade, anchoring him while the water held everything else. Along with Mateo holding him, they also added some pool noodles under his arms and some kind of float to support his head.

He surrendered to it all. His legs drifted. His fingers loosened just a bit. He closed his eyes and let the water hold him. And for the first time in years, he didn't feel trapped in his body.

When he opened his eyes, Anna was walking alongside the edge of the pool, barefoot, pants rolled up to mid-calf. She was beaming. Not just smiling—*beaming*. Her sneakers were tucked beside the bin of floaties and goggles, and her wet bare feet left faint marks on the pool deck.

Her presence moved like light across the surface of the water.

"Everyone doing okay?" she called.

Mary, floating gently with two noodles under her arms, gave a serene thumbs-up. "Like a lily on the water, dear."

Another staff member at the pool started the class, guiding everyone in some gentle movement exercises.

Frank rolled his eyes and half-heartedly splashed water as he lifted his arms. His noodle floated under one arm like a reluctant life raft.

"This is ridiculous," he grunted, flapping his arms just enough to meet the bare minimum.

Anna passed by the edge of the pool, calling out encouragement. "Looking good, Frank!"

"Yeah, yeah," he said, puffing a little. "I ran a garage for forty years, now I'm out here doing synchronized swimming with a bunch of old drama queens."

But he didn't stop.

Gabe wasn't exactly doing the same thing as everyone else but Mateo guided him through a gentle rocking motion, side to side, the pressure of water changing along his ribs and chest. The water was working some magic on him. The tension in his spine was beginning to let go.

He drifted, barely tethered, Mateo's hand always there. His head shifted slightly to the side to look at Anna. She was crouching now, close to the edge, watching him with wide, glassy eyes. She was crying. She wiped at her cheek like it surprised her.

He wanted to say something. Anything. His hand twitched in instinct but the AAC was up on the dry deck with his wheelchair. Didn't matter.

She saw him. She leaned in and whispered, "You look like you're flying."

And that's exactly what it felt like.

After a while, the class shifted to slow leg motions, assisted kicks, stretching arms and spines in the water. The air filled with laughter, the kind that echoed and bubbled like water itself. Time dripped, and flowed, and breathed.

When they finally brought Gabe back to the pool hoist and lifted him up, the world felt heavier. Denser. His body, no longer held, remembered gravity and pain.

On the bus ride home, Gabe closed his eyes and leaned back into the hum of the engine. His hair was still damp. His skin itched a little from the chlorine. His spine ached where it always did. But his chest still held the memory of weightlessness, and his arms remembered motion.

"Just so you all know," Frank declared loudly, "I may never recover. My back's shot."

"Poor baby," Ellie said flatly, without looking away from the window.

"I'm serious!" Frank said. "I've got aches in muscles I haven't used since the Nixon administration."

Anna turned around in her seat, biting back a smile. "You were doing laps by the end."

"Dog paddling for survival is not the same as laps," he muttered. "And you all laughed when I nearly capsized on that noodle."

"You screamed like a girl scout," Max said, grinning. "A *loud* girl scout."

Frank scowled at him. "Keep talking, intern, and I'll rewire your car horn to play show tunes."

Max's eyes lit up. "Wait, could you actually do that?"

Frank muttered, "Damn kids think sarcasm's a how-to manual."

13

ANNA

Anna arrived at Rosehaven the same as usual but today something was different. It took her a few moments to realize what it was. No Harriet at the entrance. Anna's stomach tensed up as she stared at the spot Harriet had always been sitting. She knew what it probably meant but she didn't want to face it.

Why did life do this? Just when she got her feet under her even a little bit, the ground shifted and knocked her off balance again. Anna felt a strong urge to get back in her car and drive away before she heard any news about Harriet.

Instead she resolved to focus on where she could make a difference to counteract the feeling of helplessness. *You're doing things differently now*, she reminded herself. *No more running away.*

She walked in and approached Sylvia at the front desk.

"Is Harriet okay?" she asked.

Sylvia sighed and shook her head. "Sorry, Anna. She went last night. There's a little service planned for this evening, if you want to go."

No tears came. No tightness of breath. No feelings of shock at all. Anna just nodded. It surprised her but maybe it was because her heart knew the truth the moment she saw the empty space by the door.

She would let her dad know she would be home late and stay for the service. But for now she should keep moving forward and focusing on what she had control over.

"I've been talking with Doris about what she still needs to be able to go home. Can I coordinate some of those things with you?"

Sylvia stared at her. "Go home? What do you mean?"

Anna felt the ground turning slippery under her feet again. "She said if she can get a few practical matters taken care of she'd be able to go back home. I have some lists." Anna started to dig into her bag.

"Oh dear," Sylvia said and her tone stopped Anna instantly. "No one told you?"

One hand still in her bag, Anna looked back up to Sylvia's face. "Told me what?"

"Doris has bipolar schizoaffective disorder and she won't take medication for it. Most families would force it but her daughter is a kind soul. She knows Doris's mind tortures her but she also wants to honor her mom's wishes and respect her autonomy."

Anna still didn't understand and her blank look must have prompted Sylvia to explain further.

"Disorders like that cause delusions. Seems a lot like schizophrenia to me but I'm no doctor. Poor Doris doesn't live in reality. Her brain created a new reality and she won't believe anyone who tells her it isn't true. She's thought up obstacles to explain to herself why she can't go home because she can't accept the real reason. She keeps solving that same problem and over and over and over. She's been doing this for at least five years. Kind of reminds you of that movie Momento, doesn't it?"

Anna didn't answer. She was only half processing what Sylvia was telling her. Delusions? A false reality? None of it was real. *None of it was real.*

She staggered away from the desk and stumbled in the direction of the resource room but she was rapidly losing her hold on the world around her. Her eyes were wide but she wasn't seeing what was in front of her. She gasped for air as a vice tightened around her lungs. She stopped moving, leaned against a wall. Her heart felt like it was going to explode and all she could hear in her eardrums was its wild, terrified pounding.

Pulling air into her lungs was getting harder and harder, she gasped in shallow breaths, each one feeling like sandpaper against her throat. She stared wide-eyed at the floor in front of her and the tiny pin-point of wood grain she could see seemed to dance and swirl together. Her fingers were trembling and numb. The pins-and-needles traveled rapidly up her arms and down her legs. She wanted to bolt but she couldn't move, trapped in her own skin.

Her heart slammed against her ribs. The lights above were too bright and too loud. It was all happening again. She was going to pass out. She was going to lose her job.

Then a hand came into her narrowing field of vision. Unmistakably Gabe's. She knew that bent wrist and the limp fingers curled in towards the palm. It shook in front of her as Gabe exerted tremendous effort to hold it out to her.

She snatched it like a rope tossed to her in a stormy ocean. His warm fingers were solid and real in her grip. With her eyes, she managed to follow the line of his arm up to his face and she saw that he was breathing very deliberately and deeply while staring intently at her. She found an anchor in his eyes and followed along with the deep breaths.

In through the nose two three four.

Hold two three four.

Out through the mouth two three four.

His eyes wouldn't let her go for a second. Her racing heart began to slow. He nodded encouragingly, continuing the breathing.

As she calmed, exhaustion took over and her legs went weak. When her knees buckled, Gabe used the hand she was still holding to gently guide her forward until she collapsed onto his lap. She closed her eyes and rested against his shoulder, feeling his chest rising and falling beneath her. She felt his breath in her hair and after a moment she felt a vibration as he began to hum.

She didn't recognize the melody but it sounded like a lullaby. They stayed that way for long minutes; his chest lifting her cheek gently up and down, the vibrations of the song like a purr against her skin, the feeling of his breath on the top of her head.

She felt as safe as she had as a child, able to fully relax for the first time in her adult life.

Finally Anna felt composed again. "Thank you," she whispered, sliding off his lap.

He smiled.

"I'm sorry," Anna continued. "I didn't want you to see that."

He narrowed his eyes and shook his head as he typed. Anna waited silently for him to finish.

Oh please. After what you've seen with me?

She crossed her arms. "I don't have the excuse of a spotlight falling on my head. I'm supposed to be okay," she retorted.

I always win that contest.

She smiled but didn't answer. He kept typing and she saw the muscles in his face tighten as he tried to force his hand to go faster but it wouldn't.

It's happened before?

"Yeah," Anna said. She pulled over a chair that was out in the hallway for no apparent reason and drew her knees up to her chest. "It was happening so much I dropped out of college. I still feel stupid for letting anxiety derail my whole future. I'm turning 30 next week and I still don't even have my degree. This is my first 'grown up' job. I feel so behind everyone else."

An eyebrow lift.

Let?

"I should be able to get a handle on the anxiety. Other people do. I don't even have anything to be upset about. I have an objectively great life. I'm just weak." Her voice broke a little as she whispered, "I don't know why I'm weaker than other people."

Gabe frowned and shook his head. He let out a a frustrated growl and then he closed his eyes and took a deep breath, centering himself enough to hum again. He kept his eyes closed and Anna watched him as she waited for the melody to reveal itself. In just a moment she recognized *Let It Be.*

It wasn't perfect; his breath wavered, but the heart of it was there, wrapping around her like warm hands holding her steady. Every note told her what he couldn't type out fast enough: *We never know what life is going to bring. All you can do is be at peace with where you are. But you're not alone. I'm here for you and with you.*

Softly she began to sing along, "...when the night is cloudy there is still a light that shines on me. Shining til tomorrow, let it be. I wake up to the sound of music, mother Mary comes to me speaking words of wisdom, let it be. Let it be, let it be, let it be, let it be. Whisper words of wisdom, let it be."

When they stopped, the absence of the music felt strange — like stepping off a boat and realizing the dock isn't swaying beneath you. She smiled. "Thank you. I think you might be better than my therapist."

A pause as he pressed the AAC.

And I'm probably hotter.

Anna laughed, relieved at the feeling. "You cheeky bastard," she muttered.

He winked.

That evening the living room transformed into a funeral home. Anna texted her dad that she wouldn't be home for dinner and quietly slipped into the back row, sitting on a hard folding chair. Gabe drove in a moment later and she moved a chair out of the way to make room for him beside her.

At the front of the room, a priest waited for everyone to find a place. Aside from the bed-bound residents, all of Rosehaven was in this room. Staff and residents mingled together on the cold metal chairs. It was strangely silent, just the creaks and shuffles that were usually drowned out by other sounds.

Finally the priest took a deep breath and began. "I didn't know Harriet in her youth. But I've heard stories. And I knew her here in her last few years as first her body and then her mind failed her. I'll always remember her as the sharp perfectionist who inspired those around her to want to be better. She didn't mince words and she had thoughts on how you could improve."

A quiet murmur of agreement rippled through the front row. Ellie gave a small nod. Frank harrumphed softly. Anna couldn't imagine the woman outside the door with the vacant stare being the person he was describing.

"When I first met her," the priest continued, "she corrected my Latin pronunciation."

Soft chuckles scattered through the rows.

"She told me she'd been a librarian and that fact explained so much about her: her love of language, of order, of stillness. Like most people, when she came here to Rosehaven, it wasn't because she wanted to. She missed her books. She missed her house. But she found other things to care about. She wasn't a saint and I won't pretend she was because I think what matters most is that we remember people for who they were, for who God made them. But she lived with dignity. And with more humor than most of us ever noticed."

There was a short ceremony next and Anna swallowed back a lump in her throat. The service was beginning to remind her of her mother's.

Helen's was Protestant, not Catholic, but the purpose was the same. Some people might say that a memorial service is meant to help people say goodbye and feel closure but to Anna they were more about making you feel like you did okay by the person who was gone, that you honored them and didn't let them down. It seemed to her that if you didn't acknowledge their passing with a ceremony, their spirit would haunt you with guilt.

Anna remembered being in the basement of her childhood church, standing beside a table covered in foil pans of food. Her mother's photograph rested in a frame surrounded by carnations. The minister's words had been different but the rhythm was the same—measured, reverent, unbearably final.

Anna remembered the way her knees shook, the way her chest locked tight, how she couldn't make herself look at her father. Everyone had come with casseroles and careful smiles, and all she'd wanted was to scream that her mother wasn't supposed to be gone. There was a mistake. A misunderstanding. Helen would come in at any moment and laugh at the joke.

Then they'd all eat together and share stories and have a nice afternoon.

But that didn't happen.

We give thanks for this woman: wife, mother, friend.

Anna pinched the soft flesh by her left thumb with the fingernails of her right, trying to use the small sharp pain to ground herself in the present. This was Harriet's moment, not her mother's. But grief never stayed in its own lane. It bled, it seeped, it found echoes everywhere.

Beside her, Gabe noticed because of course he did. He pushed his arm off the wheelchair towards her until he was able to intercept her fingernails with his hand. Anna smiled at him without a word. His eyes were soft and kind.

She looked back to the front where the priest was wrapping up his thoughts. "I believe we honor people not just by remembering what they did, but by noticing what they still leave behind. The quiet rituals. The birdsong in the morning. We carry that forward."

He bowed his head. "May Harriet be at peace. And may we be better for having known her."

As the residents slowly began to shuffle and roll their way out of the chapel, complaining softly about the folding chairs, Anna lingered near the back.

Mary hustled towards her as quickly as she could with her walker. "Anna! Come over here, I want to introduce you to Father Stephen."

She led Anna toward the front of the room, where the Father was folding his reading glasses into his shirt pocket. Up close, his features were weathered but kind, eyes warm with an alert sort of calm.

"Father," Mary said, "This is Anna Lin, our new activity coordinator."

Father Stephen smiled and offered his hand. "Miss Lin. A pleasure."

Anna shook it, a little self-conscious. "You don't have to call me that. Just Anna's fine."

"Anna, then," he said with a chuckle. "I've heard good things."

Mary interjected gently, as though letting them in on a secret. "Father Stephen baptized all my children."

Anna blinked, suddenly realizing that she didn't even know Mary had children. "Really?"

Mary nodded. "In the little chapel on Hill Street. This was long before the ramp was installed, mind you, so I had to carry my youngest up with no stroller and four others clinging to me." She smiled faintly, eyes misting just slightly. "He was so small then."

Father Stephen chuckled. "And now he's taller than both of us put together."

Mary beamed at Anna. "There's not many people left who've known my family that long. He buried my husband. Gave my daughter her first communion. He knows what we've come through."

Father Stephen and Mary looked at each other and Anna was suddenly sure that what they'd come through could fill several books. And with that, the Father gave a gentle nod and moved to speak with another resident.

Mary turned to Anna. "He comes every Tuesday. You should sit with him sometime."

And even though Anna wasn't particularly religious she said softly, "I think I will."

Anna's weekends were too quiet. After the energy of the week at Rosehaven, being at home felt empty. Maybe she needed a hobby. One that actually got her out of the house. What she really wanted was people. Noise. A place where she didn't have to carry the weight of filling every silence.

Her phone buzzed on the counter. Rachel, of course. Reminding her yet again that she had a date tonight. Maybe dating counted as a hobby. It certainly got her out and around people.

The man's name was Trevor, and he had perfect hair. That was the first thing Anna noticed as she slid into the booth opposite him at Bistro on Main. Dark, gelled into immobility, not a strand out of place.

"Traffic was insane," he said by way of greeting.

Anna smiled politely. "Yeah, it gets bad around here after—"

"And parking," he barreled on. "They want twenty bucks now. Twenty. For a cracked asphalt lot with potholes the size of bathtubs." He shook his head, stabbing the air with his fork like a man betrayed.

She nodded, sipping her water.

By the time their entrees arrived, Trevor had launched into an exhaustive breakdown of his golf handicap, complete with hand gestures tracing imaginary swings in the air. The server nearly got clipped in the jaw.

Anna poked at her pasta, fighting not to laugh from sheer disbelief.

Trevor cleared his throat. "So, do you cook?"

"Sometimes," she said carefully.

"Good." He leaned back, smug. "Women who don't cook—red flag. My ex tried to feed me vegan chili once. Nearly called it off right there."

Anna blinked. "...Right."

He launched into a new story about the injustice of condo association fees. She sat back, tuning out, her eyes wandering over the restaurant's yellow light fixtures and the couple laughing at the bar.

For a moment she pictured herself somewhere else entirely: in the nursing home living room, Mary quietly reading a book out loud to herself, Frank ranting about the Sox, Ellie critiquing the director's choices on Murder, She Wrote. Gabe watching it all, silent but missing nothing. His eyes on her.

She realized she was smiling.

"Did I say something funny?" Trevor asked.

Anna snapped back. "Oh—no, sorry. Just...thought of something."

He frowned, clearly irritated that she'd dared to have a thought that wasn't about him.

By dessert she had already decided. Next time Rachel tried to set her up, she'd fake the stomach flu. She was just going to have to wait for love to come to her naturally.

14

GABE

Mary sat primly in the upholstered chair beside Ellie's bed. Ellie, reclining with a book she wasn't reading, gave Mary a sidelong look.

"Well," Ellie said, arching one silver brow, "that boy needs more than Bingo, Wheel Of Fortune, and Patricia's bland menu rotations. He needs *life.*" She tapped her good hand on the tray beside her, where a highlighter rolled off with a clatter. "And don't give me that look—he lights up when Anna's around."

Mary tilted her head thoughtfully. There was no question that the "boy" was a certain 50-something resident of Rosehaven. "Anna does laugh more when she's talking to him. Even when he hasn't said a word."

"Exactly," Ellie said, triumphant. "You and I have both lived long enough to recognize when people are trying not to fall in love. I'm not saying we push them together like some high school prom committee, but...a little nudge here, a conveniently misfiled schedule there..."

"Eleanor," Mary murmured, eyes twinkling, "you're scheming."

"I am *facilitating joy,*" Ellie corrected. "Besides, you know as well as I do—she makes him happy. And he makes her forget to look so sad when she thinks no one's watching."

Mary nodded, lips pursed. "Then it's settled. Should we pray about it?"

Ellie waved her off. "I already did. Now we act."

The piano was wheezing its way through a warbly rendition of *Sweet Caroline* courtesy of Max's enthusiastic but somewhat untrained hands. Ellie sat nearby, offering commentary in the form of exaggerated sighs and muttered Shakespeare. Mary was settled in her usual spot, knitting something pale pink and shapeless, her eyes flicking discreetly between Gabe and the door.

Ellie leaned toward Mary. "You said she's due in about—?"

Mary didn't look up. "Three minutes. I told her I found a few old watercolors in the supply closet that she might want to salvage."

After a particularly enthusiastic chord on the piano Gabe's AAC device clicked once, the robotic voice saying:

Noise.

Max grinned without missing a note. "You love it. I can tell."

Tone-deaf.

"Rude," Max countered.

The door opened.

Anna stepped in, her canvas tote bumping against her hip and a smudge of blue already on her wrist. "You found more watercolors?" she asked, heading straight toward Mary.

Mary nodded sweetly. "Back of the tall cabinet. Terribly disorganized, I'm afraid."

"Oh, I'll go through it now."

She rose up on her tip-toes and stretched to reach the top shelf. Her tee-shirt rode up a little bit exposing a narrow strip of her back. Mary and Ellie both noticed that Gabe was looking and they smiled at each other. If it hadn't been too obvious they might have high-fived.

Ellie coughed loudly. "Well," she announced, "Mary and I need to go check on dessert for tonight. They're supposed to be using my hermit recipe. Max, could you come help us enforce it?"

"Uh, okay," Max stood from the piano, eager as a puppy to do whatever anyone asked.

Anna turned back and gave them a questioning look. Then she seemed to think better of it and returned to trying to climb the cabinets.

Gabe saw an opportunity and he followed Ellie, Mary, and Max out of the living room.

"Oh, Gabe, don't you think Anna could use your help?" Mary said. She looked strangely distraught.

He raised one skeptical eyebrow. What the hell was he going to do to help her reach art supplies in a tall cabinet?

Listen.

As he hoped, that one word was enough to get all three of them to stop and wait for him to say what he wanted to. It took all his strength and concentration but he finally typed out:

Anna's birthday. Need to throw a party.

"Oh, heavens, Gabriel. That's...that's perfect."

Ellie's eyes lit like stage lights. She leaned closer to Gabe's chair, her jewelry clinking softly. "Darling, if you wanted to impress her, you'd only need to bat those pretty eyes of yours. But a party—that's a proper production."

Mary nodded, solemn as if they were planning a cathedral wedding. "We'll need to keep it a surprise. Anna always thinks of everyone else first. She mustn't suspect."

Max nearly clapped. "Oh my God, yes, a secret operation! Balloons, streamers, cake—do we think she likes chocolate or vanilla?" "Chocolate," Mary said without hesitation. "She always goes for the chocolate pudding at lunch."

"And music," Ellie added. "Something joyful. Gabe, you'll have to pick. That's your expertise."

"I love music too!" Max said but everyone ignored him.

They began to shuffle down the hall, conspirators now, leaving Anna still teetering on the cabinet in blissful ignorance. If Gabe noticed that suddenly no one was concerned about supervising dessert for the evening, he didn't say.

Frank was grumbling. Nothing unusual about that.

"You know I can't stand being out here when the sun's right overhead," he said, adjusting his Red Sox cap. "What am I, a tomato plant?"

In the far corner of the Rosehaven garden, Ellie, Mary, and Frank were sitting around a white lattice metal table and neither of the ladies bothered to point out that Frank was fully under the umbrella with them.

There was one more empty chair at the table and a space that was somehow the perfect size for a power wheelchair.

Frank squinted at the empty chair across from him. "Why are there four chairs set up? You expecting company?"

Ellie gave him a patient smile. "Oh, no reason."

Frank grunted. "You two are up to something."

Mary's fingers resumed their slow knitting. "Well that's neither here nor there," she murmured.

Before Frank could pursue it further, the side door opened with a soft creak. Anna emerged, a plastic tray in her hands with several iced lemonades balanced carefully. She placed the tray on the table and Frank eagerly reached for one.

"Ah, that's the stuff," he said, no longer bothered by the sun.

Anna handed them to Ellie and Mary. At that moment, the door opened again and Gabe drove his wheelchair down into the garden too. Frank raised an eyebrow but said nothing as Gabe came over to the empty space at the table.

"Did you want lemonade?" Anna asked. "I wasn't sure. But I brought all the stuff just in case."

Gabe nodded. Then he said:

Stalker.

"Ha! You wish," Anna said, laughing as she clipped a cup holder to his armrest, placed a glass of lemonade in it, and guided an extra long straw to his mouth.

"Sit, sit, Anna," Ellie said, patting the empty chair that was between her and Gabe.

"I should be logging supplies," Anna said.

"Five minutes," Ellie said. "In this heat, you need some lemonade too."

Anna smiled. "Okay," she said. She sat in the empty chair next to Gabe and gratefully sipped the last lemonade.

Frank narrowed his eyes at Ellie but she looked away. "I saw a bluejay here yesterday," she said suddenly.

"How lovely," Mary said. She finished her row and turned the knitting around.

"How can you knit in this heat?" Ellie said, shaking her head.

"I like to keep my hands busy," Mary said as the length of wool scarf fell across her lap and down towards the ground.

Anna and Gabe were paying no attention to them. Anna took a sip of her lemonade and looked at Gabe.

"You don't get out enough," she said. "Your skin is so pale it's practically glowing and with your dark hair, you look like a vampire in the sun."

He smirked, then shifted his knuckle to type:

Team Edward.

Anna laughed so hard she snorted and Gabe took a satisfied sip of lemonade from the straw.

Frank stared between them. "I don't get it."

You're better off.

15

ANNA

Anna had been bracing for another ordinary Tuesday—the kind where the copier jams, the coffee tastes burned, and Patricia finds a reason to use the word *protocol* before lunch. Her ponytail swished against her neck with each step as she came down the hall, mentally ticking through the day's activity schedule.

When she walked by the living room, she stopped cold.

The room had been transformed. Streamers looped from the drop ceiling in slightly mismatched shades of pink and gold. A paper banner stretched across the far wall read *HAPPY BIRTHDAY ANNA* in cheerful, wobbly bubble letters. Someone had blown up a ridiculous number of balloons, which bobbed gently against chairs, walkers, and wheel rims.

And in the center of it all, Gabe. A cluster of helium balloons was tied to his armrests, bobbing gently every time he shifted. His eyes locked on hers—smug, satisfied—and the machine spoke before she could even breathe:

Surprise.

She blinked, looking from him to the banner to the grinning residents. "What? How?"

Ellie leaned toward her, eyes glittering. "Gabe here is quite the ringleader. Bossed us around like a Broadway stage manager."

Mary nodded primly, a cone party hat on her head didn't even wobble. "He had a vision. And we were simply the instruments of execution."

Frank snorted. "Execution's the right word. Nearly broke my back hanging those streamers."

Anna turned back to Gabe. "*You* did this?"

Underestimating me?

"I don't even remember telling you it was my birthday."

Mary tilted her head toward Anna. "Go on. Say thank you before the frosting dries."

Anna laughed, crossing the room until she was close enough to see the fine lines at the corners of Gabe's eyes. "Best birthday surprise I've ever had," she said softly.

Happy 30th, Anna.

She wanted to hug him but instead she directed her momentum into cutting and distributing cake like it was a full time job.

Later as they all lounged in a sugary stupor, Anna stretched out on the old floral sofa and looked up at the ceiling. There was a water stain that made her think of a huge pom-pom of hydrangea blossoms.

"What on earth is this?" Patricia appeared in the archway, staring at the party aftermath as though she had stumbled upon a crime scene. Anna shot up straight. Patricia continued, "This is a facility, not a carnival. Streamers on the sprinklers are a violation. Food needs to be logged. And no one authorized...this." She waved her hand at the room in general, her nose crinkled. "Whose idea was this?"

No one answered. Ellie gave her a look of theatrical innocence. Mary lowered her eyes but not her smirk.

Patricia's attention cut straight to the man at the center, balloons bobbing from his chair like taunts. Gabe's eyes held hers, unflinching. She inhaled sharply. "Somehow you always seem to be at the center of chaos, Mr. Whitlock. Don't think I haven't noticed it." To the rest of the room she said, "Get all this cleaned up."

Her soft-soled shoes still managed to slap a sound from the hardwood as she walked away. As soon as they couldn't hear it anymore, Frank started laughing. He slapped his thigh and laughed so loud and hard that tears gathered in the wrinkles around his eyes. For a moment everyone else just stared at him but then they all started to laugh too.

Ellie giggled and Mary grinned at Anna. Gabe's eyes crinkled with mischief. With a big sigh Anna pulled herself off the sofa and started to tidy up.

"You're not supposed to do that," Mary said, "It's your birthday."

"And," Ellie added, "we haven't given you your gifts yet." With a little flourish, she held out a small, tissue-wrapped bundle.

"What? There's gifts too?!" Anna stared at her.

"Every heroine deserves her sparkle," Ellie said as she pressed it into Anna's hands. "This is from my own collection, mind you. I wore it when I directed *Oklahoma!* in 1983. Try to live up to it."

Anna peeled the tissue back to reveal a brooch in the shape of a silver starburst, rhinestones catching the overhead light. Her throat tightened. "Ellie, it's beautiful."

Ellie tilted her chin. "Well, of course it is. You'll dazzle in it."

Mary was next, moving carefully with her walker, a pastel ribboned box balanced on the padded bench near Mary's knees. "Now, these aren't mine, dear. My grand-niece made them for her parish bake sale, and I bought a few for you. They're Snickerdoodles."

Anna pressed her palms together in delight. "Mary, thank you. You didn't have to—"

Mary's lips curved in that gentle, pointed way of hers. "Nonsense. Birthdays are for sweetness."

Frank grunted from his chair. "Well, hell, I didn't realize we were doing gifts. Nobody told me." He scratched at his temple, glancing around as if one might materialize. "Guess you can have the rest of my streamers. And any automotive advice you want, free for life."

The room chuckled, but Frank's eyes softened when they landed on her. "Happy birthday, kid."

Anna laughed, blinking quickly as her chest filled with something fierce and warm. She gathered the brooch and the cookies on the sofa and then went back to tidying up.

Nurse Becky appeared in the archway. "I heard Patricia ranting about a party in here?" She stepped further in. "Oh...my."

"It's Anna's birthday," Ellie explained.

"Happy birthday!" Becky immediately started helping Anna with the cleaning up. Thirty minutes later the room was completely back to normal.

"I've got to run," Becky said, "My girlfriend is picking me up in...uh, five minutes ago." She rushed out with a quick pat on Gabe's shoulder.

Frank turned to Ellie and said, "Do you think she means girlfriend or *girlfriend*?"

Ellie poked him. "None of your business, you dirty old man."

Gabe had spent most of the time they were cleaning preparing one sentence:

I'll carry those cookies to your car for you.

Anna grinned. "I suppose I can trust you not to eat them."

She fetched the gifts and put them on Gabe's lap. He drove his wheelchair out into the hall and Anna followed. She let him lead the way since his steering wasn't always super precise and people walking in front of him had occasionally been clipped by a metal footrest.

When they reached the front door, Anna pressed the accessibility button and they waited for it to swing completely open.

"Running away, Gabe?" Sylvia at the front desk asked with a wink.

"He's being a gentleman," Anna said.

"Will wonders never cease?" Sylvia murmured.

In the parking lot, Anna took the box of cookies and the brooch from Gabe and slid them into the passenger seat of her car. The brooch winked once in the sun before she shut the door, the sound echoing too loud in the open air. She leaned against the hot metal, squinting down at Gabe.

Nice car.

"It was my mother's." Anna's palm brushed the hot metal of the door, her fingertip finding the edge of a tiny chip in the paint. She let out a brittle laugh. "I never really get to talk about her. My dad—he's already barely holding it together. So I just...don't."

Gabe's eyes fixed on her, steady and intent. He nudged his knuckle against the AAC, slow and deliberate.

Tell me.

Anna rested the back of her head against the car. The metal pressed hot against her scalp, and she closed her eyes, letting the red glow of sunlight soak through her lids. "It's so hard to talk about her in the past tense. My love for her is still present tense and I keep having these dreams where she's on the phone and she's asking me to come and pick her up and when I say, 'But I thought you were dead,' she laughs and says, 'Oh, that was just a misunderstanding. I'm over at Logan, come and get me.'"

Her voice frayed and she breathed in the smell of sun-baked rubber from the tires nearby to steady herself. "And for those first seconds after I wake up, I believe it. Then I remember."

She pressed her lips together before continuing, her eyes still closed. "Sometimes the dreams get stranger. Sometimes she's calling from heaven and she says they have monthly allotted minutes." She choked out a sad laugh. Then took a deep, shaky breath and said, "I don't know how to believe in a world that she's not in. Where did she go? How can this world be the same world if she has vanished? It feels like I've somehow fallen into a parallel universe and I can't get back home. She's waiting for me back where I belong and I can't reach her."

That's when the tears came. Sudden, hot, relentless. They slid down her cheeks in fast streaks, and she let them go, made no attempt to stop or hide them.

"She was so alive," Anna whispered. "She came from this stoic, tight-lipped family, but she was all color and noise. My father...he's always been the quiet one. He loved her for her noise. She was the kite, and he was the string that kept her from flying away. And now..." Her voice thinned to a rasp. "Neither of us knows what to do without the kite."

She opened her eyes at last, lifting her hand to shield them against the glare. Gabe's gaze met hers, steady, kind, unflinching.

"I don't know if any of that makes sense," she whispered.

And once again, Gabe began to hum. Their own strange, private language. Anna leaned in, listening, holding herself steady in the moment. The melody tugged at her memory until recognition struck and she let out a half sob, half smile. *Nowhere But Here*. His song.

She began to sing the chorus along with his hum:

"If I'm lost, I'm lost with you.

If I'm found, it's only true

That there's nowhere, nowhere but here,

Nowhere but here to belong."

The hum faded and Anna felt stronger than she had in months.

So much I want to say.

Her lips trembled. "This is exactly what I needed. Thank you for being here to catch me when I finally broke."

16

GABE

That night Gabe couldn't sleep. The way Anna had spoken about her mother still rang in his mind. Colorful, bright, loud. A force of joy in a tight-lipped world. That was Anna. She filled Rosehaven's stale air with laughter, with warmth, with little bits of life no one else bothered to bring. And she didn't even know she was doing it.

He wanted more than anything to be the string to her kite. To anchor her, steady her, keep her safe when the wind pulled too hard.

Again he imagined them in another world, in another life...

The boxes were stacked in awkward towers, half-labeled, half-forgotten, the way moving days always seemed to go. Gabe braced one against his hip and shouldered it through the doorway, pretending the weight wasn't digging into his arms. Anna darted past him, hair slipping from its ponytail. They hadn't invented a hair tie yet that could contain the silkiness of her hair. She tugged open the blinds and sunlight spilled across the empty apartment like a row of exclamation marks.

"This is it," she breathed. "Ours."

Gabe set the box down and leaned against the wall, watching her. She filled every space with energy, with possibility. For a second he swore he could feel a current pulling her upward, her joy so buoyant it might carry her clean out of reach.

Instinctively, he stepped forward and caught her around the waist, pulling her against him. Her laugh startled into a soft gasp, fading into warmth as she rested there. He pressed his cheek to her temple and closed his eyes, letting her movement settle into his stillness.

And still deep in that fantasy, Gabe finally drifted to sleep.

The next morning Gabe found the living room unusually still for mid-morning. A few residents were dozing in sunbeams or quietly flipping through magazines. The heat had been intense this summer and every day seemed a bit worse. It was hard to get any energy on days like this.

Max stood by the ancient stereo cart, a gleam in his eye, and a vinyl sleeve in his hands like it was sacred scripture.

"I found this gem at a yard sale over the weekend," he announced to no one in particular. "Limited run, purple-splatter vinyl. First pressing. Absolute art."

Gabe wasn't listening to him. He was wondering what came next for the Gabe and Anna who existed in the alternative reality in his mind. Perhaps they were the Gabe and Anna who lived in the parallel universe where her mother was alive and waiting.

In his fantasy, the day was soft with the smell of spring: new earth, damp grass, a hint of lilacs drifting from the neighbor's yard. Gabe stood on the porch with Anna's hand in his, his heart beating far louder than it ever had before walking onstage. No guitar to hide behind, no lights to blind him. Just a painted front door and the sound of footsteps inside.

Anna gave his fingers a quick squeeze, her smile both teasing and encouraging. *Relax,* her eyes said. But his stomach still flipped when the door opened.

Her mother appeared first. She was exactly as Anna had described—her face fresh and happy, full of welcome. Her hair was threaded with silver but her smile was young, unguarded. She pulled Anna into a hug immediately.

"There you are," she said brightly, before her gaze shifted to him. Her eyebrows arched, appraising but playful. "And this must be Gabe. My daughter's new obsession."

"Ma," Anna groaned softly, but she was already laughing.

He held out his hand. "It's an honor, Mrs. Lin."

"Oh, don't you dare 'Mrs. Lin' me," she said, gripping his hand firmly. "It's Helen. Come in, come in. The porch isn't that special."

He wasn't going to argue even though the porch was actually quite interesting, filled with flower pots of all different shapes, sizes, and colors. Some had plants and some were empty. Each spindle of the railing was painted a different color and yet they all worked together. There was no time to look closely, as he was rushed into the house.

Inside, the air smelled of garlic and ginger sizzling in oil. A wok clattered in the kitchen, and soon Anna's father appeared, wiping his hands on a dish towel. He was quieter, measured. Short, but his posture neat as a soldier's. His eyes were sharp and Gabe suspected not much got by him.

"Dad," Anna said, "this is Gabe."

Her father extended his hand, grip strong, deliberate. Gabe met it without flinching. For a moment, they studied one another: the protective father and the man who dared to love his daughter. Then Henry Lin gave a single nod, the kind that meant *all right, you'll do...for now.*

At the kitchen table, her mother fussed with bowls and chopsticks, urging seconds on everyone even before the first bites were taken. Her voice filled every corner, bright and unashamed.

Her father said, "Anna tells us you're a musician."

"Yes, sir."

"Like, weddings? Teaching lessons?"

He smiled faintly. "Not exactly. I play in a band."

Henry's chopsticks paused mid-air. "And this is...your profession? Most people play in a band on the weekends for fun."

"It's my profession, yes."

Her mother tilted her head, unconvinced. "Forgive me, but that doesn't sound very steady."

Anna groaned. "Mom."

"What?" Helen waved her off. "A career should be stable. Music is wonderful but it's not a sustainable living, is it?"

Gabe kept his voice calm. "We're doing quite well. Band's called *Pressure Front*. We've been touring for ten years."

"Never heard of it," Helen said brightly, unbothered.

Henry cleared his throat. "Do you have another trade? Something to fall back on? A profession with security, benefits, pension?"

"I'm sure I'll think of something if it comes to that."

Anna dropped her chopsticks with a clatter. "Guys! They're *world famous*. This is ridiculous."

Her father interrupted, his tone measured. "Fame doesn't last, Anna. What happens when the noise fades?" He looked back at Gabe. "Can you keep her safe? Provide for her?"

Gabe felt heat crawl up his neck. He wanted to say, *I can give her everything that matters.* Instead, he held Henry's gaze. "I can promise I'll never walk away. Whatever the world throws at me—I'll still be here."

For a long moment, no one spoke. Then Henry gave a single, deliberate nod.

Helen sighed and muttered something about artists being too stubborn. But when she returned with a plate of peanut butter cookies, she set one in front of Gabe with the same affection as the others.

Later, while her mother washed dishes with a tune on her lips, her father walked Gabe to the door. The evening air had cooled, smelling of cut grass and spring earth. Henry studied him a long moment before speaking.

"She's like her mother," he said carefully. "Bright. Reckless. Needs someone steady."

"I know," Gabe answered, quiet but certain. "I want to be that."

Another pause, then Henry extended his hand again. "Then welcome."

Anna slipped her arm around his waist and leaned into him, whispering, "You passed. Trust me, if my mom's feeding you dessert, you're in." From the kitchen window came her mother's laughter, musical and alive.

Max dropped the needle on his new record. A guitar riff cut through the room—rich, sharp, just a little off-kilter in a way that told you something dangerous was about to happen. Then the unmistakable voice:

Don't save me, I shine better when I'm burning.

Gabe's head turned slowly.

"Pressure Front!" Max said, grinning like he'd just rediscovered fire. "Debut album! What a find! Man, they were *everything*. Angry. Poetic. Sex on strings." He air-guitared a little too enthusiastically, nearly knocking over a plastic vase of fake daisies.

I don't need your promises, don't tell me it gets better.

Gabe's AAC screen blinked to life.

Turn it off.

Max gasped. "Excuse you?! Do you not have any taste? This music is *legendary*. This is—this is sacred."

Another pause as Gabe tapped. Only the sound of the music from the record player, *If I burn, I burn smiling, because you struck the match.*

I wrote it.

Max stared. Blinked. Gabe could practically see the gears in his head turning as he tried to process what Gabe said. "What?"

Gabe didn't say elaborate, just kept looking steadily at Max. *If hope's a rope, I'll hang from it, swinging just to feel the air.*

Max's mouth fell open. "Holy *shit*." He spun around, hands in his hair. "No. No way. No *freaking* way. You're Gabe Whitlock? Like *that* Gabe Whitlock?"

Gabe's face twitched.

No, the *other* one.

Max was practically vibrating. "This is *insane*. Why didn't anyone tell me you were—like—*you*?"

Raise your glass to the ruins, we're the lucky ones still standing.

Turn it off.

This time Max did as Gabe asked, reverently lifting the needle and gently slipping the record back into its sleeve. But his excitement hadn't abated. He sat on the floral sofa and peppered Gabe with questions too fast to be answered. "I heard the band was fighting before the accident, is that true? I thought you died. That spotlight falling on you is like on the countdown of the wildest moments of rock and roll history. Were you writing a solo album? You would have killed it. Wait, wait, did you really date the bassist from Bone Trap or was that just—"

Gabe didn't even turn his head.

Jesus.

Max froze mid-sentence, one foot halfway onto the low table. "Too much?"

Gabe didn't answer. He just exhaled.

Max sank back, chastened but not entirely silenced. "Right. Sorry. Just...you're kind of my teenage hero. And now you're *here*. And I'm *here*. It's like the start of a redemption arc."

Gabe's brows lifted.

For who?

Max grinned sheepishly. "Honestly? Probably me."

Gabe raised an eyebrow and Max said, "Look, I've always been the guy who coasts. I'm late to class, late to work, half-assing my way through. My professors keep saying I've got potential if I'd just—" He waved his hands, searching. "—commit to something. But I never do. I flake. I get distracted. I let people down."

His voice softened. "And now I'm in this place where people are counting on me and I can't afford to screw up. Where showing up actually matters. And then I find *you* here—the guy I plastered on my walls in high school—and it's like...okay, story-wise? This is where I finally step up. Where I learn how to be reliable. Responsible. A grown-up worth a damn."

Gabe chuckled but didn't say anything. He hoped the story went that way for Max.

17

ANNA

Anna had a new activity prepared. Movie quote trivia.

The residents were divided into two teams, though "teams" was generous—Frank had declared himself captain and jumped in to answer first even though he didn't know anything about movies. Mary was writing the scores on a piece of printer paper, her penship elegant even with a leaking ballpoint pen.

Max fidgeted with the speaker, trying to connect his phone to queue up a round of theme songs for the bonus challenge.

Anna read off a set of notecards in her hands. "Fasten your seatbelts. It's going to be a bumpy night.'"

"That's *Gone With the Wind*," Frank said instantly.

"Seatbelts in *Gone With The Wind*? What is wrong with you?" Ellie screeched. "*All About Eve.* Bette Davis. 1950."

"Who the hell's Bette Davis?" Frank muttered.

Mary pursed her lips. "You'd know if you'd ever gone to a proper matinee, Frank."

"Next one," Anna said. "'Snap out of it!'"

Mary squinted. "That's got to be Katharine Hepburn," she said.

"Wrong again," Ellie said, leaning forward with relish. "That's Cher in *Moonstruck*."

Max nearly dropped his phone. "Wait, you've seen *Moonstruck*?"

"Of course I've seen *Moonstruck*. Everyone's seen *Moonstruck*." Ellie sniffed.

Meanwhile, Gabe's mouth twitched as Frank answered Casablanca for the fourth time in a row. Gabe didn't bother weighing in, but the look in his eyes said he was keeping score on his own.

Anna grinned. "All right, here's a bonus: name that villain—'I'll get you, my pretty, and your little dog too!'"

"Cruella De Vil," Frank blurted.

"Are you kidding me?" Ellie barked a laugh. "It's Margaret Hamilton as the wicked witch of the west in *The Wizard of Oz*. 1939. Good grief."

Frank muttered something under his breath that sounded suspiciously like, "Could've been Disney."

Mary clucked her tongue, carefully writing Ellie's team score with the neat precision of a schoolmarm tallying sins.

Anna crouched down to adjust Ellie's wheelchair footrest, still grinning at the chaos, when the older woman said, far too casually, "Dear, could you help Gabe stretch his arm out? He's been so stiff lately, and you have such nice strong little hands."

Anna blinked. "Oh," she said. "I thought Denise or Max were doing his stretches."

Ellie waved a bejeweled hand. "They *rush*. It's not the same. You're gentle."

There was a sudden silence. Mary froze. Even Frank looked up.

Anna stood slowly, a crease forming between her brows. "Are you asking because you think he needs help...or because you're trying to throw us together?"

Ellie didn't miss a beat. "Can't it be both?"

"Eleanor," Mary hissed.

"I mean it," Anna said, more serious now. "Is this some plan?"

Ellie tilted her chin. "I happen to believe in encouraging compatible people to spend time together."

Mary set her pen down a little too hard. "You're not supposed to manipulate them like they're props in one of your school plays."

"Oh please, Mary. It's not manipulation—it's guidance."

"It's inappropriate," Anna said, cheeks hot. She was trying so hard not to fall for him and now it turned out the others had been working against her.

Gabe hadn't moved a muscle. He was doing his impression of a stone statue staring fixedly at a spot on the far wall, his expression unreadable.

Mary sighed. "Saint Monica, give me patience. And a muzzle for my neighbor."

Ellie looked abashed for the first time.

Frank coughed. "You two are exhausting," he muttered. "No wonder Gabe plays dead half the time."

Gabe's AAC clicked once.

Confirmed.

At that moment someone new appeared in the doorway. He leaned one shoulder against the frame like it had been waiting for him, hand splayed just so, chin tipped up as if the fluorescent-lit hallway were a Broadway spotlight.

"Bernard Feldman," he announced, his voice carrying with stage-trained resonance. "But everyone calls me Bernie. Easier to shout from the cheap seats."

His outfit looked like it had been stolen piece by piece from a costume closet—an emerald silk scarf draped loosely over a loud paisley shirt, a velvet blazer five decades out of fashion, and plaid trousers that clashed so badly they almost circled back around to genius. Rings glittered on nearly every other finger, and the swoop of his salt-and-pepper hair was lacquered into place.

Ellie's mouth flattened as she took him in. "Oh great," she muttered. "We've got a peacock."

Mary pressed her fingers to her lips, stifling a laugh, while Bernie's grin only widened, clearly delighted to have drawn first blood before he'd even crossed the threshold. He swept into the room with a dramatic half-bow, the emerald scarf nearly brushing the floor.

"A peacock, madam?" he said, straightening with a hand to his chest. "Then I assure you, I intend to strut. Better a peacock than a pigeon, don't you think?"

Ellie raised one eyebrow. "Peacocks make a mess wherever they go."

"And pigeons," Bernie shot back smoothly, "just sit on statues and sulk. I'll take feathers and color any day."

Ellie just rolled her eyes.

Anna let out a small snort. But even as the room tilted toward amusement, there was a shift beneath it—something unspoken. Everyone here knew why there was space for Bernie, whose scarf trailed like a banner behind him. He had Harriet's bed now.

The loss still hung in the air, folded into the quiet shadows of their days. It wasn't his fault—this was life in a place where beds didn't stay empty for long.

Anna gestured toward the circle of chairs. "We're just getting started. It's movie quote trivia. Come on in."

Bernie lowered himself with a flourish, crossing one leg over the other.

"All right," Anna pulled out her cards again. "Next one. 'You can't handle the truth!'"

"Jack Nicholson, *A Few Good Men,* 1992," Ellie fired back without hesitation.

Bernie leaned forward, eyes glittering. "Delivered on the witness stand during the climactic courtroom scene: Colonel Jessup, breaking under questioning by Tom Cruise. An iconic moment in American cinema."

Ellie's eyes narrowed. "Details don't get you extra points."

"They do in my book," Bernie said, flashing her a grin.

Frank groaned. "What the hell, we got two encyclopedias now?"

Anna stifled a laugh and read out the next line, "'I'm ready for my close-up, Mr. DeMille.'"

"Gloria Swanson, *Sunset Boulevard,*" Ellie said, leaning back in satisfaction.

Bernie tipped his head, voice dropping into a flawless imitation of Swanson's husky dramatics: "I'm ready for my close-up, Mr. DeMille." His delivery sent shivers and chuckles around the circle.

Gabe's mouth quirked, his eyes glinting.

Ellie crossed her arms, looking both challenged and invigorated. "Fine. Anna, up the difficulty. Let's see if the peacock can keep up."

"I'll try." Anna flipped through the cards until she found one she thought might be more obscure. "Life is a banquet, and most poor suckers are starving to death!'"

Ellie sat forward instantly. "Rosalind Russell, *Auntie Mame.*"

But Bernie was right there with her, smacking his knee for emphasis. "1958, darling! And if you've never seen it, you've been robbed of joy."

"Here's a bonus, fill in the blank: 'You're gonna need a bigger—'"

"Boat," Ellie said at the same time Bernie said, "budget."

That broke even Frank's stone face into a laugh.

Bernie gave a mock bow. "Jaws," he conceded. "Though I maintain the budget line was implied."

Anna glanced at Gabe. He was watching with the sharp amusement of someone enjoying the absurdity and too smart to get in the middle of it. His eyes crinkled at her in silent commentary: *You've lost control of the room.*

Gabe's sister was visiting again. Anna only knew because she happened to walk by his room and saw Vicky through the open door. And when she paused, he looked up past his sister's shoulder, eyes latching onto Anna's in a silent plea. She felt an instant chill. Something was wrong.

She walked a little bit past the door and stopped, out of view but still within earshot. he paused outside his door, out of view but still within earshot.

What she heard was, "This is the power of attorney document I was talking about. Mom and Patricia can be witnesses. They'll get someone to hold your hand so you can sign. I don't know why I bother telling you, it's not like you even know what I'm saying." She sighed heavily and Anna was afraid she might be about to leave the room so she scrambled away.

Anna went to the resource room, her domain, her little sliver of happiness in the world. But it didn't make her feel any better this time. Gabe was pleading for help and what could she do?

She lowered her face flat onto the table, feeling the fake laminate wood on her forehead. Then there was a familiar voice in the doorway. Ellie had shuffled down the hall, propelling her wheelchair with her feet. "Everything all right, Anna?" she asked.

Anna looked up and was surprised to find that Ellie was looking at her with a steady, quiet calm. The theatrics were nowhere to be seen.

"No," Anna whispered.

Ellie continued into the room and stopped across from Anna, holding out her wizened hands, white with a smattering of large brown circles. "Tell me what's the matter," she said gently.

Anna took the offered hands and felt the warm pulse in them as she said, "It's Vicky. Gabe's sister."

Ellie sniffed judgmentally. "Yes, I've met the harpy."

"She's trying to get him to sign some kind of paperwork that will give her power of attorney over him."

"That woman," Ellie muttered angrily, shaking her head.

"You aren't surprised?"

"That sounds exactly like something she would do," Ellie said.

"I don't know what to do about it," Anna said, her voice breaking. "Gabe has no one looking out for him."

"Now that's just not true." Ellie smiled at Anna. "He has us."

Anna pulled her hands away from Ellie and shoved a stack of watercolor paper onto the floor in pure frustration. "What good is that? What are a bunch of old people and a college drop-out going to do?"

"You know," Ellie said, ignoring the insult, "A band as big as his was must have had some legal entanglements. They must have worked with a lawyer. If you can find their lawyer, I'd bet anything he would be happy to help our Gabe out of this predicament."

Anna's face lit up in a huge smile. "That's brilliant, Ellie!"

"Us old people aren't just here for decoration," she said with a wink.

"Can I give you a hug?"

"Of course." Ellie opened her arms and Anna ran around the table, leaning over to clasp her arms around the frail woman's bony shoulders.

The hydrangeas had bloomed early this year, their petals already beginning to spot and curl in the July heat. Henry knelt in the soft dirt, careful on his knees, pruning away browned leaves with the same slow precision he'd once used to measure a bridge span. The air smelled faintly of cut grass and something sweet turning sour.

Anna crouched on the flagstone path beside him, watching the deliberate arc of his clippers. "You know," she said softly, "sometimes letting it grow wild isn't the worst thing."

He didn't look at her. "Wild means overrun." A pause. "Overrun means decay."

She reached out and let her fingers trail along one of the blooms, brushing the edges where the blue had faded to papery beige. Anna smiled faintly, remembering her mother with dirt under her nails and sweat across her brow, planting flowers in mismatched rows because she liked the "conversation" between the colors.

"They're beautiful," she said. "But they were never perfect. Mom liked them to surprise her."

He clipped another stem, more forcefully this time. "Surprises don't last."

"They do," Anna said, "if you let them keep happening."

For a long moment, all he did was look at the flower heads in his palm, brittle enough to crumble if he closed his fist. Her mother's voice seemed to hang there, too—laughing, impulsive, always reaching for something new. Finally, he set the blooms gently in the trimmings bucket. "I suppose," he said quietly, "nothing stays preserved forever. Not gardens. Not houses. Not people."

The breeze shifted, carrying the faint sound of children playing somewhere beyond the fence. Henry set his clippers down on the grass. "The best you can do is tend what's here now. Make it the best it can be while it's yours to care for."

When he looked up at her, there was no defensiveness in his eyes, only weariness.

Anna stood back up. "I have to do something for work."

At least that made him smile.

She went into the house and opened up her laptop. It didn't take too much research to figure out who the lawyer for *Pressure Front* had been. Clint Rivera. His professional headshot on his firm's website was enough to make her want to never do anything wrong in her life.

And she had to call this man.

18

GABE

Clint Rivera walked in like he hadn't missed eleven years of Gabe's life. Same clean-cut lawyer look. Same leather briefcase. Same damn expensive shoes. But the lines around his eyes were deeper now. And he wasn't trying to fake small talk.

"Whitlock," he said with a nod. "You look like hell. But glad to see you're still breathing."

Gabe stared. His jaw would have been on the floor if he had that much control over it.

"Your friend contacted me," Clint said, pulling up a chair and sitting. It creaked under him. "Anna. She said Vicky is trying to get her hands on your money."

Gabe blinked. Anna had understood the look he tried to give her. Not only that, she had come up with a damn good idea too. If anyone could stop Vicky in her tracks, it would be Clint.

"I looked into it and it's true. She's filed a motion for full power of attorney. She's claiming you're not competent to manage your own affairs. That the brain damage—"

His knuckle slamming the screen with more force than necessary:

Bullshit.

"I know," Clint said. Calm. Flat. "But the court doesn't know you. All they'll see is paperwork and a woman in a blazer crying on cue about her poor broken brother."

Gabe's pulse pounded in his ears.

Why now?

Clint opened his briefcase. "I can't know this for sure but the company her husband works for has been plummeting in the stockmarket and I bet she's hurting financially. Vicky thinks you're alone. That you won't fight back. That you've given up."

He laid a form down on Gabe's lap, only one of the pages. "You can designate someone of your choosing as POA. I'll file it myself, but the judge is going to ask—who's watching out for you? Who do you trust?"

Gabe stared at the line. The blank space. He wanted to burn the fucking form.

Me.

"You can't name yourself. The system doesn't work that way."

Silence.

Clint continued on. "We need someone the court will trust. Someone clean, dependable, with a legitimate tie to you."

Gabe knew what was coming. He hated that he knew what was coming.

"Ray," Clint said.

Gabe turned away.

Absolutely not.

"I figured you'd say that," Clint said, no judgment in his voice. Just strategy. "You haven't seen him since the accident?"

Same with you.

Clint winced almost imperceptibly. But what he said was, "I'm not going to lie to you. If we fight this without naming someone, we could still win. But it'll be ugly. And expensive. And public."

A pause.

"And if we lose—she gets everything. Decisions. Access. The right to move you. Sell the rights to your music if she wants."

Gabe's throat tightened.

"Ray has a clean record. A stable life. He runs music schools for kids."

Gabe ground his teeth. His hand twitched on his lap. He tried to imagine Ray walking into this room. Seeing him like this. Limp. Strapped to a padded chair. Speaking through a box with a robot voice. Him. The guy who used to fuck groupies on top of an amp stack. Who used to break strings mid-set from playing too damn hard. He never wanted them to see him like this, Ray or Tommy.

But if the cost of freedom was shame?

He'd pay it.

Every goddamn time.

Okay.

Clint didn't smile. Just nodded, took the paper back, and stood. "Good to see you again, Whitlock." He gave Gabe's shoulder a firm pat.

At the door to his room, Anna was waiting. Clint handed her a card on his way out. "Any time," he said quietly. "He ever needs *anything*, call me."

After Clint left, Anna cautiously came further into the room. Gabe was staring into the distance, trying to be okay with his bandmates showing up here, his old life colliding with his new life.

"I hope it's okay I reached out to him. I didn't know what to do. It was Ellie's idea. He really does care a lot about you," Anna said.

Gabe smiled wearily.

You did good.

19

ANNA

"All duds, huh?" Rachel scrolled lazily through the dating app while stretched out on Anna's bed, her socked feet kicking in the air. She made a face, shuddering dramatically. "Man, I'm so glad I'm finished with dating. Sorry, Anna."

Anna sat propped against the headboard, arms loosely wrapped around her knees, not even glancing at Rachel's phone. Her thoughts were elsewhere, heavy and circling.

"Rachel," she said suddenly, "what do you love about your husband?"

Rachel lowered the phone, lips pursing as she considered. "That's...not what I expected you to ask."

Anna forced a shrug, like it was nothing.

Rachel stared at the ceiling for a moment. Finally she said, "There's nothing better than someone who makes you laugh. Things change: circumstances, bodies, life. But if you have someone in your corner that you can laugh with, it all gets easier."

Anna's throat tightened. She didn't want to admit she was thinking about Gabe. Not that she had told Rachel anything about...whatever that was. What she was feeling didn't make any sense. Just because he was the only man under 80 that she knew didn't mean she should be thinking this way about him.

He did make her laugh, which was impressive considering his limited communication. And she felt so relaxed around him. So *herself.* No. She could not be falling for the frontman of *Pressure Front.* She could not be falling for a quadriplegic living in a nursing home.

I'm getting my life back on track, she scolded herself, *not going even further off the rails.*

"Anna?" Rachel was looking at her intently, eyebrows raised. "You have someone in mind?"

"No," Anna squeaked too quickly. She ducked her face as Rachel narrowed her eyes. "I've just been thinking a lot about a guy at my work. But it's so inappropriate."

"Oh yeah, be careful with that. Your contract probably has a clause about relationships among staff. You're just lonely. This is why you have to keep putting yourself out there. You know what they say, you have to kiss a lot of frogs."

Anna's stomach flipped. Her brain, unhelpfully, was now stuck on what it might feel like to kiss Gabe. To lean down, to feel the warmth of his breath, the press of his lips, his stubble tickling her skin.

She pressed her palms against her flushed face. If Rachel only knew her crush was on a patient, not a staff member. "You're right," she mumbled. "I'm just lonely."

That made more sense than anything else. She used to know people, she used to have more friends. Now it seemed they had all moved on without her. All she had was her dad, her job, and this too-big house. And Rachel. Kind-hearted, practical Rachel.

Rachel brightened, already moving into solution mode. "We'll have you over for a BBQ this week. Steve wants maximum grill time while the weather holds. Summer's halfway gone."

Anna could see the gears turning behind her friend's eyes. They would invite Steve's coworkers. Eligible men.

Anna forced a smile. "Sounds nice."

By the time Rachel went home, Henry was already asleep and the house was quiet again. Far too quiet. Anna padded through the hallway, brushing her teeth on autopilot, switching off lights, setting her phone on the nightstand.

But when she slid under the covers, sleep wouldn't come. Her body was restless, her skin prickling with heat, and she knew exactly why.

Gabe.

She bit her lip hard, trying to force her thoughts away, but the images crowded in anyway: his eyes holding hers with a steadiness that made her feel anchored, the curve of his mouth when he was amused, the way he could say more with a single lifted brow than most men did in a paragraph.

Her pulse throbbed in her throat. She imagined touching him, deliberately sliding her hand into the narrow space between his body and the hard frame of his chair. She imagined leaning down, catching his mouth with hers, feeling his lips yield to her, tasting him.

Her thighs pressed together under the sheets as she tried to ease the unbearable ache between them. She squeezed her eyes shut, but it only made the fantasies clearer: her hands sliding over the planes of his chest, her cheek resting against his while he tilted his head back into the cradle of the chair's headrest, burning alive beneath her.

Anna covered her face with the pillow, shame and desire tangling until she couldn't breathe. She had to stop. She had to *stop*.

But her body wasn't listening.

When she finally drifted into sleep, her cheeks were damp, her pulse still thrumming, her last coherent thought a desperate admission she couldn't say out loud:

She wanted Gabe Whitlock.

Not because he was famous. Not because she was lonely. Not because she felt sorry for him.

She wanted him because he was already giving her more than anyone else did: laughter, steadiness, a space where she could finally stop pretending.

Deep in her heart she knew the truth. She had already fallen for him.

20

GABE

He knew they were here before they even walked through the front doors. The music was faint at first—muffled bass notes from a phone speaker, someone humming along. Then: laughter. Loud, unfiltered, obnoxious laughter.

Tommy.

The sound ricocheted down the hallway like a chainsaw at a book club. From his room Gabe heard the commotion. His bandmates couldn't have even made it past the front desk yet when Tommy shouted, "Damn, this place smells like pudding and broken dreams!"

"Tommy," Ray hissed. "Lower your voice."

But Tommy never lowered anything.

"Where's my boy Gabe? Where's my beautiful bastard?"

Gabe's chest tightened. His jaw twitched. They were here. He hadn't seen them in over a decade. Not since the hospital. Not since the accident broke his body and the silence afterward broke everything else.

The door to his room swung open without ceremony.

Tommy charged in like a storm in too-tight jeans, still wearing that godawful leather jacket from their '09 tour, his silver hair stuck up in spikes that he was far too old for. Ray followed more slowly, hands in his jacket pockets, gaze flicking around like a man walking into a confessional for the first time, looking more like a middle-aged businessman than a bass player.

"Gabe!" Tommy cried, dropping his bag on the floor. "Holy *shit*, you look terrible. Like sexy Frankenstein. You miss me?"

Gabe stared. Then blinked once.

Tommy whooped. "Still got that laser-beam stare, huh?"

He leaned over and slapped Gabe's shoulder with way too much force. Gabe winced.

Ray hovered by the door, stiff, quiet, shifting his weight back and forth.

Tommy was already spinning in place, eyes darting around Gabe's chair.

"Wait, wait. What's with this setup? What is this, NASA?" He peered closer at the AAC. Then he turned to Ray and said, "Why the hell can't he talk? This shit ain't right."

Gabe narrowed his eyes. Tapped out slowly, deliberately:

Ask me, asshole.

Tommy stopped cold. His mouth broke into a grin. "There he is."

Ray finally stepped closer, his eyes flicking to Gabe's headrest, the joystick, the AAC mounted on the armrest. His throat bobbed.

"Hey," he said, voice low. Rough.

Gabe didn't respond.

Ray rubbed the back of his neck, then reached into his pocket and pulled out a wrapped chocolate bar that must have already completely melted in the summer humidity. "Thought you might still like these."

Gabe stared at the offering. He couldn't reach out and grasp it, couldn't unwrap it, couldn't even eat it without help. His fingers twitched but that was the most he could do. This was exactly why he hadn't wanted them here. It took less than a minute for Ray to accidentally rub in Gabe's face just how very crippled he was.

Ray coughed and didn't know what to do so he put the chocolate bar back in his pocket. Tommy either didn't notice or didn't care. He plopped down in the visitor chair and stretched his legs out like he owned the place.

"So what's the plan, Gabe? We bust you outta here? Stage a riot? Or we just drink Ensure and play Bingo with the octogenarians?"

From the hallway came Ellie's voice: "I heard that, and I'm still hotter than your drum solos ever were, darling."

Tommy whooped again. "That one's got a future! Let's go Bingo, my man!"

They made their way to the resource room, Gabe reluctantly leading, self-conscious of how he must look to Tommy and Ray following behind his power wheelchair.

Bingo was a goddamn circus.

Tommy, naturally, took over as caller after five minutes. He'd grabbed the mic from Anna and started reading numbers in his best stadium voice, throwing in commentary like he was announcing a prizefight.

"B-6, and if you don't have it, blame capitalism!"

Ellie cackled so hard she nearly knocked her glasses into her apple juice.

Mary leaned over to Anna and said, "Is this your doing?"

Anna just laughed, cheeks flushed, silky black ponytail brushing against her shoulder. "Absolutely not. But I'm not stopping it."

She looked over at Gabe and smiled like she was letting him get away with something. He couldn't look away from her.

Ray, meanwhile, sat two chairs away from Gabe, quietly helping a resident who struggled to pick up her chips. He didn't say much: just placed the chips on the numbers, smiled gently, and kept scanning the corners of the room like the ceiling might drop again. Gabe watched him. Noted the fidgeting. The way his eyes avoided any sharp movement. The way he flinched at the jarring squeal of the microphone Tommy kept swinging around like a weapon. Ray wasn't having fun. He was enduring it.

The door banged open and Max barreled in, nearly tripping over a walker, face flushed with the kind of excitement that made him look twelve instead of twenty-two.

"Oh my God. Oh my God. Do you have any idea what's happening right now?" He was already halfway across the room before anyone could even think to answer. "All of *Pressure Front* in one place! This is incredible."

"Sit down, kid, you're blocking my view," Frank grumbled. Of what wasn't clear since Bingo wasn't a highly visual activity.

Max ignored him and planted himself between Gabe and Ray, putting a hand on each of their shoulders, practically vibrating as he connected them like a wire. "Do you even understand the historical significance here? I mean, Tommy Keys, Ray Delgado, and *Gabe Whitlock*—" His voice dropped to a reverent whisper, "—together again."

Tommy grinned and pointed the mic at Gabe. "What do you say, Gorgeous Gabe? Reunion tour?"

Gabe's eyes glinted. His left knuckle tapped once, twice, three times. The AAC's flat electronic voice announced:

Sure. In hell.

The room broke into laughter—Tommy whooping, Anna giggling with delight.

But Gabe didn't look away from Tommy. His throat worked once, and then the sound came—low, rough at first, like an engine turning over after years in a garage. A single note. Then another. Three, four, strung together into the middle of *that* song. The one they'd been playing the night the rigging came down. Gabe remembered the exact moment the song was interrupted and he picked it back up from that point.

Tommy froze mid-swing of the mic, letting it fall against his thigh with a soft thud. Ray's head jerked up, eyes locking on Gabe like he couldn't believe what he was hearing. Even Max's manic grin faltered.

The hum deepened, steady now, pulling in the next line, then the next. The melody threaded through the air, filling every corner of the room, soft but unstoppable.

Ellie lowered her Bingo card into her lap. Mary's lips pressed together, eyes flicking between Gabe and the men beside him. Anna's smile faded into something quieter, her chest rising and falling in time with the tune. They may not have known the significance of his choice but they could feel the sharp, haunted energy in it.

By the time he reached the last few notes, the room was silent except for him. The ending was softer than it had ever been on stage—no roaring crowd, no crash of cymbals—just a breath and the fading echo of what was lost.

Gabe let the final note die, the silence afterward stretching thin as glass.

"Holy shit," Max whispered. Then he did what he did best and stated the obvious. "That's the song. That's the one that you never finished that night."

Tommy let out a sharp laugh that wasn't really a laugh at all. "Kid, you don't just say that out loud." He shoved a hand through his silver hair, eyes darting anywhere but Gabe. "Je-

sus...I can still feel the damn lights in my face from that night."
His voice cracked on the last word, and he quickly cleared his
throat, snapping the mic cord against his palm like he needed
the sting to ground himself, forced a grin, and said, "N-42, and
you know who you are."

The Bingo game continued. Ray finally looked up, met
Gabe's eyes, and gave the smallest nod. No smile. Just a quiet
acknowledgment. Then he pushed his chair back, murmured
something to the resident beside him, and slipped out the side
door without another word.

The game stumbled on, numbers being called without con-
viction, laughter muted to a polite hum. Gabe stayed where
he was for a while, watching the door Ray had gone through.
When enough time had passed that it wouldn't look like he was
chasing him, when most of the room's attention had gone back
to their cards, Gabe eased the joystick forward.

The door opened with a slow creak, and the heat of the
garden spilled in. His wheelchair bumped roughly down the
short wooden ramp into the gravel of the garden path.

The Rosehaven garden wasn't much. Some raised beds,
mostly overgrown. Two benches. One patch of half-dead hydrangeas that someone tried to revive every spring with manure
and months later, it still stank.

Ray stood at the edge of the raised bed, staring down at a
ceramic frog half-buried in over-grown clover.

He didn't turn when he heard Gabe's chair.

Just said, "I used to hate the noise. Now I chase it. You were the one who never stopped moving, never shut up. I used to hate it but now I hate being without it." He rubbed the back of his neck, eyes fixed on the frog like it might blink.

Gabe didn't answer. Let the chair hum to a stop beside the bench. He hadn't been that person in a long time.

Ray turned back to Gabe; looked at his face, then down at his body strapped to the wheelchair, then back up again. The wind caught the edge of Ray's windbreaker. He dug out a crumpled pack of cigarettes, lit one with shaking fingers and took a drag.

"Surprised you came out here," he said quietly.

Surprised he came or surprised he *could* come out here? Gabe wasn't sure. If Ray was trying to escape him, there were other places he could go that Gabe wouldn't be able to follow. Gabe tapped on the AAC slowly and Ray watched, his face looking sader and sader with every shakey movement of Gabe's hand:

Not done with you.

Ray nodded, then lowered himself onto the bench. Sitting made them nearly eye level, but his gaze stayed on the cigarette between his fingers. "I know how this sounds," Ray said with a sigh, finally looking at Gabe again. "But I'm going to say it anyway. All of this has been really hard for me."

Gabe's eyes opened wide, his eyebrows raised, clearly intending a sarcastic "for YOU?"

"Yeah, I know, I know," Ray said. "Nothing happened to me. I shouldn't be struggling with it so much. You're the one who lost everything in that moment. I lost everything more slowly."

Gabe raised an eyebrow again, this time more of a question. Ray pulled in on the cigarette and blew the smoke behind him towards a bush. "You were standing *next* to me. Same goddamn spot we stood every show. And I've gone over it so many times in my head. Why you and not me? Why not both of us? Why not someone else entirely? Just a few inches could have changed everything."

He flicked ash onto the pavement. Didn't look at it. "I couldn't cope with it. I started drinking. Like for real. Not fun drinking, escape from life drinking. Elaine left me."

Gabe didn't know how to respond to that. Part of him wanted to roll his eyes and say "cry me a river." What Ray and Tommy lost was nothing compared to what Gabe lost. His career, his friends, one hundred percent of his independence, and his literal goddamn voice. He could no longer even use music to exorcise his demons.

Then again, why compare at all? The accident had been horrible all around. It impacted everyone who was there that night, and everyone who knew them, rippling out further and further. Gabe was the epicenter but the quakes shook apart other people's lives too.

He never thought Elaine and Ray would split up. He knew how much Ray loved his wife. That alone was a devastating impact of the accident.

Ray roughly wiped a tear from his cheek with the back of one hand. "I shouldn't be saying this to you of all people," he said. "I just...I never said I was sorry. Not for something I did, but for what I couldn't stop. I replay that night like a bad track on loop. My hands on the bass, your voice in my ear, and then—" He broke off, shoving the words away with another drag from the cigarette. Then he looked down at the glowing tip and a shadow passed across his face. With a strange, innocent sincerity he held it out towards Gabe, offering.

Gabe's brow furrowed like he was about to refuse, but then—slowly—he gave the smallest nod. Why not? Ray hesitated, then stepped in close, one hand steadying the cigarette, the other bracing against the back of the wheelchair, trying not to drop ash on him.

"All right," Ray muttered. "Just like the old days."

The smoke hit Gabe's lungs with a burn so sharp it made his eyes water. He coughed. Once, twice. Then he doubled over, caught only by his seatbelt, gasping as his body shook in spasms.

"Shit, shit, Gabe," Ray's voice pitched high with panic, cigarette hitting the dirt as he grabbed the wheelchair armrests. He looked like he was about to start shaking Gabe by the shoulders but was afraid he would just break him worse. "Breathe, man. Come on, just breathe."

Gabe's coughing eased into a rough wheeze, then into laughter, low and ragged. He awkwardly pushed himself back up with his fists against the wheelchair seat and his knuckle tapped the AAC until its voice said:

Easy there. Trying to kill me again?

Ray froze, then let out a choked, relieved laugh. "You asshole."

Gabe grinned, then he tapped:

Next time, bring whisky.

"You got it," Ray said, sinking back onto the bench and pushing his hand roughly through his hair.

The chair's motor gave a low hum as Gabe adjusted slightly, letting physics move his body for him. He took a few deep breaths to test if his lungs were functioning again. They were.

Then Ray said, seemingly from nowhere, "Anna is a sweet little thing. I think she really likes you."

Gabe's brows pulled together. A slow blink.

Ray didn't look at him, just shoved his hands into his jacket pockets and stared at the garden like it might offer him an easier conversation. "Not that it's my business. Just...nice to see someone paying attention. You were always better with people than you thought."

Gabe's knuckle hovered over the AAC for a long moment before tapping out:

Why are you saying this?

Ray shifted, cleared his throat. "When I saw you in there, finishing that song...it hit me how much I've been avoiding you. Avoiding this." He gestured vaguely toward the chair and everything that went with it. "I didn't know how to look at it. At you. Without feeling like I should've done something that night."

Gabe's jaw tightened, but he stayed quiet.

Ray gave a short, bitter laugh. "Guess I'm saying, if there's someone who can make you forget about all this shit for a while...don't push her away."

For a moment neither of them spoke. The air was thick with the smell of damp earth and cigarette smoke. Somewhere inside, Tommy's voice boomed another Bingo number, oblivious to the weight out here.

"I'm sorry," Ray said. "We should've come sooner."

No shit.

Finally Ray smiled a real smile.

Clint arrived an hour later with the paperwork. "Everything good?" he said, stepping into Gabe's room like he'd been here a hundred times. His suit jacket smelled faintly of rain and expensive coffee.

Gabe gave him a small nod.

Ray was already there, leaning against the wall with his arms folded, like he might bolt if this turned into something heavier than signatures. His eyes flicked to the folder under Clint's arm. "So that's it, huh?"

"This is it," Clint said, putting a slim stack of papers onto a desk against the wall. He laid a pen beside them, then paused. "You're sure about this, Gabe? No coercion, right? We both agree this is the best course of action?"

Gabe's gaze shifted from Clint to Ray. No hesitation. He tapped once.

Yes.

Clint glanced at Ray. "Alright. Then we'll make it official." He gestured for Ray to sit down at the desk. "Durable power of attorney. This gives you authority to make financial and legal decisions if Gabe can't."

Ray shifted his weight, rubbing a hand over his jaw before picking up the pen. "Feels weird," he muttered. "Like I'm stepping into something I shouldn't."

"You're stepping into what he asked you to," Clint said evenly.

Ray glanced back at Gabe again. "You really trust me with this?"

Gabe's knuckle tapped.

Vicky is circling

Ray's throat worked. "Well I don't mind sticking it to that bitch," Ray said. "...pardon my language."

He bent over the paper and signed, his name neat and deliberate despite the slight tremor in his hand. Clint flipped to the next page, explaining each section in that calm, methodical lawyer voice.

When it was done, Ray set the pen down and let out a slow breath. "Guess that's that."

Clint gathered the documents, slipping them back into the folder. "That's that. I'll file these with the court this week." He gave Gabe a brief nod. "It's a good choice."

When Clint left, the room felt quieter. Ray stayed in the chair for a long moment, looking at the now-empty desk. "You know this means I'm in charge of your money, right? First thing I'm buying is a hot tub."

Gabe tapped.

Only if I get to drown you in it.

Ray laughed, shaking his head. "Yeah. That's the guy I remember."

"Yo, Ray, we going?" Tommy's head appeared around the doorframe. "You do the thing?"

"Yeah, it's taken care of," Ray said. He clapped a hand to Gabe's shoulder. "We'll visit again soon."

Gabe let his head fall back against the headrest and tilted his chair back, eyes fixed on the ceiling. The papers were gone, yet their weight seemed to linger in the air, like a conversation that hadn't entirely ended. He was exhausted and it was still hours until bedtime. What a day. He didn't even know where to begin processing all that had happened.

The door opened again, softer this time. He knew it was Anna even without raising his wheelchair or turning his head because of the smell of paint that always clung to her like perfume. She closed the door behind her.

"I saw Clint leave," she said. "Guess it's official now."

Gabe's eyes tracked her as she came closer. He blinked once, too tired to do anything else.

She sat on the edge of his bed and said, "How does it feel?"

He tried to raise his left knuckle to type but gave up almost immediately. His hand fell down into his lap.

"Ray's a good choice," Anna said gently. "He came back for you. Not everybody does that."

She reached out, resting her fingers lightly over his right hand on the armrest. "You don't have to figure out how you feel about it all today. You've got time."

She let the silence linger for another beat, then looked toward his window. "By the way, Tommy's been telling Ellie and Mary about how he once got mistaken for Elton John. With sunglasses and a boa. And Mary kept saying 'Isn't that something?' like she's just being polite but you can see her dying inside."

One corner of Gabe's mouth lifted.

"And Ellie," Anna went on, "is taking notes for her memoir. Which I think is mostly just a list of people she's judged."

That pulled an actual sound from him—half a hum, half a laugh.

Anna just looked at him for a long moment. "You look tired," she said softly. "Do you want to get into bed for a while?"

He closed his eyes for a moment and nodded a small nod.

Anna's eyes darted to the lift by his bed, and the flicker of uncertainty in her face was unmistakable. "Uh...I have no idea how to work that thing."

He arched a brow and tried to give a look that expressed that it was way too complicated to explain. That seemed to work because she said, "Okay, then we'll do it the old-fashioned way."

Her voice had that forced brightness she used when she wasn't sure of something.

But even if he had only known her for a short time, he already knew that she had more determination than anyone he had ever met. He had total trust that she would find a way to do absolutely anything she decided to.

Gabe tilted the wheelchair back up and drove it closer to the side of the bed. Anna fumbled with the seatbelt but got it undone. He felt her fingers against him and a shudder of desire ran through him that he tried to ignore.

She crouched beside him. Her arms slid behind his back and the warmth of her body seeped through his clothes immediately.

He tried to help—lifting his left forearm just enough to hook it awkwardly against her shoulder, a faint push of his elbow to shift his weight toward her. It wasn't much, but it was all he had, and he saw the flicker of gratitude in her eyes when it made the lift even a fraction easier.

He could smell her shampoo—something faintly citrus—and underneath it, the clean sweat of someone who'd been moving around all day. When she shifted to lift, his chest pressed against her shoulder, his cheek close enough to catch the stray hairs that had fallen from her ponytail.

"Okay...here we go," she murmured, half to herself. She pivoted awkwardly toward the bed, It wasn't graceful. She had to stop, readjust, brace her feet before lifting again. The movement jostled his legs, his torso, everything he couldn't help her with. The helplessness bit, but her closeness dulled the edge.

She got his butt onto the bed then lowered the rest of his upper body to the mattress. His arm twitched in a small, useless attempt to adjust himself. She pushed hard to get him fully onto the bed, then bent down to lift his legs up swing them up onto the bed too. Finally she rested, breathing heavily, her forehead against his chest. Her fingers brushed his arm as she stood back up; light, but enough to make the air between them feel different.

"Not bad for a rookie, right?" she whispered.

With the AAC device still on his wheelchair and out of reach, Gabe didn't bother to try to communicate anything about liability and how much trouble Anna would probably be in if she dropped him.

Gabe knew Clint's plan had worked because of Patricia. He had suspected that his sister was good friends with the executive director and the way Patricia was behaving proved it beyond a shadow of a doubt.

The change wasn't loud. That wasn't her style. She didn't throw tantrums or slam doors. But she stopped pretending. No more fake smiles when she passed him in the hallway. No more over-articulated greetings like, "How are *we* today?"

Now?

She didn't look at him at all. She walked past him without looking, tablet in hand, posture tense. She muttered instructions under her breath. And she spoke to Anna like she was a temp and her days were numbered. Clearly it didn't escape Patricia's notice that Anna had played a role in this coup. Gabe hated that it was going to hurt her. If he could undo that, he would. Maybe he could still find a way to take the heat completely off her. He had been a trouble-maker long before she showed up. But he had to admit she had helped light the spark in him again.

If I burn, I burn smiling, because you struck the match.

And when Ray came in last Tuesday to drop off notarized copies of the POA, Patricia's face had gone pale in a way that made Gabe almost laugh.

Almost.

She recovered quickly, greeted Ray with a flat "We appreciate you advocating for your friend" but it was just a beat too slow.

That's when Gabe *knew*. Knew Vicky hadn't just been working the legal system. She'd been working the damn *building*. And Patricia—rigid, precise Patricia—had been in her pocket the whole time. Probably sold it to herself as following procedure. Probably let herself believe she was "protecting a vulnerable resident" or whatever institutional euphemism helped her sleep at night.

Now, when she looked at him, she saw a problem she no longer had permission to solve. And through her, his sister was going to get the message loud and clear: *You don't own me anymore.*

21

ANNA

Ray and Tommy were visiting again, so Anna canceled the planned cornhole tournament in the living room and let the energy take them wherever it wanted to go. She may have even been the one to suggest this particular day, knowing that it was Patricia's day off.

The room was chaos in the most beautiful way: folding chairs haphazardly arranged, coffee cups balanced on every available surface, and at least two guitar cases. Sylvia took one look, muttered something about "OSHA violations," and fled back to her desk. Frank had stationed himself near the door with arms crossed like a bouncer, as if someone might try to sneak in without paying cover.

Bernie, already holding court on one of the side sofas, popped up the second he saw the guitars. "Gentlemen," he said, sweeping a hand like he was introducing royalty. "At last, some class in this place."

Ellie rolled her eyes. "He's going to work his way into the set, just you watch. The man needs a spotlight like plants need the sun."

Bernie ignored her entirely, striding toward Ray and Tommy like they were lifelong friends. "You boys need a triangle player? Kazoo? Backup dancer?" He gave Tommy a wink and clapped Ray on the shoulder. "I'm available for all positions, day or night."

"Flirt with someone else," Ellie called out. "Or better yet—don't."

Bernie grinned and pivoted toward Anna, who laughed and shook her head.

Ray plucked a low note that vibrated in everyone's chest. "We're gonna do this old-school," he said.

"You're not singing?" Tommy asked.

Ray smirked and tilted his head toward Gabe. "Nope. Lead vocals right there."

A few chuckles rolled through the room. Max whooped with delight. Gabe raised his brows like, *Really?* His AAC lit up with a slow tap: **You're insane.**

Max turned to Anna and said, like a narrator in a bad documentary, "They've never performed together without him. Never replaced him, despite the pressure. Tommy went to another band. Ray started teaching."

"C'mon," Ray coaxed. "You still got the timing. You hum, we'll fill in the rest."

Anna, perched on the arm of Mary's chair, grinned. "I want to hear this."

Bernie clapped his hands. "Me too! If I faint from sheer musical bliss, just leave me where I fall."

Ellie gave him a withering look. "We can only hope."

Gabe narrowed his eyes at Anna—*traitor*—but when Tommy hit the first familiar chords, something in his shoulders eased. The melody came back to him like muscle memory. His mouth stayed closed and the hum rose up, low and rough, a little shaky at first, then stronger. Not a stand-in for his voice but something alive, threaded with every mile he'd traveled to get here.

The room shifted. Conversations stopped. Mary's hands folded over her walker. Ellie leaned forward like a critic at opening night. Even Frank, at the door pretending not to care, tilted his head. Bernie had gone still, the first time anyone had seen him quiet.

Ray grinned, bass locking into step with Gabe's rhythm. Tommy, eyes closed, followed him down every turn of the melody with a portable drumset. By the second verse, Anna was softly singing along, Max had his phone out, and Bernie was swaying like he was in the front row at Madison Square Garden.

They tried to write us off in ashes,
Said the fire had burned us down.
But every mark on our skin
Is the proof we're still around.

When they stopped, the silence broke into applause loud enough to draw a frown from Sylvia in the hallway. Gabe's smiled.

Not bad for OSHA violation.

After five more songs, the impromptu concert ended but no one left. The folding chairs stayed scattered, coffee cups forgotten, the air still buzzing with the aftershock of the music. Gabe sat in the middle, flanked by Ray and Tommy like it was 2008 and they'd just come off stage. Anna leaned forward eagerly, soaking up the stories spilling out of them.

"I swear to God," Ray said, grinning like a man half his age, "he once climbed out a third-floor window to avoid a girl he'd been dating—and her *mother*—showing up at the same hotel. In Denver."

Anna's eyebrows shot up. "He what?"

"Oh yeah," Tommy said, tapping a plastic spoon like it was a snare drum. "Slid down a fire escape with his guitar strapped to his back like some leather-jacketed Spider-Man."

Bernie pointed at Gabe like he'd just solved a mystery. "Ah-ha! That explains the energy. You're the type who could get me into trouble and somehow make it my fault."

Ellie snorted. "Bernie, everything *is* somehow your fault."

Ray laughed and kept going. "Didn't even grab a shirt. Press was waiting out front too. That was the first time *Rolling Stone* called him 'Gorgeous Gabe.'"

Anna's eyes opened wide. "That was real?"

"Oh, yeah," Ray said with a smirk. "Started as a snide caption on a photo, but it stuck. Fan signs, tee-shirts, whole Tumblr pages. Our label loved it. Played it up. The bone structure, the hair, the moody eyes. He hated it."

Tommy chuckled. "He used to grumble every time someone said it. One time a radio host called him Gorgeous Gabe Whitlock on air and he ripped the mic cord out mid-interview."

Gabe groaned and Ray laughed harder. "You were so dramatic about it. 'I'm not a fucking boy band.'"

Bernie slapped his knee, grinning. "See, *that's* the kind of rockstar tantrum I can respect. A man with boundaries."

Ellie muttered to no one in particular, "He's been here five minutes and thinks he's part of the band."

Anna laughed and the way he was looking at her was so full of affection it made his heart ache. "You were a menace," she said, a teasing tone in her voice.

Still am.

Tommy raised his eyebrows dramatically. "You've got the eyes of a menace. The rest of you's just...parked."

Bite me.

Bernie whistled low. "Careful, sweetheart, that's an invitation I might accept."

"Bernie," Ellie said, "go flirt with the vending machine."

The whole room cracked up again, but Anna's smile lingered even after the laughter faded. Ray's tone softened and he looked right at Anna as he said, "He always had that spark. Even before the band. Pure chaos wrapped in leather. We just gave him a microphone and turned up the volume."

22

PART TWO

ANNA'S

SKETCHBOOK

self portrait

Gorgeous
Gabe

RuthMadisonBooks.com/Anna

Rachel

Me & Gabe

You stitched me together
with nothing but light...
—Pressure Front 2010

Pressure Front 2006

"I don't need a future
if the moment keeps
bleeding"

Gabe and Ray in the garden

Ray

Tommy

23

GABE

The heat had been thick for days, clinging like a fever that no one could shake. The box fans scattered around Rosehaven did little more than shove hot air from one corner to another. The air smelled of sweat, boiled peas, and something vaguely metallic like heat had scorched the wiring in the walls.

But today it was the worst it had been.

Gabe lay in his bed. Sweat slicked his temples, sliding along the curve of his cheek and pooling in the hollow behind his shoulder. He could feel it, but he couldn't wipe it away. His body was being even more stubborn than usual; his hands twitching without control, spasms raking up his chest like electrical wires shorting out.

He tried to lift his left knuckle toward the AAC pad on his wheelchair next to the bed. After several attempts he finally tapped it on and used all his remaining strength to press:

Help.

But even at the maximum volume, he knew it wasn't loud enough for anyone to hear outside his room.

No one came.

From the hallway, a sudden *thud*. Then a yell.

Becky. "Call 911! Doris is down!"

Footsteps pounded. Doors slammed. Denise's voice—rushed and worried—"Get the AED, just in case. Max, help me roll her—Max!"

They were gone in seconds.

The air in the room thickened. His vision blurred slightly at the edges; not panic, not fear—just too much heat. No airflow. Sweat soaked the pillow behind him. His mouth was dry. He tried to make a sound but nothing came.

He didn't pass out. That would've been easier. He just waited, listening to the chaos down the hall. Someone's sandals slapping the floor. A gurney being rushed in. A beeping heart monitor. The faint whine of a siren.

The heat folded over him like a weighted blanket soaked in bathwater.

When Anna finally appeared in the doorway—red-faced, more hair out of her ponytail than in, gloves still on—she looked straight past him at first, scanning the room for supplies.

Then she looked again.

And froze.

"Oh my god, Gabe!"

She was at his side in a blink, pressing cool fingers to his forehead, already grabbing the fan cord and yanking it closer, activating an ice pack she was carrying and jamming it under his neck.

"I didn't see you. I'm so sorry—I didn't—fuck—okay, I've got you." Her voice cracked but her hands were steady.

He blinked, slow and heavy. His mouth was too dry to even moan. But his eyes locked on hers and wouldn't let go.

"I've got you," she whispered again.

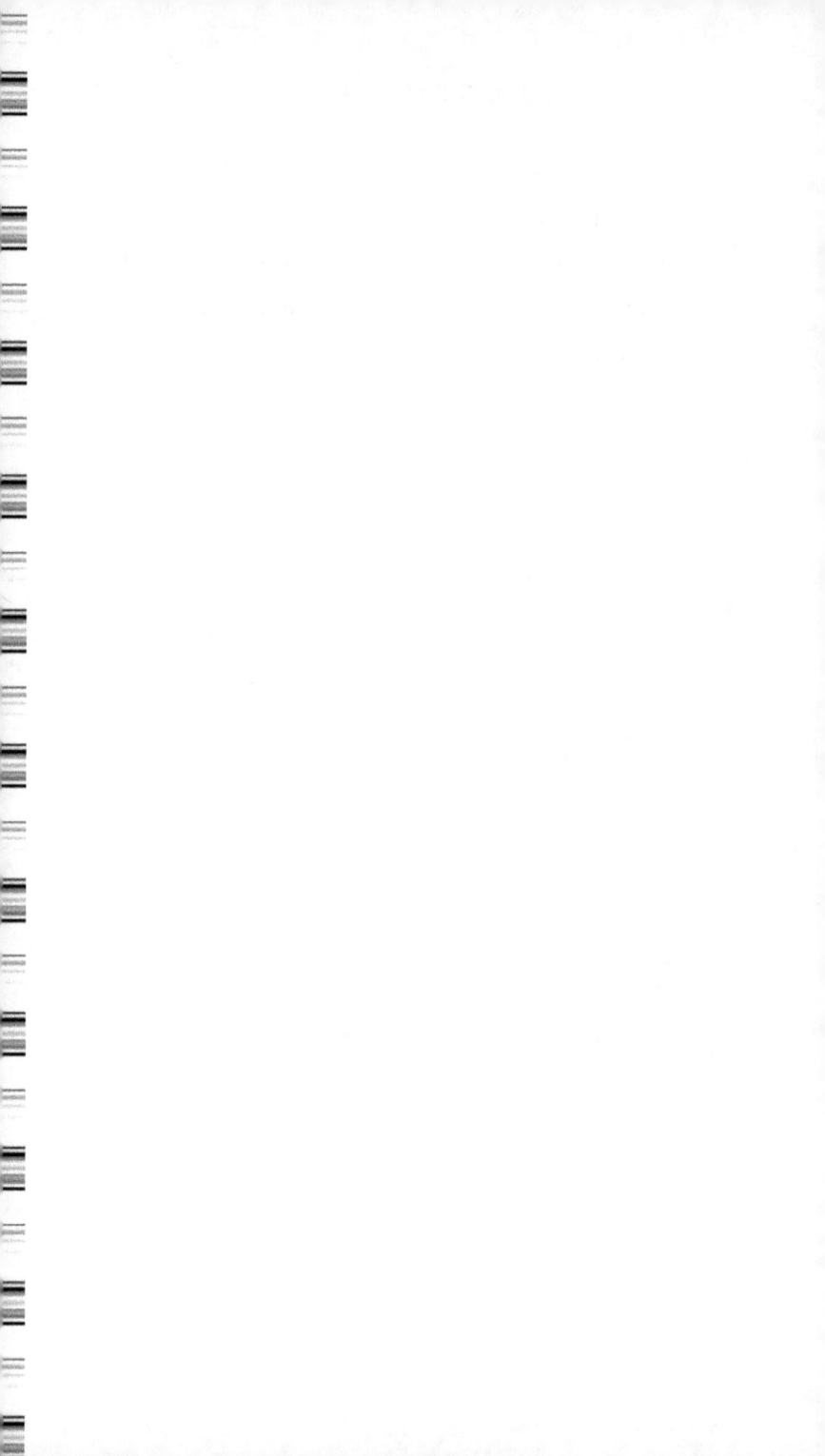

24

ANNA

"Becky!" she shouted, voice high and cracking. "Becky, I need help in 217 now!"

No answer.

Of course not. The whole wing was still focused on the emergency with Doris.

Anna turned back to Gabe. His lips looked dry and dull. The front of his tee-shirt was soaked, and his body gave a full-body jerk: an involuntary spasm that sent a horrifying ripple through his rigid frame.

"Okay," she whispered, breath coming fast now. "Okay, okay. Stay with me."

She didn't stop moving. Yanked the drawer open, found the alcohol swabs, tore one free with shaking fingers and ran it down the sides of his neck. It wasn't much. But the evaporation would help.

"You're overheating," she muttered. "Of course you are. God, I should have noticed."

She looked around, heart pounding. No call button. Only the AAC with its conversational volume. He'd been stuck. For hours maybe.

Her throat burned with guilt. His eyes met hers. There was no accusation in them. Just resignation.

"No. No, don't look at me like that. You fight. I am here now, okay? I'm here."

She grabbed his wrist and felt for the pulse. It was weak and far too rapid. He blinked slowly again and struggled to focus his eyes on her.

A shadow passed the doorway.

"Max!" she screamed.

He stopped mid-run. "Oh God—what—?"

"Tell Becky or Ken we have a second emergency. He's in heat exhaustion or worse. Go!"

Max vanished, his sneakers squealing as he took the corner too fast.

Anna turned back to Gabe. "They're coming. You're going to be okay. Just hang on."

She grabbed a clean towel and soaked it with the last of her water bottle; dabbed his face, his chest, his arms. Her fingers brushed along the groove of his collarbone, and she saw his eyes squeezing closed, not from pain but from something else. Emotion.

"Don't you dare leave me," she whispered fiercely.

The sound of wheels came at last; Becky, huffing, with Denise right behind her, one pushing a gurney and the other carrying supplies.

"Christ," Denise said when she saw him. "How long's he been like this?"

"I don't know. At least twenty minutes since I found him so could be much longer."

Becky moved to check his vitals while Denise took over with cooling packs.

"He's spiking," Becky muttered. "Pulse is 130, temp's high as hell. We need to move him." She called for another gurney and EMTs rushed in moments later.

Anna watched as they lifted him. It wasn't easy. Gabe was stiff and shaking, spasms still rippling through his body. Anna stayed by his head, speaking low and steady even as her own sweaty shirt clung to her and her hands shook.

"You're safe. I'm with you."

As they wheeled him out, she followed. She was not letting go; not when he needed her most. They were going to need someone who could communicate with him, who understood every tiny change of his expression.

The paramedics loaded him into the ambulance, voices clipped and urgent. She caught one last glimpse of his eyes: wide, glassy, locked on hers as if he could pin her there by will alone.

"I'm right behind you," she promised, even though he couldn't hear her through the siren already winding up. The doors slammed shut.

Anna's little Toyota felt like a toy car in the chaos of traffic as she trailed the ambulance. Her knuckles ached from clenching the wheel, her heart battering her ribs. Every red light was an insult, every slow driver a threat. She whispered nonsense prayers to herself—please, please, please—her voice trembling as if sheer desperation could hold him alive.

At the hospital, the automatic doors yawned open into a blast of cold air and harsh light. She rushed inside, nearly tripping over her own sneakers, but the gurney was already gone, swallowed into the labyrinth of corridors.

So she put her name in at the desk and sat on a hard plastic chair in the ER waiting room. She could still feel the scorch of sun on her skin, still hear the guttural rasp of his breath as the heat swallowed him. Her whole body vibrated with leftover terror, like she'd been wired to a current and no one had unplugged her.

Minutes crawled. Her fingers clenched and unclenched in her lap. People passed in and out—families whispering, a man arguing at the desk, a child wailing—but it all blurred together. All she saw was him. The slackness of his face when they tilted him back, the way his body had shook, the way he had looked at her, terrified but still fighting.

When a nurse finally called her name, she almost stumbled in her rush to stand up. She followed down a long white corridor that had giant photos of local fauna mounted all along it.

And then they turned into a small room and there he was. Not gone. Not lost. Resting against crisp hospital sheets, skin pale but steadier, his chest rising and falling in uneven but certain breaths. A band of monitors hummed beside him, wires snaking across his still body. His hair was damp, plastered to his forehead, and his eyes opened when she stepped inside.

The nurse left and Anna walked to the edge of the bed. Gabe's eyes tracked her, heavy-lidded but sharp, and the relief that poured through her nearly knocked her off her feet.

Her throat tightened. "I thought I was going to lose you," she said, her voice breaking. A few tears escaped the corners of her eyes and ran rapidly down her face. Her eyes blurred.

She reached out carefully, brushing the damp hair back from his forehead. He didn't flinch.

"I don't know what I'm doing," she whispered, voice barely audible. "I didn't come in here to—God, I don't know."

Her hand lingered near his cheek. His skin was warm but not dangerously so anymore. He looked at her. Not just at her, into her. His gaze was unguarded in a way that it rarely was. No sarcasm. No shield. Just him.

She felt herself lean in a little. Stopped.

And then she closed her eyes and kissed him.

For a breathless moment she thought she had misread everything. Maybe it was only her, pouring herself into him, desperate and foolish. But then the angle of his mouth shifted, pressing back into hers. Not with smooth ease. Not with the hungry control of the man he used to be. But with everything he had now.

The sensation burned through her: the hesitant catch of his lips against hers, the tremor of his jaw as he fought to hold it. He couldn't lift his arms to pull her in, couldn't seize her, but his effort was there, trembling against her mouth.

She clutched the side of his bed, bracing herself against the surge of feeling. Every hum of the monitors, every sterile beeping around them faded into the background. All that was left was this: the living, undeniable weight of him kissing her back.

The kiss grew ragged, not careful now, not tentative. He was kissing her back, really kissing her, as though he'd been waiting for this too. A small sound escaped her, half sob, half moan, muffled against his mouth. She tried to swallow it back, but the truth of it was there; she wanted him, wanted this, had been holding back for too long.

When she finally tore herself away, gasping, his eyes were locked on hers—so brown they were almost black. She cupped his face with one hand, her thumb grazing his cheekbone as his strength gave out and he slumped back into the pillow, spent but grinning.

Her chest swelled with relief so fierce it hurt. She bent her forehead to his, breathing him in, and whispered, "Never do that to me again. I can't lose you. Not now."

She lowered her forehead to his chest and silently felt the rise and fall of his breath for a long time.

She didn't want to move.

But it was late and she'd already pushed every boundary she could for the day.

Her voice was barely above a whisper. "I don't want to go…"

His gaze didn't waver. Tired, yes. But locked on hers.

She smiled through the ache. "…but I have to go home."

A flicker of something passed through his face. Disappointment, maybe. Resignation. But also understanding.

She brushed her thumb along the line of his jaw, a feather-light touch. "I'll see you soon."

And as she stood, he hummed again. Not a melody, just a soft and beautiful sound.

It followed her out the door.

On the drive home Anna couldn't stop thinking about the kiss. It was everything she had been trying not to want, and now it sat in her chest like a secret ember, glowing, dangerous.

Dangerous because it jeopardized everything.

This job wasn't only the best she'd ever had, it was the first real chance she'd had to get her life back on track. After years of panic attacks, of false starts and failures, of nights lying awake hating herself for never finishing what she started, Rosehaven had been different. The residents needed her. She had ideas that mattered, things she could build. She wasn't useless here.

And her father...her father had gone out on a limb for her, pulling strings to help her get the position. If she lost it, she wouldn't just be ruining her own life again. She'd be letting him down in a way he wouldn't forgive.

The thought made her press harder on the gas, as though she could outrun her own choices.

By the time she turned into the driveway, the porch light was already on. Henry stood in the doorway, a dark silhouette against the glow of the kitchen. She shut off the car and forced her shoulders back, bracing.

"Where have you been?" His voice wasn't raised, but the tone made her feel twelve years old again.

"There was an emergency at work," Anna said quickly, hoping her voice didn't shake.

Henry studied her, face shadowed, unreadable. Finally he gave a short nod. "I'm glad to see you so dedicated to it."

Dedicated. She swallowed. If he only knew. She managed a smile, too wide, too brittle. "Yeah. Me too."

But the words rang hollow. Because beneath her father's praise was the truth: she was standing on the edge of blowing it all up. One slip, one rumor, and this shot at rebuilding her life would crumble. And Henry—who had already lost so much—would look at her not with quiet approval but with disappointment she wasn't sure she could survive.

She stepped past him into the kitchen, the familiar scent of coffee and soil from his gardening shoes wrapping around her. He asked if she wanted tea, as though nothing unusual had happened. And she said yes, pretending she could still live inside that ordinary rhythm. But her chest ached with the knowledge that she had already crossed a line, and no amount of tea or polite routine could ever undo it.

A half-eaten box of supermarket muffins sat in the middle of the table, their plastic wrap crinkled. Staff crowded into the mismatched chairs—Becky still in cartoon scrubs, Denise with her arms crossed tight, Max bouncing one knee like he was responsible for generating all the electricity in the building.

Patricia stood at the whiteboard. Her bun was tighter than usual, her voice clipped. "First, I want to commend everyone on your swift action during this week's heat emergency. Thanks to your attentiveness, both residents are recovering well."

Anna blinked. Attentiveness? She saw again Gabe's pale face, the frantic scramble for ice packs, Frank slumping against the couch, Doris unconscious on the floor. Attentive wasn't the word.

Patricia clicked her pen like punctuation. "Of course, these situations test our resilience. It's reassuring to see our protocols work as intended."

A murmur of agreement went around the table; reluctant, tired.

Anna's hand went up before she thought it through. "With respect, the protocols didn't work. People nearly died."

The room went still. Max's eyes widened. Denise lowered her gaze, jaw tight.

Patricia's smile was thin as a blade. "Miss Lin, emergencies happen in every care setting. We responded quickly, we stabilized, we transferred as necessary. No one died. That's the definition of protocols working."

"That's the definition of barely scraping by," Anna said, her voice trembling but firm. "We need real changes. Air conditioning. Cooling stations. At minimum, a stockpile of fans and ice packs ready, not scrounged from the break room."

Patricia adjusted her glasses, unruffled. "Central A/C is not in the budget. As for fans, we have what's required by the state. Residents' families are, of course, welcome to bring additional comforts if they wish. A heatwave like that in Massachusetts is quite rare. There's a reason many homes still don't have central air here."

Anna leaned forward. "Comforts? That's not comfort, that's survival."

Patricia's tone sharpened. "Our responsibility is to meet state-mandated standards. And we do. You may not like the constraints, but this is the real world of long-term care. We cannot indulge every idealistic impulse."

Silence pressed in. No one met Anna's eyes. Max's leg had stopped bouncing. Becky studied her hands.

Patricia clicked her pen again, signaling the meeting was over. "Now, let's return to work. And remember, panic doesn't serve our residents. Stability does."

Chairs scraped as staff filed out. Anna stayed seated, fists clenched in her lap, the word stability ringing in her ears like a cruel joke. A few moments later Mary poked her head around the door.

"Are you okay, dear? Everyone else came out but I noticed you didn't."

Anna stood up and crossed to the doorway. "Thanks, Mary. It means so much that you noticed." Anna smiled but it was weak.

"Tell me what's going on. And don't try to sugarcoat anything, I didn't get to be this old by being delicate."

"It's just that I think we need some big changes to keep everyone safe and Patricia is not on the same page." Anna sighed. "That's just how life is, I guess."

"Hmm, maybe," Mary said but her eyes told a different story. She had an idea.

The day began like the others: thick with heat, nerves frayed to threads. Anna had come in early, prepared to sneak extra hydration rounds with Max and Denise while avoiding Patricia's gaze.

But when she turned into the staff lot, she stopped short.

There were cars everywhere.

Not the usual tired sedans and staff Hondas, but Subarus and minivans and pickup trucks with bumper stickers like "Plant Joy", "No Farms, No Food", and a faded "Bernie 2016." The air buzzed not just with heat, but with activity.

All over the place, sunhat-clad women unloaded box fans and small window units, mason jars full of lemon-mint water, bags of donated cooling towels, even potted herbs and wind chimes "to freshen the air."

Anna spotted Sylvia trying to direct traffic, completely outmatched by a spry 80-something in orthopedic sandals shouting, "Bev, grab the dolly! I've got two more from Home Depot in the trunk!"

At the center of it all was Mary pushing her walker proudly behind a woman in a floral apron and a *Retired But Still Raising Hell* tee-shirt. She had a new basket carrying a handheld misting fan and a ziplock bag of frozen washcloths.

"Don't look so shocked, dear," she murmured as Anna gaped. "The **Pioneer Valley Gardeners' Fellowship** knows how to organize better than most war rooms. And *we* remember how to act when someone's in trouble."

"But how—?"

Mary's smile was beatific and absolutely guilty. "I may have made a few calls from the church phone tree last night."

Anna could only stare as two old women roped Max into helping them install a window air conditioning unit in the living room. There were enough units lining the front hall to go in every resident's room.

Then Patricia appeared at the edge of the hallway like an approaching storm. Her lips were pressed into a line so thin it looked carved.

"Who authorized this?" she asked.

Mary turned to her with the calm of someone holding all the cards. "Oh, they're just delivering donations. Can you believe someone wanted to donate all of this to our own little Rose-haven?"

Patricia stared at her, speechless for once.

By mid-afternoon, the front hall looked like the tail end of a country fair. The window units were humming like a chorus of bees, basil plants lined the windowsills, and residents were propped comfortably with icy washcloths, lemon-mint water in hand. Even Frank looked halfway peaceful, muttering something about "finally not baking like a goddamn turkey in here."

That's when Patricia reappeared, shoes smacking down the hallway. She paused just inside the lobby, taking in the entire transformed space.

"Wonderful," she said, voice bright and brittle. "Exactly the kind of proactive, community-centered initiative we've been hoping to foster this summer."

Anna blinked. "We?"

Patricia clasped her hands behind her back. "Of course. I've been in conversation with local community organizations for months about seasonal involvement. I must say, I'm pleased to see our plan gaining such...traction."

Mary raised one thin eyebrow, but said nothing. The matron in the *Raising Hell* tee-shirt snorted loud enough to make a nurse look over.

Patricia continued, undeterred. "We'll be putting out a press release soon highlighting our commitment to holistic care and intergenerational outreach. A real win for everyone."

She turned toward Anna then, her smile sharpening by a degree. "Thank you for helping bring it together, Anna. I'm sure you'll agree, it's best when we all work within the same vision."

Then she pivoted and walked away, spine straight. Anna stood in stunned silence until Max leaned in and whispered, "That woman could gaslight a solar panel."

Anna laughed. That was one way to put it.

The fans kept spinning. The building, for the first time in days, felt like it could breathe again.

25

GABE

Denise pushed Gabe's empty powerchair toward the front doors, and that alone drew attention. Frank lifted his head. Mary paused mid-step with her walker. Ellie wheeled herself out of the living room, her bracelets jangling.

By the time the transport van rolled up outside, a cluster of residents had gathered at the windows. The back doors swung open, and there he was on the stretcher, pale but alive.

"About damn time," Ellie announced, her voice carrying.

Mary pressed a hand to her chest and whispered, "Thank God."

The stretcher rattled down the ramp, aides guiding him carefully toward the doors. Gabe's gaze darted over the crowd, startled at the sudden applause and cheers. When they pushed him into the lobby, a cool current of air brushed his skin. He blinked, surprised. The humming box units in the windows sent steady gusts across the room, cutting the heavy summer heat.

They stopped the stretcher beside his chair. Denise and another aide leaned in together. "Okay, Gabe," she murmured, slipping her arms beneath him. "We're going to do this nice and steady."

He hated this part, the indignity of being hefted like fragile cargo. His muscles spasmed once in protest, his body unco-operative as ever. But the aides counted down—"Three, two, one"—and in one strong, careful motion they lifted him from the stretcher to the seat of his wheelchair. The cushion took him, the headrest catching the weight of his skull.

Denise adjusted his arm on the rest, checked all the straps, then gave his shoulder a firm pat. "Better."

Now with the AAC at his side, he pressed his knuckle to it and typed:

Doris?

Ellie said, "Oh she's right as rain. Or as right as that crazy brain of hers ever is."

A ripple of laughter moved through the crowd.

And then Gabe saw her. Anna, half-hidden at the back of the group, twisting her fingers in the hem of her shirt. When his eyes found hers, the noise around him blurred. Something sharp and wordless pulsed between them—longing, fear, heat. She glanced quickly away, cheeks pink.

He pressed the device again.

Rest.

At once, the group shifted aside, clearing the path. He drove his wheelchair towards his room and Denise followed. He pulled up next to his bed and Denise pulled the lift into position. The steel frame loomed, its sling draped across the arm like a folded flag.

Denise bent to slide the fabric beneath him, tugging it carefully behind his back, then threading it beneath his legs. "Okay, big guy. Up we go."

The motor groaned when she pressed the button, raising him inch by inch. His body swayed in the straps, every muscle screaming at the loss of ground. His head lolled slightly until the harness caught him—suspended like a marionette without strings to pull.

"Easy," Denise murmured as she anxiously watched the sling move along its track until he was over the bed. She lowered him slowly, keeping one hand on his shoulder. The mattress pressed against his back, cool and firm. Relief shuddered through him when the straps released, his body finally still.

"There we go," she said, straightening the sheets around him. She adjusted his head with a practiced gentleness, then fussed with the blankets until she was satisfied.

Before leaving, she angled his wheelchair close to the bed so the AAC screen faced him. She adjusted the armrest mount until the buttons were within reach of his left knuckle.

"There. That should do it." Her tone softened. "Call if you need me."

When the door clicked shut behind her, silence settled.

But moments later, the door eased open again. Anna slipped inside.

"So," she said, voice low but edged with a tease, "did you actually want to rest? Or was that just an excuse?"

His eyes caught hers. He raised his eyebrows in invitation.

Anna turned the lock on the door.

She crossed the room and sat on the edge of his bed. The mattress dipped, the faint shift pulling him toward her without touching. Then she let her hand rest lightly against his chest, fingers splayed over the cotton of his soft, threadbare tee-shirt. The warmth of her palm bled through the fabric.

"Is this crazy?" she whispered.

His eyes crinkled. He nodded.

"You know what?" she said. "I don't care."

Her fingers slid higher, tracing the ridges of his forearm, slow and careful. Every inch she covered made his pulse hammer harder in his throat. She lifted the bottom edge of his shirt and began to pull it up. The fabric dragged against his skin, baring him inch by inch. His chest tightened, not from fear but from the electric shock of being revealed, exposed in a way he hadn't been in years.

She leaned closer, pulling the shirt over his shoulders and head, careful not to jar him, careful not to rush. When it was free, she tossed it aside. Her hand returned immediately, exploring his bare chest, tracing down over his sternum, fingers light enough to make his skin tighten beneath the touch.

He remembered a time he was proud of his body, when women would gasp in delight at the strong cut of the muscles in his chest and abs, and shiver as they touched his pronounced hip bones. It was very different now and yet he didn't feel embarrassed as Anna's fingers dragged across soft muscles and a pronounced belly instead. Because she knew him. She knew what his body was like. She had known him far longer than any other lover in his life had. In fact the average time between introduction and sex used to be about two hours.

She bent toward him, her breath warm against his throat before her lips followed. The first press of her mouth made his pulse leap, a shiver running through him like an old amplifier sparking back to life. She lingered there, tracing his throat with slow, deliberate kisses, and he felt each one thrum against the place where his voice used to live.

When her lips reached the hollow of his collarbone, he groaned. She kissed the sharp ridge then grazed it lightly with her teeth. The sensation was almost unbearable—his body, usually so muted and stiff, suddenly alive under her touch.

Her mouth drifted lower, over his chest. She kissed him where his heart beat steady and insistent, the wet warmth of her lips searing into his skin. A strand of her hair brushed his ribs, delicate as a whisper, and it made him ache with wanting.

His left hand trembled violently as he fought it towards the AAC device. Finally, the voice broke out, flat and metallic:

Hold the bar.

Her head snapped up, lips parting. "What?"

His eyes shifted upward—deliberate, insistent—to the steel rod above, the bar of the lift.

I want to taste you.

A flush rose in her cheeks instantly. Her eyes widened, shock and heat all tangled together. "You mean...like now?"

His gaze didn't waver. As she stood, he could hear her heart pounding, almost in sync with his own shallow breaths. When she peeled her pants down, her hands shook. Pale thighs, soft hips, unveiled inch by inch. She stripped slowly, as if the act itself were a kind of offering, never breaking eye contact until she lifted her shirt over her head and he saw that she wasn't wearing a bra. Small, round boobs appeared and the nipples stood out so firm it looked painful.

Naked, she climbed back onto the bed and reached up to grip the lift's bar, testing her weight against it. She held herself there, steadying her body above him. Then she lowered herself carefully, her thighs framing his face.

His chest clenched. His pulse roared in his ears. The heat of her was immediate and the scent—raw, sweet, intoxicating—rushed over him. He strained his neck, pulling every ounce of strength into the small forward motion he had left, and pressed his mouth to her.

At first it was clumsy. His angle awkward, his lips grazing her inner thigh searching for the wetness he craved. But then he found her center and she gasped. Her grip on the bar tightened, her body lowering toward his mouth even more.

His tongue worked carefully. Every flick, every stroke, deliberate. He couldn't hold her hips, couldn't guide her—but she understood, moving just enough to let him reach deeper. She moved to direct him exactly where she wanted him.

Her taste flooded his mouth, salty and sweet. He drank her in like a starving man, jaw aching, neck burning with effort. Pain streaked down his shoulders, but he clung to it, transformed it, kept going. Above him, she trembled. Her thighs pressed against his cheeks, her soft moans breaking into raw whimpers of his name. The most beautiful sound in the world.

The metal bar creaked faintly as she held herself there, body shaking with need. He didn't stop. Until suddenly, her body locked tight above him. She gasped, choked, shuddered apart, release crashing through her as her legs trembled violently around his face. Her strength faltered. She let go of the bar and collapsed forward, draped across him, skin damp, breath ragged.

"You..." she whispered, voice shattered and awed. "You..."

He couldn't speak, of course. But he was hard beneath the blanket, throbbing with a pulse he hadn't felt in years.

Anna froze when she felt it, her breath catching. She shifted to the side of him in the bed and her fingers trembled as she folded the blanket back. The air was cool against his bare skin, making goosepimples rise across his stomach. His cock stood rigid, flushed and eager. She reached out and gently brushed her fingers along the length and it jerked towards her with an ache that was almost unbearable.

She kissed her way down, soft lips pressing into his stomach, then the jut of his hip where his tattoo was, then the thin skin of his inner thigh. Each touch of her lips dragged heat deeper into his groin. Finally, she wrapped her hand around him: warm and solid. She stroked, slow and steady, watching his face as if every change in expression were a sentence she could read.

He couldn't arch. Couldn't thrust. His jaw clenched, his throat tight with unspoken sound, his chest straining with shallow breaths. The intensity gathered inside him anyway, winding tighter with every drag of her hand.

She paused to lick her palm and slid it over him again, smoother, firmer. His eyelids fluttered, his breath fractured into gasps.

The muscles in his legs seized, his hips trembling helplessly. And then—like lightning cracking open a summer sky—the release broke through him. His hips jerked once, so violently that his foot almost kicked her, and heat spilled across her hand in sharp pulses. He moaned, ragged and raw, shuddering with the aftershocks, every nerve in his body trembling.

Slowly, the tension drained, leaving him slack, spent, his chest rising in uneven waves.

Anna sat back and grinned at him.

He dragged his knuckle to the AAC, hand clumsy with exhaustion.

Sorry so fast.

She laughed. "It's been a long time, hasn't it?"

He managed the smallest nod.

"For me too," she admitted. She leaned down and kissed his temple, lingering. "But we have time. For fast, for slow, for all of it."

She slipped away for a moment to fetch a washcloth, humming under her breath, then cleaned them both up.

He woke to the sound of plastic wheels squeaking outside his door and a distant voice calling for someone who wasn't him.

The light through the curtains was pale purply gray, the color of early morning before shift change, before breakfast trays and linen carts and checklists.

He wasn't sure at first if it had all really happened. Did he dream the encounter with Anna? Had it happened only in that elusive parallel universe where everything happened as it should and there were no disappointments?

But then he shifted his head and the faint soreness in his neck reminded him. Yes it had. Anna had touched him and he had tasted her.

He could still feel the echo of her hand, her mouth, her body trembling above his. He could still hear her soft gasp, the whisper of his name like a song half-forgotten and rediscovered. It was all there beneath his skin, layered into the weight of his limbs.

Gabe's eyes drifted toward the ceiling. He looked at the curved metal track of the lift. Last night, it had made him a lover again.

The thought was staggering.

He'd spent years trying not to think about sex. About *touch*. About pleasure. It had been too painful. Too humiliating. A ghost limb of the past. His body betrayed him too often for him to believe it could still give him something beautiful. What it could still do had been reduced to the sniggering of aides when he had a reflexive erection.

Anna never looked away. She didn't hesitate. She ran towards problems, trusting that a solution was going to materialize in her hands by the time she arrived. And because she believed that, it usually did.

She had no fucking idea how special that was.

And for the first time in over a decade, he had come with someone watching him, someone wanting him, someone saying yes to him, giving their whole self to him.

Footsteps approached.

He tensed.

Not Anna's gait. Too quick. Too heavy. Denise, maybe. Or Becky. The morning med pass. Whoever it was, they didn't pause at his door. Just kept going.

He exhaled softly.

He didn't know how long they could keep this hidden. He didn't know what would happen if Patricia found out. Or Vicky. But for now, he had the memory of her shuddering above him with his name on her lips.

The Gabe in his fantasy could never understand the weight of that moment. That man had never known loss. That Gabe heard women cry out his name every day and he expected it, took it for granted. What that other Gabe wouldn't give a second thought to, this Gabe recognized as the miracle it was.

He had mourned the life that man still lived in his mind. But now, with Anna's touch still burning across his skin, he saw the truth: that man would never feel this. He would never know what it was to be emptied out, to have everything stripped away, and then to be given something back.

For the first time, Gabe didn't want to trade places with him. Because this—this fierce, hard-won joy—was his. And no fantasy of who he might have been could ever know the kind of wild joy that came after clawing your way back from hell.

26

ANNA

The TV hummed in the background while residents dozed in their recliners or picked half-heartedly at lunch trays. Denise flipped through the channels until a headline caught her attention.

Right to Die Legislation Gains Public Support. Victoria Whitlock-Pierce, sister of former rock musician Gabe Whitlock...

Anna was wheeling past with a cart of paint supplies when the name stopped her in her tracks. She came into the living room. On the TV the camera cut to Vicky—poised, makeup flawless, her voice syrupy with concern.

"We have to talk about dignity," she said. "About what people like my brother have lost. He was vibrant. Creative. Full of life. And now...he's trapped. It breaks my heart, but I truly believe we need to allow people in his situation to choose their own peace."

Gasps rippled through the room. Even Frank lifted his head and muttered, "That's cold as a busted radiator in January."

It might have sounded reasonable if they didn't all know Gabe. Everyone turned to look at him. His jaw was clenched so hard the muscle in his cheek twitched. His eyes were locked on the screen. A pulse beat furiously above his eyebrow. His left knuckle jabbed the AAC.

Fuck her.

Then again. Harder.

Fuck. Her.

The machine stuttered on the second playback, the voice garbled, but he slammed the switch once more, his whole arm trembling with the effort. For a moment Anna thought he might break the device, rage rolling off him in waves so strong she swore she could feel it in the air.

"Okay, okay," Denise said quickly, fumbling for the remote and shutting the TV off, her voice pitched too high. "That's enough."

But Gabe was still staring at the blank screen, chest heaving, fury burning so hot it scared Anna. She hovered, uselessly wanting to touch him, but afraid.

Then Mary's voice cut through, sharper than they'd ever heard it. "Should have known that witch wouldn't take it lying down. She's just mad you got one over on her."

Gabe blinked. After a moment, the jagged edge of his breath softened. A small, reluctant smile tugged at his mouth.

"That's the god-honest truth of it right there," Ellie added. She fixed her gaze on Gabe, her hand trembling a little on her armrest, but her words were steady as stone. "She loves having control and now she's fighting to get it back. But you're OUR sulky musician, and we're not letting you go anywhere."

Bernie gave a sharp clap, rings clicking together. "Hear, hear! The diva tried to upstage the leading man, but I assure you, the audience isn't buying it." He shot Gabe a sly smile. "You've still got the crowd, darling. And that's how you win."

Gabe's eyes flashed darkly at the word "win."

Everyone else began talking over each other about all the issues around "right to die" legislation but Anna kept her eyes on Gabe and she saw something hardening in his face. Shots had been fired and Gabe was about to go to war.

Max, who had been hovering by the doorway, suddenly burst forward. "She doesn't get the last word." His voice cracked with urgency. "You need to answer her. Like, publicly. Press release, interview, something. I can help—we could draft a statement, or a video, or—" He broke off, flustered but determined, cheeks flushed. "People need to hear *you*, not her."

He stopped but no one said anything. Gabe looked down at the AAC. They were all thinking the same thing—how?

Knowing how difficult it was for Gabe to speak his mind, Anna worried all the way home about how he was going to stand up to his sister. After dinner with her dad, she went up to her room with her laptop to do some research about his AAC device. Just to see if there was anything they could do to make it even a tiny fraction easier for him to use.

What she actually discovered stunned her.

The touch screen AAC was old news. People online were demonstrating eye-tracking devices.

She leaned closer to the screen. One woman was lying in bed, blinking slowly at a digital keyboard on a monitor. Words appeared in perfect sync with her gaze. Smooth. Natural. Fast. It didn't require a knuckle or a fist or a trembling reach.

Just eyes.

Anna sat back, the weight of it hitting her like a slow punch to the chest.

Gabe didn't have that. Every time he'd cracked a joke with one word. Every time he'd told her something quietly vulnerable with a pause between each phrase. He'd *fought* for those words. Every single one.

And now, she realized…he didn't have to. There was something better. Something easier. Something he deserved.

She grabbed her phone and found Ray's number. He answered on the third ring, his voice low and tired. "Anna? Is Gabe okay?"

"Ray, you have to hear this! There's a whole new kind of AAC, the machine Gabe uses to speak. They have eye-gaze technology. He wouldn't have to beat his knuckles against that old thing anymore. He could just…look. At the words. At the letters. And it speaks. Full sentences. Anything he wants."

For a heartbeat she thought he'd sigh, tell her she was over-stepping. But instead there was a sharp inhale.

"Wait—really? You're saying he could...?" His voice cracked. "God, Anna, I saw him fight that box like he's still on stage trying to keep the crowd from slipping away. And all he gets out is three words before he's spent. It kills me to watch."

Anna's throat tightened. "This could change everything for him. But it has to come from you. You're his power of attorney. If you request an evaluation, they have to bring in a speech language pathologist. They can't say no."

On the other end of the line, Ray laughed, but it was ragged, thick with tears. "Send me the links. All of them. I'll make the call first thing in the morning. If this can give him back even half his voice, I'll bulldoze whoever I have to."

"Done!" Anna gleefully texted everything she had found to Ray. "Thank you."

"No, thank *you*. After all these years...things are moving again. And it's because of you. He's lucky to have you on his side."

Anna didn't know what to say to that. She hadn't done anything special. Just when she saw someone she could help, of course she did. What else was she going to do?

The Pioneer Valley Gardeners' Fellowship arrived at Anna's house on Sunday afternoon. Anna had asked Mary for a favor after they had helped so much in the heatwave. Today it was three women, each bearing a different contribution. Bev, wiry and brisk, had a spade slung over her shoulder like she meant business. Jean, softer, with silver curls escaping her visor, carried a flat of pansies for underplanting. And Dolores, tall and lean in her faded UMass sweatshirt, brought a thermos of lemonade that sloshed with every step and the funny single branch that was somehow going to grow into a whole pear tree.

Anna led them around to the backyard where the spot had been marked. Henry was there already. He stood with his hands clasped behind him, surveying the chosen patch of lawn like it was an engineering project.

"This is the spot?" Jean asked. "Where she would have wanted the tree?"

For a long moment Anna thought he'd stay silent. But then he said, "Yes. She liked to read here. Said the breeze was softer on this side."

The women exchanged a quick, approving look, and set to work. Bev dug with brisk, efficient strokes. Dolores spread the soil out. Jean crouched with the sapling, murmuring encouragement as though it were a child about to take its first step.

Henry lingered at the edge. Anna watched him. She wanted this project to bring them together, to be a step towards closing the past and moving forward together. But her father had never been a fan of metaphors. Perhaps her intention was lost on him.

Then Dolores, without looking up, said, "What did she read out here?"

Henry smiled finally. "Poetry. Dickinson, Mary Oliver, sometimes Frost. It might sound funny..." he hesitated as though he might be about to disparage his beloved wife. "But she liked to read to the flowers."

The women smiled, and Bev said, "No wonder things grew so well."

Something in Henry eased and stories about Helen began to spill out of him. He told them about the spiral-bound journal she kept, tracking which bulbs broke through the soil first each spring. She insisted that the daffodils came up earlier the year Anna was born.

He told them how he often found pressed flower blossoms hidden in his scientific journals. Only a few days ago, a perfectly preserved Rose of Sharon had fallen into his hands from a book of the collected works of Thoreau he wanted to re-read. Like she was still sending him little love notes through the flowers.

Anna stood very still, hardly breathing, afraid if she moved she might break the spell. It was so rare for her father to open up like this, rarer still to hear her mother's name spoken anymore.

Next he recalled the way Helen used to hum while she worked—tuneless, absentminded—and how Anna had the same habit when she was absorbed in drawing. More than once, he'd found mother and daughter side by side at the kitchen table, one writing, one sketching, both lost in their own worlds, both humming without realizing. A memory rose up in Anna's mind, just a fragment. Her crayon rolling across the table, almost falling off, while her mother's pen scratched on paper.

There was the time Helen insisted on repainting the kitchen a bright sunflower yellow, even though Henry worried it would be "too much." He remembered coming home to find Anna, no more than eight, with a streak of yellow across her cheek and a roller in her hand, declaring, "It feels like the sun lives here now."

Anna remembered how Helen had let her paint whatever shapes she wanted to since it would all be covered as they went. Anna had painted a heart and a princess. And at the end of the project Helen painted over them, telling her they still lived underneath the layer of paint.

Henry smiled faintly as he told how Helen always carried a little notepad in her purse, scribbling down turns of phrase she overheard or bits of poetry she loved. "Anna does the same thing, only with sketchbooks," he said, as though only just now realizing it. "Different tools. Same impulse."

And then he said, more quietly, "Helen believed in keeping evidence of joy. She thought life gives us scraps, little fragments, and it's our job to notice them, to save them. Anna has that same...instinct toward joy."

Anna pressed a hand to her chest, blinking hard. Finally Henry looked right at her for the first time since the garden club had arrived. "You're just like her," he said, his voice surprisingly steady. "And we'll always have a piece of her spirit because she gave it to you."

She stared at him, rooted to the spot, until Jean gently pushed her shoulder and said, "Oh come on, you two, time for a hug!"

Anna threw herself into Henry's startled arms, laying her head on his shoulder like a child. He held her, his arms strong against her back, and tears leaked from her eyes into the soft fabric of his khaki button-up. After a few moments Anna turned her face, keeping her head on his shoulder, to watch as they put the stick that would become a tree into the ground.

Bev tamped down the soil and Jean turned on the hose that Dolores was holding. The fresh little new tree drank in the water, getting the best start in life that it could.

Jean poured lemonade into paper cups and distributed them around.

"She would've liked this," Henry said.

Bev raised her cup. "To Helen," she said simply.

They all drank.

27

GABE

He didn't know why everyone was acting weird.

Mary kept patting his shoulder like someone had died. Ellie rolled in dramatically late, wearing a silk scarf with stars on it. "For the occasion," she said, which clarified nothing. Even Ray looked suspiciously pleased with himself.

And Anna?

Anna wouldn't meet his eyes at first. Her hands were clasped together. Nervous energy practically shimmered off her. Her ponytail was crooked in the way it got when she'd been distracted for hours and didn't notice. But her smile—God, that smile—was too soft to mean anything but good.

"You ready?" she asked.

He blinked once even though he didn't know what he was supposed to be ready for. Did this have something to do with the speech therapist they had insisted he talk to?

Ray pulled up a case that looked like it might have held an instrument and placed it on a table in front of him. Inside was a thin monitor, a mount, and a bar of sensors.

What was it? Gabe looked around at the excited faces. Raised an eyebrow.

"It's an eye-tracking AAC," Ray said, his voice trembling with glee. "You don't have to touch it to speak. You just look and it registers where you're looking and it speaks. The voices sound a hell of a lot better than that robot too."

Gabe stared at him.

"Yes, I'm serious," Ray said before Gabe could ask. "Let's get you set up."

Becky rushed over to help before Ray broke anything. Together they unhooked his current device and mounted the new one. They figured out which direction the sensors were pointing and how to line it up with Gabe's line of sight. Becky turned on the screen and moved through some of the settings.

While they worked, Gabe moved his eyes to Anna. She was bouncing on her toes like she did when she had too much energy and nowhere to put it. He knew she was behind this in some way.

"You'll need to calibrate it," Becky said. "Let me get it to the right screen."

She punched some buttons on the touchpad of the device and it began its calibration, asking him to look and hold in certain places. Then it was ready for him to try.

Hello.

A deep British voice spoke from the device and Gabe gave Becky a look. She giggled. "I couldn't resist. You can change it in the settings down there."

Gabe realized he could use the eye-gaze sensors to control the settings too and he changed the voice to something a little closer to his real one.

This feels like cheating. In the best possible way.

Everyone laughed. Ray whooped like a teenager. Even Frank, who'd wandered in just to complain about the coffee, let out a bark of surprise.

Gabe grinned. He practiced more. Each sentence got easier. Smoother. Faster.

Now you're all in trouble.

But he knew who was actually about to be in trouble.

Get Max to my room.

The ring light Max had dragged in glared against the wall behind Gabe, too bright for a place like this, and highlighting a spot on the wall where a gas light fixture had been removed and the painted patch didn't quite match.

Max's phone was perched on a spindly tripod, and his usual frenetic energy had trimmed down to a single nervous focus. Anna stood with her arms crossed behind Max, watching. Gabe was glad she was there. He was going to say his piece either way, but it felt good to have her listening.

"Okay...rolling when you are," Max said.

Gabe flicked his eyes around the screen on the AAC.

My name is Gabe Whitlock. You may know me from my music. But that's not why I'm speaking.

The voice wasn't his but it was closer. Less robotic. Almost human in its cadence if you didn't listen too hard. His gaze locked on the lens of Max's phone for a moment, unflinching. Then his eyes returned to the AAC screen.

Last week, my sister spoke on national television. She said I had lost everything. That I would be better off dead.

A twitch in his mouth. Not a smile. The caged burn of fury.

She's wrong.

Again he paused to look directly at the camera recording him.

I have a voice. I have thoughts. I have feelings, both positive and negative. The same as anyone else. My body is limited. My life is not.

The voice smoothed the words, but every single one was the strike of a hammer he was finally able to swing.

Disability is not the same as despair. Death should never be sold as dignity when what we lack is support, care, and respect. Before you offer me death, offer me resources.

Max exhaled behind the camera, too loud, but Gabe didn't stop.

My sister will try to tell you I don't understand what's happening. That I'm confused.

He paused, let that land. Then his eyes continued to move across his screen.

I am not confused. I am not broken. I am not a tragedy. Don't use people like me to sell your fear of what it means to be human.

Silence fell sharp and heavy. Even the hallway noise seemed to retreat.

Max stopped the recording. When he spoke, his voice cracked. "That was…That was incredible, Gabe."

Get it to the news outlets. If they don't respond within 24 hours, put it on YouTube.

"On it!" Max fumbled the phone from the tripod, nearly dropping it in his rush. A moment later he was gone, his footsteps echoing down the hall.

Silence closed in, thick with meaning. Anna stepped closer to Gabe's wheelchair. Her eyes searched his face as though weighing everything he had just set in motion.

"He's right," she said at last. "That was incredible." She picked up his hand and held it in hers, tracing the back of his knuckles with her thumb in gentle swirls. "You ready for the consequences?"

Bring it on.

The first consequence came far swifter than he anticipated. He knew this particular click of heels on the wood floor making their way towards his room even though he hadn't heard them in years.

Constance Whitlock filled the doorway like she'd been expected all along. Hair silver and sculpted, pearls at her throat, a jacket tailored so perfectly it didn't dare wrinkle when she moved.

"Oh, Gabriel," she breathed, the vowels crisp, the sigh carefully measured. "You've caused such an upset."

Movement stirred behind her. He caught it in the corner of his vision, Ellie, Mary, Bernie, and Frank—who was scowling as if Constance's perfume personally offended him—were crowded near his door. Spies, the lot of them. Too curious to see what his mother was like and eager to report back to everyone else. Well, it would be an interesting report, at least.

"Do you know how distressed your sister is?" Constance went on. She lowered elegantly onto the chair in his room, staying near the front edge, her back ramrod straight and her legs crossed just at the ankles. "She's poured herself into looking after you all these years, and then you...humiliate her. Publicly. Do you realize what people must think?"

He wanted to look away, but his eyes locked on her pearls, the way her hand rose every few seconds to touch them, smoothing her worry into jewelry.

She sent you?

"Of course not, darling. But when I see how much she does to help you...I just had to step in." Her voice dropped into that cultivated softness, the one meant to imply intimacy. "You're lucky you have a sister who cares as deeply as Victoria. Not many people here have someone advocating for them." She sniffed the air as though it stank of poor. "And here you are being ungracious. That's not how we raised you. She's only ever tried to do right by you and you always gave her a hard time. You could be gentler."

He could have said it. The words were hot, pushing against his chest: *You always cared more about her feelings than mine.* But what difference would it make? The pearls would still shine, the residents would still whisper in the hall, his mother would still be unable to comprehend why her words hurt.

The silence stretched. Then Ellie's voice, sharp and teacher-strong despite her strokes, carried from the hall, "Some people could stand to remember whose life it actually is."

Constance flinched—just barely—and slowly turned her head to the peanut gallery in the hallway. And Gabe, without meaning to, felt his mouth twitch toward a smile.

"Excuse me?" Constance said, her voice as calm and steady as ever.

"You heard me," Ellie shot back.

"I would think a mother would be proud her son still has a mind sharp enough to tell the world what he thinks," Mary added.

Bernie snorted. "Amen. I'd rather live with my own choices than have someone else polishing my coffin lid before I'm in it."

Constance blinked. Her gaze skated over them like they were unruly schoolchildren. "Really," she said at last, voice cool, "I don't think it's appropriate for…residents to meddle in private family matters."

Ellie wheeled herself forward a few inches, her left hand braced on the rim of her chair. "You should know: we look out for our own here."

Instead of answering, Constance turned back to Gabe. "Oh, Gabriel. I can see how difficult this must be for you. Surrounded by...riff-raff. It's hardly a dignified environment. I should have said something to Victoria long ago about the sort of people you're mixed in with here.

"I may have to report this...unruly behavior," Constance went on, her tone still precise, as if she were commenting on the weather. "Honestly, it borders on harassment. I cannot imagine how the staff allows it."

Frank muttered, "Riff-raff's better than a snake in pearls."

Constance's smile didn't slip, but the pearls twisted between her fingers twice before she caught herself. She searched Gabe's face as she said, "They're using you, darling. Can't you see that?"

We're done here. You can find your own way out, I trust.

His mother rose as though floating upwards without using a single muscle. "Next time, darling," she said, and kissed the air by each of his cheeks before walking out of the room, past the entire rag-tag group gathered in the hallway, without giving any indication she saw them.

"Way to stick it to her, Gabe!" Max cheered. Gabe hadn't even seen him arrive.

Thanks, everyone.

He smiled as he pressed the button to close his door. He'd choose the riff-raff who stood up for him over his old-money family any day of the week. Still, he didn't think Vicky was out for the count quite yet. She had powerful allies, including their parents. And publicly humiliating her was just poking a bear. He had to be ready for her to retaliate in some way.

28

ANNA

Anna was still juggling her bag and thermos when she saw Patricia standing in the hallway, arms crossed.

"Good morning," Anna started.

"Anna. A word."

The tone stopped her short. Anna shifted her bag higher on her shoulder and followed her into an alcove near the admin office.

"I didn't think it needed to be said," Patricia began in her clipped, neutral tone, "that relationships between staff and patients are highly inappropriate. But given recent revelations, perhaps it does."

Anna blinked.

"To find out that you have been engaging in a physical relationship with a patient who has severe brain damage is shocking and disappointing to say the least."

Anna felt like the floor had fallen out from beneath her. "It wasn't like that. He—he's not—"

"There's no need to try to explain," Patricia cut in, lifting a hand with institutional finality. "The decision has been made. Security has been notified."

Anna's breath caught. "You can't—you don't even know…"

"You will not be permitted contact with any residents, especially Mr. Whitlock. Any attempt to do so will be considered a breach of facility safety protocol and may involve legal action."

Anna's mouth opened, but no sound came. Not even the practiced deep breathing could anchor her now. She couldn't see Gabe? Couldn't talk to him? Couldn't even explain what was happening?

A soft voice interrupted.

"I beg your pardon," Mary said, her walker easing into view as she rounded the corner. Her silver scarf fluttered slightly as she tilted her head. "Is this really the best place for a termination conversation?"

Beside her, Ellie's wheelchair was angled just enough to give her a full view of Patricia and Anna. "I'm sure there's a policy about public humiliation," Ellie added, with acid sweetness. "Unless that got replaced with a new code of shame-and-dismiss."

"This does not concern either of you," Patricia said tightly.

"It concerns us," Ellie said, her voice sharper now, "when the one staff member who treats us like actual human beings gets marched out like a criminal."

Anna stood frozen, the weight of the moment pressing down on her chest. Her vision blurred as her eyes stung.

"I need you to leave now, Ms. Lin," Patricia said quietly but firmly, stepping aside. "Your presence is no longer authorized."

Anna turned—heart racing, throat tight—and began to walk. Her feet moved but her brain didn't catch up. She drove all the way home in a haze, on auto-pilot, no thoughts forming. She walked past Henry and quickly headed for her bedroom before he could ask her why she was home early. She sat on the edge of her bed, unmoving and numb. Each time her brain tried to form a thought, something within her cut it off.

Every thought was too scary right now. They tried though.

Lost your job...

Screwed up again...

Never see Gabe ever again...

Suddenly she bolted to her bathroom and riffled through all the old bottles of medicine. She found a bottle of Nyquil and she didn't know how many doses were left but she swallowed the whole thing. Anything to shut down the world for a few minutes. She wasn't trying to hurt herself. Only to turn herself off for a few minutes of relief.

It did put her to sleep but her dreams were as tense and scary as real life. She woke at midnight choking with sobs. She texted Rachel even though it was late.

Then she grabbed the only lifeline she knew, a sketchbook, and tried to lose herself in the point of the pencil against the paper.

Early the next morning, Anna was asleep with her face on the sketchbook when Rachel burst into her bedroom. Blearily Anna opened one eye. "All right," Rachel said, eyes sharp, "explain. I get a cryptic text at midnight about you being fired, and then nothing? That's not how best friends operate."

Anna slowly lifted her head, the paper sticking to her cheek for long enough that she knew she had charcoal smudges over her entire face. She swallowed hard. "It's bad, Rach."

Rachel sat down beside her. "How bad?"

"You know when I asked you about what you loved about Steve?"

"And I thought you were thinking about someone in particular? Yes, I remember. The guy at work."

"He's not staff. He's a resident." Anna covered her face with her hands, afraid that Rachel might give up on their friendship right then and there and walk out in disgust.

"Holy crap. That's—okay, I was not expecting that." Rachel shook herself and regrouped. Then she leaned in, voice dropping to an almost gleeful urgency. "Tell me everything. How did you manage to fall in love with a resident at a nursing home?"

Anna peeked between her fingers and groaned. "You don't get it. I lost the job, Rachel. Dad already thinks I'm barely holding it together, and now...now I've just proved him right. I haven't even told him yet and I'm so scared to let him down.

And Gabe...I can't even see him anymore." Her voice cracked. "They're not going to let me back in."

Rachel reached out, prying Anna's hands away from her face. "Hey. One disaster at a time. You're not in trouble for caring about someone. Start with him. Tell me."

Anna's throat tightened. "He's...he's sarcastic. Funny. He can make you laugh with just the way he moves an eyebrow. But more than that, he really listens. He hears me, he remembers things. He centers me and he calms me. He even helped me through a panic attack."

Rachel's expression softened. "Oh, Anna."

"I know it sounds crazy," Anna whispered.

"What's crazy is you burying the lede, why is this dude living in a nursing home?"

"Do you remember the band *Pressure Front*?"

"Non-sequitur. Okay. I like it. Yeah I think so, they were big in the early 2000s, right?"

"He's the lead singer."

"Of *Pressure Front*?"

"Right. There was an accident on stage eleven years ago. It disabled him. Like really badly. He's been at Rosehaven ever since. And I keep thinking maybe I made things worse for him, dragging him into this mess. I feel guilty for everything: losing the job, making Dad worry, maybe screwing up Gabe's life, too."

Rachel squeezed her shoulder. "Or maybe you made his life better. Maybe you made each other's lives better. Look, I've known you since we were fifteen, you don't throw yourself into something unless it matters. And the way you're looking at me right now? It matters."

Anna let out a trembling laugh. "I miss him already. It's like someone shut off the sun."

Rachel pulled her into a quick, fierce hug. "Then don't let this be the end. Screw the job, screw your dad's nerves. Figure out a way to see him. You deserve this, Anna. For once, you deserve to want something and not apologize for it."

The kitchen was too quiet.

Anna stood by the sink, her hands clenched around the dish towel she wasn't using. The plastic donut magnet on the fridge stared at her with its googly eyes like it knew. Like it had watched her whole life lead to this moment.

Henry sat at the table with a Scientific American magazine open beside his tea. He hadn't looked up yet. Just kept stirring the mug with the same deliberate motion, like precision could hold the world together. He was pretending to read but he hadn't turned the page in at least five minutes.

Anna's voice barely made it past her throat. "I got fired."

The spoon paused.

Then clicked softly against porcelain.

He didn't look at her.

"I'm sorry," she added, quickly, stupidly. "I didn't want to tell you like this. I just...I didn't want you to hear it from someone else."

Henry set the spoon down with gentle care. Then finally looked at her.

"You lost the job I put in a good word to get you?"

"I'm sorry." She swallowed. Her heart thudded like a slow, sick drum.

He stood up. Not abruptly. Just with that same deliberate, measured calm he used when pruning back a dying rose.

"So what happened?"

"I fell in love."

His eyes snapped to her, his gaze sharp, looking at her like he did when he found a structural flaw on a blueprint. "Anna. You don't throw away stability for..." he faltered, his mouth tightening, "for some crush."

"It isn't a crush," she whispered.

"You don't understand." His voice was measured, low. "After everything—after your mother, after the panic attacks, after years of struggling just to find your footing—you finally had a chance. I pulled every favor I had left to get you that job. And you..." His breath came out in a slow hiss, sharp through his nose. "You squandered it. Reckless, Anna. That's what this is. Reckless."

Her throat ached. She wanted to defend herself but the words sat like stones in her chest. Because he wasn't wrong. Reckless was the perfect word to describe how she went through life. "I wasn't reckless. I..."

His eyes narrowed, waiting.

"I love him," she said.

Silence.

Then Henry's jaw set in a way she knew too well. "Who?"

Her chest felt like it might crack open. "Gabe."

"Gabe," he repeated, the name flat, meaningless. "Who's Gabe?"

She hesitated, but only for a second. "Gabriel Whitlock. He's—" She drew in a breath that scraped her lungs. "He's one of the residents."

Henry searched her face like he'd misheard. "A resident."

She nodded.

Something hardened in his expression. "Older man?"

"Early fifties?"

Henry sighed. "And what's wrong with him?"

The way he said it was a punch in the gut but Rachel had reacted better than expected, maybe her father would too. Either way, he was bound to find out the truth eventually. "He has a traumatic brain injury and damage to his spinal cord."

Henry stared at her.

She stumbled on. "Yes, he's disabled, he uses a wheelchair and a speech device. But—"

"But nothing," Henry snapped. Anna had never seen him this angry. All of a sudden her father was someone she didn't recognize, someone she had never met. "You're telling me that the man you've risked everything for is lying in a bed in that place, unable to move or speak?"

"No, not exactly," Anna said carefully. "Not just lying there. Watching and listening. Living."

Henry's fist pounded against the table. "My God, Anna." He shook his head once, sharply, as if to throw off the thought. "Do you hear yourself? You've chained your heart to a man who can't..." his voice cracked, then dropped to a whisper, "who can't give you a real life."

"That's not fair."

"Fair?" His voice rang off the kitchen tiles, louder than she could ever remember hearing it. "Do you want to talk about fair? Fair would've been your mother not dying when she did. Fair would've been you finishing college instead of collapsing under the weight of panic attacks. Fair would've been me not having to hold your whole life together with both hands while you—" his breath caught, his face flushing with something raw, "while you drifted from one half-plan to the next, depending on me to steady you."

Anna's throat tightened. "That's not true."

"It is true." His palm flattened hard against the table. "Every time I give you freedom, you make bad choices. I'm always chasing after you trying to stop you from ruining your life. And...and...I can't run that fast anymore."

"He's not a bad choice. He's a man. A man I love."

Henry's face twisted. He sank back into the chair. "You think you know what love is. But you don't. You don't know what it will cost you to tie yourself to someone who can't walk beside you, who will always need more from you than you get back."

Tears blurred her vision, but her voice was quietly steady. "He gives me things too. Things you can't see."

Henry let out a sound that was half laugh, half sob. "Things I can't see? Anna, I see everything. I see the way your life keeps shrinking every time you think you've found a new path. And this—" he turned back to her, eyes bright with anguish, "this isn't a path at all. It's a dead end. And you're running straight into it."

The room seemed to vibrate with the force of his words. Anna's hands clenched at her sides, her chest rising and falling. She wanted to scream, to break through that wall of fear he'd built around himself and around her.

She stepped forward. "You think I've failed you. I know. I dropped out. I stayed home. I watched Mom die in pieces. And now I'm loving someone you think is broken because he doesn't fit the box *you* built for me."

He turned away. Picked up the magazine. Set it down again.

"I wanted you to have a future," he said softly. "Not a burden. You need someone strong, Anna. Someone who can take care of you."

Tears slipped down her cheeks. She didn't wipe them. "You mean I need someone to take over your job, holding onto me so tight I can never even try to soar. Because I'm just like *her*. And you kept her safe too, *didn't you*? On a nice tight leash."

Henry flinched like she'd struck him. She had gone too far but she didn't care.

He opened his mouth, closed it again. For the first time in her life, he looked old to her. Tired. Like the fight had cost him something he couldn't get back.

"You're throwing your life away," he said quietly.

"Then let me throw it exactly where I want."

29

GABE

Gabe's eyes were on the door to the resource room. It was closed, dark and locked. Anna was late. Not morning-was-chaotic-and-someone-peed-on-the-Bingo-sheets-late. Late-late.

Had he mis-remembered when the weekend was?

Instead of the sound of Anna's sneakers on the floor he got Mary and Ellie moving in slow tandem like old queens gliding into court. If they were here, it must not be a weekend.

She's late.

Mary spoke first. "You haven't heard."

Gabe narrowed his eyes, tilted his head in a question.

Ellie took over, her voice brisker than usual. "Patricia fired her. This morning. In the hallway. It was brutal."

The words landed like punches.

Gabe's eyes locked on Ellie's.

Why?

Mary answered instead. "Improper conduct, they said." Her lips pressed into a thin line. "With a resident."

Ellie didn't sugarcoat it. "With *you*."

Gabe's jaw tightened.

She didn't.

"We know," Ellie said immediately.

Mary's voice was quiet. "It was cruel. Cold. And not private."

"They made a show of it," Ellie muttered. "Because Patricia wanted to look powerful. Because Vicky's been whispering in her ear. That's my guess."

Mary's hand lightly touched his shoulder. "She looked back," she said softly. "I thought you'd want to know that. She looked back down the hall. Toward your room."

Silence swelled in the hallway. It wasn't a distant silence. It was *close*. Choking. Like trying to breathe through syrup.

I need her.

Mary squeezed his shoulder once, with a reverence like prayer. "We all do, dear."

Ellie cleared her throat. "We'll find a way. We always do, don't we?"

Mary nodded agreement. "We look out for our own here."

The thing about Tommy was: he never knocked. He *announced*. Today, it was with a shouted "Open sesame!" followed by the sound of the door banging against the wall and something plastic crashing to the floor.

"Hey, G-money," Tommy said, already halfway into the room, "I brought you a genius idea and half a burrito. But mostly the idea."

Gabe blinked. He was not in the mood for whatever scheme Tommy had in mind.

Tommy was carrying a laptop, a backpack, and what looked like an ancient cassette recorder wrapped in duct tape.

Gabe's AAC whirred to life beneath his gaze, faster than knuckle-typing, but still too slow for chasing Tommy's verbal acrobatics. Still, he was getting better.

Do I want to know?

Tommy beamed. "You are going to love this!"

He dumped the contents of the bag across the nearby table like he was performing an exorcism. Headphones. Cables. Thumb drives. One mini tape deck that might've survived the apocalypse.

"I've been going through all our old interviews. Dude. Hours of crap. But you—*you*—had some *golden* one-liners. Like, pure chocolate syrup-level sweetness. And I thought: what if you made a message for Anna? Like a song made of words. But all your old ones. You know, so it sounds like *you you*. I heard about what happened to her and I just knew that you would want to get a message to her."

Gabe's chest tightened.

That's actually genius.

"Thank you, thank you," Tommy bowed to each of the walls around them.

Tommy was the perfect person to sneak a message to Anna. No one expected him to have enough executive functioning to put on his own shoes. They'd never suspect him of espionage.

They worked for hours. The speaker played back old audio clips: Gabe's younger voice, raspy and reckless, full of ego and fire.

"*I think love is like distortion pedals,*" Past Gabe declared from an old radio interview. "*Messy. But you feel it in your spine.*"

Tommy paused the playback. "That's a yes?"

Gabe smiled.

Keep that one.

They found another:

"*You ever fall for someone and it's like...suddenly everything else is background noise?*"

And another:

"*If I wasn't doing this, I'd be holed up in some tiny house with someone who sees through all my bullshit.*"

Tommy laughed so hard that it was a good thing he was already sitting on the floor.

After months of trying to say the right things to Anna, one laborious word at a time, here he was building a message for her out of his old chaos. But it needed a touch of the man he was now.

Add this:

The accident took my voice but you heard me anyway.

Tommy was quiet then. Really quiet. For a whole three seconds.

"Jesus, man," he said finally, eyes a little red. "You're gonna wreck her."

I just want her to know...

He paused, uncertain if he wanted to say what it was he wanted her to know. But at this point there was nothing left to lose.

...that I love her.

"Yeah, man." Tommy nodded like he already knew. He probably did. "I'll get it to her. It's all gonna be okay in the end."

I hope you're right.

He didn't ask Tommy which end he meant. Nothing was truly the end until you died.

30

ANNA

The knock came just after dinner, sharp and deliberate against the quiet of the house.

Henry looked up from rinsing dishes. "Expecting someone?"

Anna shook her head. She was curled up on the couch with a sketchpad in her lap, trying to stop thinking about Gabe's lips. Gabe's arms. Hands. Eyes. Damn it.

When she opened the door, two uniformed officers stood on the porch. The younger one, all hard lines and clipped professionalism, asked, "Anna Lin?"

Her stomach dropped. "Yes?"

"You're under arrest for sexual assault of a vulnerable adult."

The words didn't make sense. They hung in the air like a foreign language. Her pencil slipped from her fingers and rolled across the floorboards.

"No—wait—what? No, you don't understand. That's—there's been some mistake."

The older officer stepped forward. "Please place your hands behind your back."

Henry's voice cut in, flat but edged with steel. "What the hell is going on here?"

Anna stumbled back a step, shaking her head. "Daddy! I didn't, it's not what it sounds like. I promise."

"Hands behind your back, ma'am. You have the right to remain silent. Anything you say can be used against you in a court of law. You have the right to an attorney," he intoned flatly. "If you cannot afford one, one will be appointed to you."

Henry was still holding a dish towel. "You can't just come in here and—"

"We have a warrant," the younger officer interrupted, holding up a folded sheet of paper without looking away from Anna.

The cold bite of the handcuffs snapped shut around her wrists. She flinched.

Urgently Henry said, "Anna, say nothing. Do you hear me? Nothing."

She twisted toward him as they steered her out the door, tears streaking her face. The world beyond the porch had gone dark, the streetlamps cold and unforgiving. Neighbors' curtains shifted.

Her father stood rigid in the doorway, shoulders squared like a soldier at parade rest, but his eyes were wild.

How was she ever going to explain this mess to him? He had been right after all. Her way always ended in disaster. She couldn't be trusted to make the decisions in her own life.

Processing.

The smell hit first—like bleach and metal and the ghost of old sweat.

The fluorescent lights were too bright. Everything buzzed.

She stood in a concrete room with a fingerprinting machine and a desk. Her wrists still tingled from the cuffs. Her mouth was dry. She couldn't swallow.

They asked her questions. She tried to answer. Her voice didn't sound like hers.

"Ever been arrested before?"

"No. I—no. I didn't—"

A glance exchanged between the officers. A file slid across a desk.

She sat in the hard plastic chair and felt her body tipping into the familiar spiral: the cold in her chest, the tingling in her fingers, the shallow, hiccuping breath.

No no no no not here not now not again—

She clenched her fists. She pressed her feet hard into the floor.

And still it came.

Her vision narrowed. Her hands trembled. The fluorescent lights flickered.

She wanted her mother. She wanted her bed. She wanted Gabe.

And then—

She closed her eyes and remembered sitting in Gabe's lap and feeling his chest rise and fall as he hummed a tune without words, calming her panic attack. And just as though he were really there, she stilled. Her fear eased enough for her to breathe.

She didn't know what was going to come next but all she could do was handle each thing as it arose. If she could share a song with Gabe right now it would be *Que Sera, Sera*. Whatever will be, will be.

31

GABE

I don't know what to say.

Max's phone was trained on him again. It was the same stunt again but they were out of ideas.

"I still think you should say who you are first," Max offered. "You're famous. That matters. It'll make people listen."

Gabe's gaze moved lightning fast.

If they only listen because I'm famous, then they're not really listening.

Before Max could argue, a sharp knock echoed at the door. Sylvia.

Not her usual clipboard-and-clarity self. She hesitated, looking around at the group assembled in Gabe's room. When she spoke, it was gentle. "There's news," she said. "About Anna."

What now?

Mary spoke first. "What kind of news?"

Sylvia looked directly at Gabe. And then away.

"She's been arrested," she said. "Taken from her home this morning."

Ellie's voice went cold. "For *what*?"

"Sexual assault of a vulnerable adult. No bail."

No!

He could feel the anguish twisting his face. He had to stop this insanity. She didn't deserve any of this. His whole body tensed. The spasm hit hard. His back arched against the chair, his arms slammed into his sides, only the seatbelt at his waist kept him from falling. His neck was forced sideways by the wave of muscular contraction and his head jerked upwards. His breath came in ragged gasps. The AAC beeped, off-target now, blinking red as his gaze skittered helplessly across the interface.

"Gabe!" Max lurched forward.

"Don't," Ellie snapped. "Go get Becky. She's trained for this."

Mary reached out, laying a gentle hand on Gabe's forearm. "Breathe, sweetheart. Just breathe."

His chest rose in sharp, jerky pulls. Both his hands twitched in his lap. His legs shook themselves straight up into the air.

But slowly the spasms released, like a vise unclenching by degrees. By the time Max returned to say that Becky wasn't in today, Gabe was still. He sagged wearily but he had some control back. He refocused the cursor on the AAC.

Vicky's gone too far.

"Understatement of the century, I'd say," Bernie offered.

Gabe swallowed hard, breath still unsteady.

Get me in front of a camera.

"No," Sylvia said sharply.

They all turned.

She stepped farther into the room. "You don't understand," Sylvia said. "This isn't about image anymore. This is legal now."

Gabe's eyes locked on her.

"Charges have been filed. This isn't some HR violation we can counter with a video. Anything you say now could hurt her legal defense. Irreparably."

Ellie scoffed. "So we're supposed to sit on our hands while Vicky crucifies her in the court of public opinion?"

"You're supposed to stop making her more vulnerable than she already is." Sylvia's voice cracked with something unexpected. "Do you think a viral video from a vulnerable adult claiming the relationship was mutual is going to *help* her in a courtroom?"

That stopped everyone.

Sylvia continued. "She's being accused of sexual abuse. This is textbook ammunition. They'll twist every word, every frame. *Look,* they'll say. *Even he didn't know he was being taken advantage of.*"

Gabe flinched. But he knew she was right.

Max shifted awkwardly. "But we have to *do* something—"

"We are," Sylvia said. "We're calling your laywer."

Ellie narrowed her eyes. "You trust him?"

"I trust what he knows about the law," Sylvia said simply. "And I trust that Gabe does."

Mary finally said, "Do you believe she's innocent?"

Sylvia looked at Gabe, then at the others. "I believe in the woman who came early to decorate the dining hall with hand-made paper cranes. The one who argued to get the Wednesday hymn books back even though they weren't in the budget. The one who paid for that water aerobics class out of her own pocket." A flutter of gasps. None of them knew Anna had paid for that herself. Sylvia continued, "I believe she would rather cut off her own hand than hurt that man."

Gabe looked back to his screen.

Call Clint.

Sylvia nodded. "Already on it."

As she turned to leave, Ellie stared after her. "You surprise me, Sylvia."

Sylvia didn't turn around. "I surprise myself," she said.

And then she was gone.

When Clint arrived, he didn't waste time with pleasantries. His suit jacket was rumpled from travel, his tie tugged slightly askew, but his eyes were clear. Focused. Dangerous in the way that only the right kind of lawyer can be.

He closed the door behind him, didn't bother to ask why there was an entire circus's worth of people in Gabe's room waiting for him.

"She made her move," he said simply.

No one needed to ask who *she* was.

"Vicky filed the report herself," Clint continued. "She claims she witnessed signs of grooming and coercion. But that's just the legal framing. The truth is, she's not getting what she wants. So she escalated."

Gabe's jaw twitched.

Ellie, seated by the window, didn't even try to hide her disgust. "You mean to tell me a woman who barely visits her brother suddenly cares enough to report 'coercion'? How convenient."

Clint nodded grimly. "It's not about justice. It's about control. She thought she could isolate him, pressure him to sign over his rights. But when the guardianship was blocked—when Ray became POA instead—she lost her leverage. So now she's targeting the one person he cares about most."

He looked directly at Gabe. "She's not done," Clint said. "If we keep reacting, we'll always be one step behind."

Gabe's eyes flicked across his screen. The words came faster now, practiced, decisive.

What's the next move?

Clint didn't hesitate. "We get you out of here."

The room went still.

Mary was the first to speak. "Out of Rosehaven?"

Clint nodded. "Immediately. Ray is your legal proxy now. That gives him full authority to make medical, financial, and residential decisions. The fastest way to take power away from Vicky is to remove you from her playing field."

Ellie leaned forward. "And where exactly will he go? It's not like you can just book a Motel 6 with a hospital bed."

"I've already started the paperwork," Clint said. "There's a fully accessible apartment available through a short-term lease downtown. Wide doors. Roll-in shower. Electric doors. Ceiling lift tracks already installed from the previous tenant. Units like this aren't easy to come by so we need to seize this opportunity immediately."

He turned back to Gabe. "Ray's name will be on the lease. You'll be the resident. I'll cover the deposit myself if I have to."

I can't live independently. I need help.

"I'm on it," Clint said. "Private agency that provides aides, not tied to any facility. We'll schedule coverage for transfers, activities of daily living, meds, everything. You'll have full control over who comes in and out. You won't be alone."

Max, standing in the corner quietly until now, cleared his throat. "Won't Vicky just show up there?"

"Not legally," Clint said. "We'll file a protective order barring contact. The minute she tries to interfere with Gabe's care again, she'll be violating court protocol. And she'll know it."

But Anna is in jail.

Clint nodded. "I know."

Get her out.

A pause.

Clint took a breath. "We will. But first, we get you out."

Gabe's eyes narrowed.

She's alone.

"She's not," Clint said carefully. "She has counsel. I've already connected with her public defender—useless, by the way—but

I'm working on getting someone better in. I spoke to her father. But if I step in now without stabilizing *your* position, they'll tie us both up in a conflict of interest."

I'm not the one who's vulnerable.

"Yes," Clint said, sharper now. "You *are*."

He stepped closer, lowering his voice.

"They're building a case around capacity and consent, Gabe. If they can prove that you weren't able to meaningfully agree to the relationship, then *any* affection, any touch, any intimacy becomes a weapon."

Gabe's throat tightened.

No one saw.

Mary, who'd remained by the window in quiet sorrow, spoke gently. "Is that true?"

Ellie's mouth flattened into a hard line. "I hate to ask this, but...who knew about it? About the two of you?"

Gabe stared ahead. The answer came slower this time:

I don't know. You did. You two encouraged it.

He flicked his eyes between Ellie and Mary.

Mary nodded. "That is true. But if it's only suspicion—"

Clint shook his head. "That's not the problem."

He turned to face Gabe fully.

"Patricia filed an incident report six days before she fired Anna. Not specific. Just said she had concerns about boundary violations. Then two days later, she quietly requested internal access to facility surveillance logs."

Gabe blinked, once. Then again. Slower.

Ellie's brow furrowed. "Wait. You mean the hallway cameras?"

Clint hesitated. "Not just hallways."

"What?" Max said, startled. "There aren't cameras in the resident rooms."

"There aren't supposed to be," Clint said flatly. "But Patricia may have had access to testing feeds from the fall safety pilot. Rosehaven applied for a tech grant last year—new AI fall detection system. Some of those motion sensors come with visual monitoring options. Supposed to be anonymized. But I've seen facilities abuse that before."

Gabe's screen flared again:

She watched? That's sick.

Clint sighed and pinched the bridge of his nose. "Please don't tell me what you two did in here."

Mary looked ill. "Dear God."

Frank perked up. "Do you think they'll play pornography of you in court?"

"Ugh," Bernie said, "Someone gag him, please."

She violated us.

Clint didn't argue. He just nodded. "I know. And I'll go after her for it. But right now we don't even know what footage she has, if any, or how she's presenting it. What we *do* know is that you're still technically her patient. And that makes you easy to manipulate."

He stepped forward, firm. "Get out of Rosehaven. Then we fight."

Gabe closed his eyes briefly, the weight of everything pressing hard against his spine. His muscles twitched slightly, but he forced his gaze back to the screen.

Then move fast. She doesn't belong in a cell for caring about me.

Clint nodded. "Let's give her something to come home to."

Mary looked toward Gabe, her expression gentle but aching. "Leaving here...it's a big change."

Gabe met her eyes.

It's time.

Ellie exhaled, one hand pressed to her chest. "Damn right it is."

"You better come visit, though," Max said, as though he were as stuck in Rosehaven as the residents.

Clint was half way out the door already. "I'll have the moving team here in forty-eight hours. Ray's flying back in tonight."

Gabe blinked once, slow and deliberate.

Tell him I'm ready.

The automatic doors whooshed open, and Ray stepped inside with a duffel bag slung over his shoulder and a folded stack of paperwork tucked under his arm.

He looked out of place in the sterile lobby, his dark jeans, leather boots, and worn denim jacket making him seem more like a roadie who wandered into the wrong building. But his expression was deadly serious. Controlled.

Patricia was mid-conversation with Sylvia at the front desk when she turned—and froze.

"Mr. Delgado," she said crisply, recovering fast. "If you're here to visit, you'll need to—"

"I'm not here to visit," Ray said. "I'm here to discharge a resident."

Patricia blinked. "I'm sorry?"

He stepped forward, dropping the paperwork on the desk with a heavy *thwack*. "That's the updated Power of Attorney. Medical and residential. Signed. Witnessed. Filed. Clint Rivera is en route to retrieve the final copies from the court clerk. But you'll find everything in order."

Patricia picked up the stack and began flipping through it. Her lips tightened as her eyes scanned the signatures.

"Gabe Whitlock," Ray said clearly, "is leaving this facility. Today."

The silence was thick.

Sylvia's eyes flicked between them but said nothing.

"I wasn't informed of this transfer," Patricia said, voice going brittle. "This is highly irregular and—"

"What's *irregular*," Ray cut in, "is you filing a misconduct report, accessing surveillance that was supposed to be deactivated, and colluding with Victoria Whitlock-Pierce to paint him as an incompetent, helpless victim while targeting the only person who treats him like a goddamn human being."

Patricia's eyes narrowed. "That is an unfounded accusation—"

"Is it?" Ray leaned in, lowering his voice. "Then why's Anna Lin sitting in a jail cell while Gabe is in a room you have under digital surveillance?"

Patricia opened her mouth but Ray was already turning away.

"I don't need your approval," he said. "Just the release paperwork. You can stall, but you'll be stalling against a court order, and Clint is very good at lawsuits."

From the hallway, a low mechanical whir grew louder—Gabe's chair. He drove into the lobby with a packed bag in his lap.

Sylvia, still seated at the desk, glanced at Patricia then stood.

"I'll print the discharge papers," she said quietly, and walked away.

Ray looked at Gabe, his voice softening. "Ready?"

Get me the hell out of here.

Ellie's daughter, Janet, burst into the nearly empty dining hall so fast the door smacked the wall. Her phone was still clutched white-knuckled in her hand. "It's on the news, Mom. Your nursing home is on the *news*." Her voice trembled, pitched too high. "They said a staff member was arrested for sexually assaulting one of the patients. Here. Where you live. Where you're supposed to be *safe*."

Ellie's head snapped up, her silver hair trembling with the movement. "Anna. Her name is Anna. And you will not stand there and slander her."

Janet's face broke, sharp edges dissolving into something raw. "Do you even hear yourself? This isn't about a *name*! It's about the fact that you could be next. You're sitting here defenseless while predators walk your hallways. They paraded her out in handcuffs, Mom. I saw the footage. Do you know what that does to me? To think of you in here, with *that* happening around you?"

Ellie's good hand curled into a fist against the table. "She would never hurt anyone. Not me. Not Gabe. Not a soul in this place."

Janet shook her head. "But how can you be so sure? Everyone always says, 'Oh, they seemed so nice, so caring,' right until the moment it isn't true. How am I supposed to sleep tonight knowing my mother is living in the middle of this nightmare?"

Ellie's voice rose, shaking with fury and pain. "Because I *know* her. I know the way she looks me in the eye and sees me. I know the way she fights for us when no one else will. You don't get to stand there with your headlines and your fear and call her a monster."

Bernie, the only other person in the room, had been unchar- acteristically quiet. But now he moved closer.

"She's terrified," he said gently to Ellie. He sat beside her, took her hand, and looked up to her daughter with not a hint of theatrics. "And who could blame her? Of course she's scared for you. She loves you. But fear doesn't make Anna guilty. Fear just makes us desperate for someone to blame."

Janet swiped angrily at her tears, still trembling. "I don't care. If they can't prove this place is safe, I'll take you out myself. I can't—I *won't* let you be in danger, Mom."

Ellie reached out with her trembling left hand, almost pleading. "Don't you take me from my home over a lie. I won't let you. You mark my words, Anna is going to be running this place one day."

Janet groaned and sank into a chair at the table. "I don't know what to do."

Bernie inserted himself again. "We do foolish things when our love makes us panic. Have patience. Let's see how this all plays out. Our Anna may yet be vindicated."

Ellie sniffled and nodded agreement.

32

ANNA

The cell was too bright and too loud. Every sound echoed—shoes scuffing linoleum, a cough from the next block, the constant buzz of fluorescent lights that never turned off.

Anna sat on the edge of the bench, arms wrapped around herself, wearing a uniform that smelled like disinfectant and bleach. Her hair was tangled. Her mouth tasted like metal.

She hadn't cried. Not since the cuffs clicked around her wrists and she saw her father's face go pale in the doorway.

But now, here, in the endless hum of nowhere, the tears kept rising behind her eyes, pressing for release. She blinked them back.

Over. And over.

She had no phone. No watch. No clock. Just time that stretched and curled like smoke, impossible to hold.

They'd told her a public defender would see her "soon." They hadn't said when. She wouldn't be able to tell anyway.

She thought she'd be able to explain. To tell someone—any-one—what really happened. But the officer who processed her barely looked up. The nurse who did intake asked her if she "understood boundaries" before sticking a thermometer in her mouth. Her cellmate was a woman with smeared mascara and eyes like knives who hadn't spoken once.

They'd called it **sexual assault of a vulnerable adult.**

Her stomach churned every time she heard the phrase. Like they were talking about someone else. Like she'd done something grotesque, something shameful and violent.

He's not broken, she wanted to scream. *He's brilliant and sharp and funny and kind and I love him.*

But all she could do was sit here, in this too-bright box, and wonder if Gabe was okay. If they'd taken his device. If they'd made him say something or sign something. What if he thought she'd abandoned him?

What if they told him she confessed? What if they made him doubt her?

The door clanked suddenly. She flinched.

Not her.

The officer passed by without stopping.

She buried her face in her hands.

I didn't hurt him. I would never.

The memory surged up fast and hot—his eyes locked on hers, the slow smile that always came just for her, the way his knuckles moved so deliberately toward hers. That time his hand trembled with effort and she held it like a promise.

She pressed her palms harder into her eyes.

What if she never got to see him again?

What if they kept her here forever? This might be her life now.

What if that moment in his bed—the two of them lying together and laughing—was the last real thing she was ever going to have?

No one told her what was happening.

No one told her that Gabe had already left Rosehaven.

That Ray had shown up like an avenging angel with legal papers and defiance in his boots.

That Clint was already cutting through red tape like a blade, setting up her defense with the precision of someone who knew exactly how to dismantle Vicky's game.

No one told her that Gabe had insisted with everything he had:

Get her out.

No one told her she wasn't alone.

So she sat in silence.

Waiting.

Praying that this wasn't the final chapter of her story.

Anna sat at the metal table, the plastic chair cold through the thin jumpsuit. Her fingers were red from biting at her cuticles. Her legs ached from trying to sleep curled on a bench that hated human bodies.

She looked up when the door buzzed.

A woman in a charcoal-gray suit stepped in, her heels muffled by the concrete floor. Sleek hair. No public defender's shuffle and over-stuffed briefcase. Just a slim leather portfolio and the kind of posture that didn't bend for anyone.

"Anna Lin?"

Anna stood automatically, unsure why. "Yes."

The woman offered a small, tight smile as she sat across from her. "I'm Natalie Chen. Clint Rivera brought me in. I specialize in disability and medical rights cases—especially when there's overlap with abuse allegations."

Anna blinked. "Clint? Wait—he's—?"

"Yes," Natalie said gently. "And Gabe is okay."

She cried out with relief. "He's really okay?"

Natalie nodded. "He's no longer at Rosehaven. He's in a temporary apartment now—accessible, safe, and under the care of aides selected by his legal proxy."

Anna stared, dazed. "They moved him."

"They protected him," Natalie corrected. "And now we're going to protect *you*."

Anna gripped the edge of the table. "What happens now? Am I being tried?"

Natalie opened her folder. "There won't be a trial. At least, not a criminal one. The charges are being suspended pending the outcome of a competency hearing."

Anna frowned. "What does that mean?"

"It means the focus has shifted. Not onto whether you assaulted him, but onto whether Gabe is capable of *consenting* to a relationship. If the court finds he is competent—emotionally and cognitively capable of making his own decisions—then this case collapses."

Anna blinked fast. "So it's not just about me anymore."

"No," Natalie said, voice calm but unwavering. "It's never been about just you. It's about both of you. And proving that Gabe isn't a helpless shell. That he's an autonomous adult with a voice—and that someone just didn't want to hear it."

Anna's throat was dry. "Vicky."

Natalie didn't confirm. She didn't have to.

"There will be a judge," she continued. "Probably a medical examiner. Possibly even a neuropsychologist assigned to Gabe for evaluation. They'll be looking at communication logs, therapist notes, witness statements—anything that can confirm Gabe's capacity to understand, reason, and consent."

Anna swallowed. "He's going to have to testify, isn't he?"

"Yes," Natalie said. "In his own way. And he wants to."

Tears pricked again, sudden and fierce. "He's doing this for me?"

"No," Natalie said gently. "He's doing it for both of you. You both have the right to make your own choices for your lives and this case is about defending that right."

Anna looked down at her hands, trembling. She was pretty sure Henry would like to declare her incompetent to make her own life choices if he could.

"Am I allowed to talk to him?"

"Not yet," Natalie said. "But we're working on it. If we can show that your relationship was not exploitative—and we will—you'll be out of here soon."

Anna looked up again, eyes full of exhaustion, fear, and something like hope trying to claw its way back in.

"Thank you."

Natalie nodded.

"What can I do?"

"Nothing right now. It's up to Gabe. If the competency hearing doesn't go the way we want, then we'll plan next steps."

33

GABE

The courtroom was cold in the artificial way institutions always were: neutral carpet, neutral walls, neutral everything. Gabe sat rigid in his power chair near the front, head cradled in the padded headrest, AAC device mounted in front of him like a shield and sword both. He could feel the sweat under his collar despite the air conditioning. His body ached and a familiar burn was starting behind his shoulder blade. But he held still.

Next to him, Clint sat poised, papers in one hand, the other resting on the table.

Across the aisle, Vicky sat with that trademark saccharine smile that made Gabe's skin crawl. Her power suit was navy today. Classic. Authoritative. "Responsible guardian" costume, accessorized with their parents seated stiffly on either side of her. Mother's pearls. Father's disapproval. The whole tableau. She was representing herself which seemed insane but that just went to show how stupidly over-confident she was.

"...the assistive communication device is eye-tracking based," the neurologist was explaining from the witness stand. "It responds to very specific movement patterns that are not replicable involuntarily. There is no question that Mr. Whitlock's responses come directly from his cognitive intention."

"Can he understand complex decision-making?" the judge asked.

The doctor smiled faintly. "If I may be blunt, he understands it better than most."

Gabe expected a reaction but he saw nothing, not even a hint of a smile on Clint's face. The judge also remained serious. Since it was a closed hearing and not a trial, there wasn't an audience for any kind of joke.

Vicky's rebuttal was clinical. "With all due respect, my brother is not the man he once was. He suffered extensive brain trauma. I've read the MRI results. He is...limited. He can't care for himself. He can't possibly assess risk. It's not that I don't love him—"

Bullshit.

The judge snapped, "Mr. Rivera, contain your client."

Clint put a hand over Gabe's arm and whispered sharply into his ear, "Do I need to put a blindfold on you? Shut the fuck up and let me do my job."

The judge looked down at her notes. Then at Gabe.

"Mr. Whitlock," she said, "We've heard from several experts about your cognitive capacity and the technology that you use to speak. I'd like to hear from you. What would you like the court to know about your circumstances?"

The synthesized voice rang out, startling even in its calm tone.

I am still here.

His mother's pearls clicked faintly as she shifted. His father sat stiff, hands folded military-tight on his knees. Vicky's painted mouth bent into that practiced curve of concern.

The judge's eyes stayed on him. "Go on, Mr. Whitlock."

The words spilled out faster now, his gaze darting in sure, sharp flicks.

I know who I am. I know what I want.

Clint sat frozen beside him, but Gabe could feel the charged steadiness radiating off him: *Good. Keep going.*

The judge leaned forward slightly. "Your sister argues you can't make rational choices about your affairs. What would you say to that?"

Gabe's jaw clenched. His eyes moved.

She wants my money.

His mother inhaled sharply. The pearls at her throat shifted as her hand rose and then stilled. His father's jaw flexed, eyes fixed on the table in front of him.

Vicky's smile held, but just barely. "Gabriel," she said softly, carefully, as though soothing a child, "that isn't fair. I've managed your finances for years because you can't—"

The machine cut across her, merciless.

I can. And I will. Stop talking for me and over me.

"That's enough, Ms. Whitlock-Pierce. Please refrain from adding your commentary to the testimony. Mr. Whitlock, do you believe that your sister is motivated by your best interests?"

No. This is another in a long line of control tactics she has used against me over many years.

Vicky was fuming but managed to remain quiet, sitting on her hands.

"Mr. Whitlock," the judge continued, "can you tell me, in your own words, what you want the court to decide here?"

I understand risk. I lived it. On stage. Every night. I chose my life then. And I still get to choose now.

The judge leaned back in her chair, pen still. All eyes in the sterile room hung on her, but she looked only at Gabe. Finally she said, "This court has heard testimony from medical professionals, from legal counsel, and now from you, Mr. Whitlock." She folded her hands on the bench. "The question before me is not whether you can walk. It is not whether you can feed yourself or dress yourself. It is whether you have the capacity to make decisions about your own life."

Vicky straightened, about to say something, but the judge raised a hand, silencing her.

"I find that you do. The clarity of your responses, the technology that allows you to communicate, and the consistent testimony about your cognition leave no doubt in my mind."

She leaned slightly forward, her tone firm. "You are competent. Your rights remain your own." The judge's gavel came down once, sharp against the block. "This matter is settled."

Vicky glared at him for a moment, her mask dropping. Then their parents hurried her out, shielding her like she was the victim in this mess. Gabe sighed. That was a lost cause if he ever saw one. Clint's hand settled on Gabe's arm, quiet, grounding.

Let's go get Anna.

Gabe knew immediately that the man already standing in the jailhouse parking lot was Anna's father, there to pick her up just as Gabe was. He had never met Henry, but he was exactly as she had described—stoic, careful posture, clothes neat despite the heat, hands folded with an engineer's precision. And she had his forehead. The same long, stubborn slope.

As Gabe drove up near him on the asphalt, Henry glanced at him once, then turned and looked again. His eyes lingered on the chair, the headrest, the machine mounted at the side like some alien appendage. His jaw tightened, but he didn't speak.

For a long minute, the only sound was the cicadas shrilling from the trees beyond the parking lot.

Finally, Henry cleared his throat. "You're him." His voice was low, flat. "The one she lost her job over."

Gabe moved his eyes to the screen.

I'm Gabe.

Henry gave a short, humorless laugh. "I know who you are. Hard not to after this mess." He turned the hat in his hands, brim twisting between his fingers. "She always did fall too hard, too fast. For everything."

You think she's falling?

Henry's eyes flicked to the machine, then back to him. For a moment, the sharpness in them cracked, revealing something rawer beneath.

"You love her," Henry said quietly.

Yes.

The word came quick, without hesitation.

Henry swallowed. His throat worked, but his words came out steady. "I don't know what that means for her. I don't know if it's enough."

Gabe nodded. He could be defensive but he understood exactly what Henry was saying. So instead he admitted:

I don't know either.

Henry turned away, staring at the concrete at his feet. "She's everything I've got left. You have to understand. And she—she's reckless. She doesn't see the cliffs until she's already over the edge. I've spent years trying to keep her safe. And now she's..." He didn't seem to know how to continue.

Gabe remembered how Anna described her mother as a kite and her father as the string. But sometimes the string didn't trust the wind enough, stayed short and close, afraid to reach for the greatest heights.

She's stronger than you think. And if she falls, I'll be there to catch her. I've got lots of lap.

He winked and looked down at his long legs that formed a significant lap. Henry actually gave a weak laugh.

She wants to fly. She wants you to let her. To believe in her and let her try.

"Every time she tries, she ends up broken on the ground and I'm picking up pieces."

Gabe thought for a long moment, then his eyes moved on the screen again.

But maybe she gets to keep trying as many times as it takes. And you can retire from picking up the pieces. You don't have to be the string to her kite anymore. You can be the wind.

Henry's lip wavered for a moment as though he might cry but he shook himself firmly instead. Then he smiled at Gabe and said, "I see why she likes you."

34

ANNA

The heavy metal door slammed shut behind her, and the brightness outside nearly blinded her. The air hit her first, thick with sun and exhaust, so different from the flat, chemical chill inside. She squinted, lifted a hand to her brow. Her eyes adjusted slowly. Then she saw them.

Two shapes waiting at the edge of the lot. One small and rigid, hat clutched in his hands, every line of his body familiar as her own. The other in a wheelchair, eyes fixed on her in a way that stole the air from her lungs.

Her father. And Gabe. Both of them. Together.

Anna froze mid-step, her pulse quickening. Her mouth went dry. They hadn't spoken before. She'd been dreading what would happen when they did. At least they didn't appear to have tried to murder each other yet.

As she approached, she braced for the lecture from her father, the disappointment, the way he always tried to steer her life back onto rails she hadn't chosen. But when he looked at her, the hardness wasn't there. His eyes were tired, yes. Worried, always. But softer.

"Dad," she whispered.

Henry's face folded, relief cutting through the steel she was so used to. "You're all right."

She nodded, though her throat ached. "I'm all right."

He wrapped her up into a tight hug. She let him hold her steady for several long minutes.

Then finally she turned to Gabe who was patiently waiting.

"Hey, you," she said softly.

The device spoke a beat later.

Hey, you.

Her laugh broke on a sob, and she leaned closer until her forehead brushed against his. "I missed you," she whispered.

"Okay, okay, love birds," Henry said, shooing at them with his hands. "We can't stand in the sun all day."

Gabe's eyes danced across his screen rapidly, eventually the voice caught up:

I have a new apartment to show you. But maybe you should go home with your dad and get some rest first.

As if on cue, Anna yawned. "That sounds good."

They all made their way to Henry's car, Anna's hand on Gabe's shoulder.

"How are you getting home?" Anna asked.

Clint will be back out in a minute. He's my ride.

"Okay. Talk to you tomorrow?"

Absolutely.

The moment Anna got home she fell into a deep sleep and woke refreshed in the morning. It actually felt like the start of a new life. At least a new chapter.

She lay still for a long moment, staring at the faint cracks in the ceiling paint, listening to the hum of her father moving around downstairs. A new chapter. She had thought her first day at Rosehaven was a new chapter. Maybe it was. Maybe she wasn't supposed to be waiting for one single lightning bolt of transformation that would set her on a smooth and clear path for the rest of her life.

Maybe it was supposed to be smaller than that, a series of gentle endings and new beginnings over and over. Books had lots of chapters. Why wouldn't life, too?

And if that was true, then maybe she didn't have to figure out her whole story right now. Maybe all she had to do was get up, take the next step, and see what this chapter had in store for her.

She padded into the kitchen, hair still mussed, and found her father at the stove.

Henry was always precise when he cooked, movements as deliberate as when he'd drawn bridges on drafting paper. The pan tilted just enough for the yolk to slide without breaking. He didn't look up when she entered, but his shoulders softened.

"Sit," he said simply. "Coffee's ready."

She obeyed, wrapping her hands around the warm mug. He set a plate in front of her: toast cut into neat halves, eggs arranged like he used to when she was little. Only then did he meet her eyes. "He's not what I imagined."

"No?"

"No." But Henry didn't elaborate. Instead he nodded to her plate. "Eat before it gets cold. You've got somewhere to be."

After breakfast, she realized that she didn't even have contact information for Gabe and so she had to reach out to Clint to get his phone number. But then she was on her way to Gabe's new apartment.

It was about an hour's drive away in Worcester but the roads were beautiful. The end of summer was bleeding into the beginning of autumn, the most beautiful time of year in Massachusetts. Though most of the trees were still deep, rich green, a few scattered leaves were already golden and red.

The apartment building was newer, the plain architecture standing out against the historic brick buildings around it. There was a long ramp that led up to the front door at a gentle angle and three working elevators inside. She rode up to the third floor and knocked on his door. A moment later the latch clicked and it swung open electronically. Gabe was inside in his wheelchair and her heart leapt immediately into her throat when she saw him. He was fresh from the shower, his dark hair still wet and a towel draped over his shoulders.

"Hi," she breathed.

Welcome to my place.

"Your place. God, that sounds good."

Hop on board the tour bus.

She laughed and eased herself onto his lap, looping carefully around the mounted AAC. Her weight pressed against him, her thigh brushing the joystick. She steadied herself, looping her arms around his shoulders, sinking into the soft warmth of his body.

He kissed her temple, lips dry and lingering, then nudged the joystick. The chair hummed alive beneath them, rolling forward. Anna clung to him, her cheek pressed against the solid line of his jaw, feeling the faint scratch of stubble on her skin.

It was a short tour. The apartment wasn't grand but it was big enough for him to maneuver his chair with ease, with a roll-in shower in the bathroom, and extra wide doors. The final stop was the bedroom. Gabe pulled up next to the neatly-made queen-size bed and she shifted until she was straddling him, her knees pressed to the outside of his thighs, and her palms braced on his shoulders. His breath hitched, audible in a shaky rasp, as her weight settled fully onto him. She bent to kiss him.

His mouth opened beneath hers, warm and insistent. He pushed his lips into her kiss with raw urgency. The world shrank to breath and pressure. The wheelchair headrest creaked faintly as he tried to hold his neck upright. She threaded her fingers into his hair, tugging just enough to keep their mouths pressed tight together as his control wavered.

Anna breathed in the faint antiseptic smell of the chair's vinyl mixed with the soap from his shower. She kissed along his jaw, down to the bristle at his throat. Her body rocked against him, the friction making his eyes squeeze shut. His lips parted again, tongue meeting hers, desperate and greedy.

When she pulled back, panting, their foreheads rested to-gether, sweat dampening her hairline. His mouth hung open, trembling, as though a voice might slip free if only his body allowed it. His eyes flicked to the bed behind her. A question.

Her grin answered.

She slid off his lap, muttering against his ear, "I promise I'll learn to use the lift, but until then..."

As she had done once at Rosehaven, she strategically used her body to leverage gravity and shift him from his wheelchair onto the bed. His breath was hot on her neck and she shivered, desire rippling down her body. His weak arms clung loosely around her neck, his trembling legs holding as steady as they were able. With a soft grunt she guided him down, feeling his weight ease into the mattress. She adjusted his twitching legs to lay flatter. His eyes tracked her, fierce and unblinking. He raised a suggestive eyebrow.

Her shirt came off in one swift motion, tossed to the floor. His gaze devoured her and she reveled in the desperately hungry look in his eyes. She came for his shirt next, peeling it from his chest. His skin was warm beneath her fingers. She kissed the hollow of his throat, the hard ridge of his collarbone. His breath shuddered out, his whole frame trembling with effort.

She leaned over him, kissing him again, slower this time. Her hair brushed across his cheek and he tried to angle his head, matching her. His hand twitched against the blanket. She reached down, tugging at the waistband of his sweatpants, sliding them carefully down his hips. His body jerked with spasms as she moved his legs, but she murmured soothing words, easing him through until the fabric was gone.

He was already hard—thick, alive, undeniable. Her breath caught. "God, Gabe..."

His eyes locked to hers, fierce and vulnerable.

She stripped quickly, climbed astride him, her knees sinking into the mattress on either side of his hips. She kissed him again, deeper, while her hand slipped between them, guiding, steadying, making up for what his body couldn't. She held him steady with her hand, guiding his cock to her entrance that was wet and waiting. Slowly she eased him in until she felt the first sweet stretch of him inside her.

Anna braced her palms on his chest and lowered herself down, inch by careful inch, until he was buried deep in her. His mouth fell open, a strangled sound breaking in his throat, his whole body seizing for a moment in response. The spasm shoved him deeper, sharp and uneven, and she gasped, clutching his shoulders. His jaw clenched, his face twisted with effort and pleasure tangled together.

"You feel so good," she whispered, rocking against him.

His chest heaved, his eyes squeezed tight, she felt every tremor in the muscles of his legs beneath her. He tried to thrust up into her, but the motion was stilted. His hips jerked again. She adjusted her body to catch each spasm, letting his unpredictable movements become the rhythm.

He lifted his left arm, trembling with strain, until the backs of his fingers pressed her hip. Awkward. Intentional. She leaned into his touch, grinding harder, faster. She bent over him and her hands slid over his shoulders, into his hair. She kissed him again, swallowing his breathless sounds, her tongue moving against his. He was hot and solid inside her, his cock pulsing as she tightened around him.

"Look at me," she whispered against his lips.

His eyes snapped open, blazing. His whole body arched beneath her, spasms jerking his hips off the mattress, driving him inside her so deep she cried out, her fingers digging into his shoulders. His face was twisted with effort and need, every spasm and twitch magnified by the intensity of being joined. She shifted the angle, lifting herself higher, then dropping back down hard, drawing a guttural groan from his throat.

His eyes were wide open now, locked on hers, pleading, commanding.

"Yes," she gasped, moving faster now, tangling her fingers in his chest hair. "I've got you. Come with me."

And he did—hips trembling, cock pulsing, spilling inside her in wild, uncontrollable shudders. A load groan vibrated through his throat. She clung to him, moving through it, feeling every pulse, following as her own orgasm shook through her. Her body clenched around his, every muscle tensed, her voice crying out in ecstasy.

When she collapsed onto him, both of them were shaking. His chest heaved under her, his arm still twitching against her hip like he refused to let go. She pressed her face to his neck, kissing the damp skin there. Breath mingled. Heartbeats pounded. Sweat cooled slowly between them.

Sliding carefully off him, she kept her hand on his thigh, grounding him, grounding herself. His hips jerked once, an aftershock that made her thighs tremble in answer. She smiled, her body still aching and humming with satisfaction.

She slipped into the bathroom to clean herself, then returned with a fresh towel for him. Her touch was tender, unhurried, as she wiped him down, careful not to rush. His eyes tracked her every movement, heavy-lidded but intent, following the glide of her hand

When she was finished, she moved to his legs, lifting and stretching them the way Becky had shown her. Her palms pressed into his hips, steady and firm, coaxing tight muscles to yield. His body fought her, spasms tensing his muscles against her hold. His mouth parted, a faint sound caught in his throat, his brows drawn together. She bent close, whispering, "I know, I know. Let me help."

His eyes flicked to hers, sharp with frustration, then softened as though surrendering. Bit by bit, the tension drained from him. She slid pillows beneath his legs, tucking others along his sides until he was supported. He smiled gratefully.

Anna smoothed a damp strand of hair from his forehead then she climbed back into bed beside him, curling her body against his. She picked up his arm and pulled it around her like a blanket.

After several quiet minutes, her phone dinged from the pocket of her pants on the floor. She leaned down and scooped it up while his knuckles traced a gentle line along her lower back.

Rachel: *Hey, Steve's going to do the BBQ thing before the summer is totally over. Bring your new guy.*

Anna showed Gabe the text. "Do you think we can do that?"

He looked over to the AAC screen on his wheelchair, his eyes moving deliberately across it.

We'll figure it out.

Anna texted back that they would be there and then she and Gabe strategized about how to get a ride over since his wheelchair wouldn't fit in her little car, and what Rachel and Steve's backyard was like. Ordinarily they did the grilling on the back deck but since that would involve stairs, Anna asked Rachel to move the grill down to the backyard and have dinner on the grass instead.

Rachel's backyard smelled of charcoal and sunscreen, the air alive with the crackle of the grill and the shrieks of their toddler running barefoot in the grass. Gabe drove his wheelchair across the lawn, a box of cookies on his lap, and Anna followed behind him. Anna was a little nervous how this was going to go but mostly just excited to finally be able to bring Gabe into her world.

"Hey! You made it," Rachel called, wiping her hands on a kitchen towel as she came down the deck steps. She hugged Anna, then looked at Gabe nervously.

Thanks for having us.

"It's so good to finally meet you."

"Beer?" Steve asked, lifting a cold bottle from the cooler. He glanced at Gabe, then at Anna. "I've got soda and sparkling water too."

Beer. Please.

Steve grinned, popped the cap, and held the bottle out. Anna took it, then rummaged in her bag for the cup holder attachment for the wheelchair and a long silicone straw. She set up the drink and guided the straw to his lips.

That hits the spot.

Steve laughed. "Right on, man," he said.

As Anna suggested, everything had been moved down from the back deck to the grass. While Steve grilled, everyone else sat around the outdoor table under a wide, green umbrella. Lena had a half-eaten bowl of mac & cheese that she occasionally returned to for a single bite and then ran off again.

"I would say I've heard a lot about you," Rachel said to Gabe, "But I honestly only found out about you when Anna lost her job. So that was what, a month ago? We've been best friends since I forced her into it when we were fifteen yet she kept this secret from me." Rachel glared playfully at Anna.

Anna straightened, defensive but calm. "I had a reason."

Rachel turned her attention back to Gabe. "So, should I take this personally? Or were you both just worried I'd run my mouth?"

Gabe looked to Anna.

She talks a lot?

Rachel barked a laugh. "Okay, point to you. Yes, I do. But it's usually good advice!"

"I had to keep it secret," Anna said. "You saw what happened when people found out."

Rachel shook her head ruefully. "Thank god that's over."

Gabe interrupted:

She thought you'd judge.

That quieted Rachel. Her frown softened as she glanced between them. "Well...she's not wrong. I probably would've said something. Maybe not fair, but...yeah." She leaned back with a sigh. "Alright. I'll take my licks. Still doesn't mean you're off the hook for keeping me in the dark. You don't pull punches, do you?"

His eyes narrowed with a flicker of amusement.

Too much effort.

Rachel let out a laugh, short and rueful. "Okay, I'll give you that. Efficient and brutal."

When the food was ready, Steve slid a burger onto a plate and set it in front of Gabe before hesitating, looking uncertain. "Uh... should I...?"

Anna leaned in smoothly. "I've got it." She cut the burger into neat pieces, added some potato salad, then offered the fork casually to Gabe as though she'd done it a thousand times before. He leaned forward just enough to take the bite, his eyes flicking to hers: gratitude, but also that teasing spark.

Rachel pretended not to notice, but her glance lingered a second too long before she redirected to Anna. Gabe distracted her with a question since he could chew and speak at the same time.

How did you and Steve meet?

Rachel blinked at him, then smiled, pushing her glasses up. "College. Freshman chemistry. He stole my lab goggles."

Steve grinned sheepishly. "Mine were fogging up and hers weren't. I figured—"

"You figured wrong," Rachel cut in. "He spilled hydrochloric acid on his notes five minutes later."

Anna laughed, passing Gabe another bite of burger. "Romantic."

"It worked," Steve said, shrugging. "She kept yelling at me until I asked her out just to shut her up."

"Accurate," Rachel admitted, eyes warm on him despite the dry tone.

Better story than mine.

Anna arched a brow. "Oh, I don't know. 'Famous rock star sulking in a nursing home until he fell for the activities girl' has a certain flair." She slipped him another bite, seamless.

Sulking until activities girl forced him to paint.

Rachel laughed. "Classic Anna. Meets a rockstar and the first thing she says is, 'Oh, hey, do you like watercolors?'"

Gabe crinkled his eyes at Anna and his gaze was full of affection. She felt warm and comfortable. This was the life she had been waiting for.

Steve finally relaxed enough to lean back in his chair. "*Pressure Front*, right? Man, I used to play your CD in my first car. I think I drove my roommates crazy blasting it."

Lena banged a plastic truck against Gabe's wheel and announced proudly, "Big car!"

Gabe arched a brow and typed with his eyes:

Bigger than yours.

Steve choked on his beer.

After Lena wandered away again, they all relaxed into the evening. Rachel talked about juggling work and a toddler, Anna told a story about speed dating, Steve asked about the new AAC technology and actually listened as Gabe explained the basics.

Finally the sun was setting and mosquitoes were starting to come out.

"We should get back," Anna said. She got up and made sure the path was clear for Gabe to back out.

"Okay, I have to say it," Rachel said. "You two are disgustingly cute. He looks at you like you hung the moon. Don't think I don't see it."

I prefer sun. Hotter.

Anna pressed her palm to her face, laughing helplessly, while Rachel whooped and raised her glass. "Cheers to that."

As Anna and Gabe waited by the street for the accessible van to arrive, Gabe said:

Listen. I need to tell you something.

Anna frowned, suddenly worried, but she waited patiently to hear what he had to say.

I love you. I think that that's obvious. But that doesn't mean it's right for us to have a relationship.

Anna opened her mouth but Gabe cut her off.

No. Don't say anything yet.

I am never going to be able to drive. I am never going to be able to do dishes. I am never going to be able to take out the trash. I am never going to be able to mow the lawn or grill hamburgers or run out to the store.

She forced herself to stay quiet through each excruciating sentence.

You should have a partner in life and that means someone who helps out. I need you to give that real, serious thought.

Anna wanted to wave these concerns away and say they didn't matter. But he was right. They did matter and these were big issues. Everything in her was telling her that Gabe was worth it, that he *was* a partner, but she had to seriously consider what he was saying.

She thought quietly about it the whole ride back to Gabe's apartment.

Finally, in the parking lot back at his building, they looked at one another in the dusk. It was time for Anna to get back in her car and drive the hour back home. He was looking at her sadly, like he thought this might be the end.

Anna picked up one of his hands and held it in both of hers. "I've thought about it," she said. "The truth is that I can hire someone to take out the trash and mow the lawn. I can hire someone to deliver things from the store. I can hire someone to do just about anything...except love me. I could never hire someone to love me."

Gabe swallowed hard.

"I love you and we are in this together. Partners in every way."

35

EPILOGUE

Rachel examined Anna carefully, her nose scrunched in concentration. Finally she moved the veil just a quarter of an inch and stepped aside so Anna could see herself in the mirror.

The dress Anna wore was her mother's off-the-rack from Macy's wedding dress, simple and plain but perfect. She stared at herself, still unable to believe it was her wedding day.

Then Henry knocked on the door. "It's time."

Anna took his arm and he led her to the sanctuary entrance. The moment she saw Gabe at the front of the church, her vision blurred with tears. His brand-new wheelchair could unfold itself, straighten out, and raise him into a standing position so he was upright with the dark wheelchair behind him like a mech suit. Straps across his chest and knees made his suit bunch up and wrinkle in those places but the overall effect was that he was standing, as tall as his former self.

Anna clung to her father's arm and he steadied her down the aisle, subtly wiping a tear from his own cheek.

Gabe held out his hands to her. His arms were still shaky and his fingers curled against his palms. She quickly took hold of his hands and felt him release the strain and weight of his arms onto her.

Anna looked out to the crowd and saw so many people that she loved. Her father was sitting in the front row with her aunt. Cut-out pews made space for Ellie's wheelchair. Bernie was beside her, his arm over her shoulders and his hand holding hers. Mary, Max, and Frank sat together. Sylvia was behind them. On the other side of the aisle, Clint and his wife sat. Tommy was behind them. Steve was chasing Lena around the back of the sanctuary. Rachel was beside her at the front and Ray was next to Gabe across from her. More friends and family filled every seat and all Anna saw looking back at her was love.

The minister began. "Gabriel Whitlock, do you take Anna Lin as your lawfully wedded wife? To have and to hold, in sickness and in health, for as long as you both shall live?"

His eyes danced across his AAC screen but the voice that came from the computer wasn't the one Anna was used to. She gasped as the voice that answered "I do" was his own. He hadn't spoken the words, the device had, but it was using the sound of his real voice. Before she could figure out if this was a party trick for just two words, it was her time to answer.

"Anna Lin, do you take Gabriel Whitlock to be your lawfully wedded husband? To have and to hold, in sickness and in health, for as long as you both shall live?"

She squeezed his hands. "I do," she said.

The minister paused. "You've prepared your own vows. Gabriel, would you like to read yours first?"

Again, the voice that came from the AAC was a close imitation of the real voice he had lost. Someone had reprogrammed the device using clips of his voice.

We're a team. You're on my side no matter what, fighting for me, figuring out solutions. I don't promise you easy. But I promise you real. Every hard day. Every good day. All of me. Always. Let me be the string for your kite, holding you steady, keeping you safe, and letting you fly.

Anna's tears were flowing freely now. She sniffled and took back one hand to rub the wetness from her cheeks. She had never heard anything so beautiful.

"I can't believe you remembered the kite," she whispered. He smiled back as if to say, *of course I did.*

The minister turned to Anna and her hands shook as she unfolded the small paper she'd rewritten a dozen times. Her voice wavered, but she didn't hide it.

"When I was little, I thought love meant rescue. Someone to swoop in and fix the broken things. But then I met you. And I learned love isn't rescue: it's seeing someone, fully, even in the hardest places. And choosing them. Every time."

She looked at him, blinking back tears. She continued, "You've taught me that broken doesn't mean less. That quiet doesn't mean empty. You've taught me that being afraid doesn't mean I can't be brave. So here's my vow: I will stand with you in every fight. I will sit with you in every silence. I will love you, not in spite of who you are, not because of who you were, but exactly as you are. And I will keep choosing you—every day, every hour, every heartbeat—for the rest of my life."

The paper slipped from her fingers as she reached for his trembling hands again. He gripped back with all the strength he had.

"You may kiss the bride," the minister concluded.

For a moment, everything was still. Now that Gabe was standing, he was far taller than Anna and she couldn't reach his lips even on the tips of her toes. The crowd was hushed. Then he pressed the controls on the chair and, with a mechanical whine, it lowered him into more of a crouch position until he was low enough for her to reach.

A wave of laughs and cheers went up from their friends and family as Anna leaned into him and pressed her lips to his.

They had tried to hire a DJ but Tommy had immediately vetoed that idea. Now he held court at the sound system, alternating between '80s synthpop and old *Pressure Front* hits, grinning whenever the crowd roared in recognition.

Anna and Gabe sat at the head table watching the crowd. She cut into the chicken marsala, taking a bite herself before spearing a smaller piece and holding it up for him. He leaned forward, mouth opening with trust, and she slipped the fork between his lips. Guests came by, leaning down with hugs for Anna, squeezing Gabe's shoulder, raising glasses in toast.

Ray appeared in the middle of it, cheeks flushed, tie loose around his neck, looking both disheveled and delighted. "Man, you looked good up there," he said, shaking his head. "Scared the hell out of me when you rose up in that contraption. Thought you were gonna sprout wings and fly off."

Gabe's eyes gleamed.

Next album cover.

Ray barked a laugh, clapped Gabe's shoulder, and melted back into the crowd.

The night went on. Cake ended up smeared across Max's cheek because he leaned too close to the slice meant for the newlyweds. Ellie, regal in her wheelchair at the center of her table, had half the room belting out *Guys & Dolls,* their voices ragged but joyful. Rachel swooped in behind Anna just as a hairpin threatened to slip, fixing it with deft fingers and muttering, "Prom night, round two." Anna laughed, blinking back the prickle of tears that kept sneaking up on her.

By the time the candles had burned low and the dance floor blurred into a whirl of laughter and motion, Anna found herself perched on Gabe's lap, his body warm and steady, her hand wrapped around his. The noise of the reception swirled around them—clinking glasses, bursts of laughter, Tommy hollering into the mic—but between them, a quiet pocket opened.

His eyes were on her, luminous in the low light.

Never thought I'd get this.

Anna leaned in and kissed the edge of his jaw, catching the mingled taste of cake frosting and the salt of his skin. "Me neither," she whispered. "I don't know how I got so lucky."

Around them, their unlikely family kept celebrating; dancing and laughing late into the night.

THE END

Thank you for reading! If you enjoyed this book I hope that you'll consider **leaving a review** wherever you purchased this book and/or Goodreads. It helps a lot :)

You can get **bonus scenes, character art, and more** at my website: https://ruthmadisonbooks.com/bonus(Including a honeymoon short story for Gabe & Anna!)

There is also a discussion guide and other extras at: https://ruthmadisonbooks.com/bookclubs

www.ingramcontent.com/pod-product-compliance
Lightning Source LLC
Chambersburg PA
CBHW050029030726
47506CB00001B/191